THE LAST WOLF

MARIA VALE

sourcebooks
casablanca

Published by Sourcebooks Casablanca, an imprint of Sourcebooks, Inc.
P.O. Box 4410, Naperville, Illinois 60567-4410
(630) 961-3900
Fax: (630) 961-2168
sourcebooks.com

Printed and bound in the United States of America.
LSC 10 9 8 7 6 5 4 3

*To M, H & G, who make my life
and the world better.*

Prologue

Titnore Woods, 1668

THIS WOULD BE ÆLFRIDA'S FOURTH AND LAST ATTEMPT. THE
Pack at Essex had refused, as had Anglia. Even the
tiny remnants of the Pack at Gyrwe had sent her away
empty-handed. Now staring at the strong and plentiful
wolves of Wessex, her heart sank. She'd even caught
sight of a pup staring at her from under a dead oak, the
first she'd seen in England in over a decade.

Her own Mercia Pack hadn't had a pup since
Halwende, and he was almost an adult. As she waited
to be announced, subordinate wolves circled Mercia's
Alpha, sniffing her curiously and gathering her scent to
take back to the dominants. Others, still in skin, watched
from a distance.

"*Ælfrida, Alpha of Mercia. Wessex þu wilcumaþ swa
beódgæst.*"

Ælfrida, Alpha of Mercia. Wessex welcomes you as
table guest.

She'd made sure her wolves had learned the English
of humans years ago. It was ridiculous to pretend that
the Packs were still the top predators. That title belonged
to humans now, and Ælfrida studied them as carefully
as deer studied her.

"Greetings, Wulfric, Alpha of Wessex, and many
thanks for your hospitality."

"*Sprecest þu ne Englisc?*" the huge man growled, though that was one of the ambiguities of the Old Tongue: it sounded growled, whether one meant it to or not.

"This *is* English, Wessex." She brushed her hand against her breeches, feeling scaly bits of fur there. "Is Seolfer here?"

"*Seolfer? Min nidling?*"

"Yes, *your nidling*." She was distracted momentarily by the scabrous clumps in her hands. Sniffing her palms to be sure, she wiped them against a tree trunk. These wolves might look well fed, but some, at least, had mange. Maybe all was not well in Wessex. Maybe Wulfric would listen to her.

For now, though, the old Alpha scowled.

"*Ic þearf wealhstod,*" she said, even though she actually didn't need a translator. Ælfrida was an Alpha who issued commands and was obeyed. This bluntness had not served her well when dealing with the other Alphas, and Ælfrida hoped that Seolfer would know how to translate that bluntness into something the conceited oaf Wulfric might find more acceptable. Besides, she liked the young woman and had looked forward to seeing her again.

"*Seolfer!*" Wulfric yelled without bothering to look.

The woman who emerged from behind Wulfric's lodge had dark-blond hair, typical of silvers when they were in skin. A runt, she was destined to life as a *nidling*, a bond servant to her Alpha pair.

Many moons ago, looking for something more than a life of endless submission, Seolfer had made a desperate run all the way to Pack Caledonia. Unfortunately, wolves tolerate neither weakness nor strangers, especially not with resources so strained. Caledonia, Essex, Northumbria, Strathclyde: all of them had sent her away with nothing but a bite to her pastern.

Then she arrived at the Forest of Dean and planted her short legs and shook her shredded hide and challenged the famously fierce and powerful Alpha of Mercia for a place in the Pack. Ælfrida took one look at the runt and laughed. Then took her in. Not because she had any room for weakness, but because she saw in Seolfer a kind of strength that Packs almost never had: the courage to face the unknown.

The runt was, as wolves say, strong of marrow.

Unfortunately, the great Forest of Dean was falling fast to the humans' rapacious desires for lumber and grazing and iron, and with her Pack on the edge of starvation, Ælfrida had sent Seolfer back to Wulfric. She knew what waited for the girl, but submission was better than death—at least that's what Ælfrida told herself.

Seolfer said nothing; her head was bowed low.

"How are you, Seolfer?"

"As you see, Alpha."

"Hmm. I don't need you to translate. I need you to make what I say palatable to the old fart. *Gea*?"

The Seolfer that Ælfrida had known would have laughed, but not this one. She just nodded and bent her head lower, trying to avoid Ælfrida's attempt to catch her eye. She didn't have much time, so Ælfrida coughed a little and started her set speech. "The time of the wolves in this country is over. It is now the time of the humans."

She waited for the girl to translate. Wolves, both wild and in skin, came close to listen to the rugged cadences

of the Old Tongue. Ælfrida wrinkled her nose and
sniffed; even human, she could smell the sick sweetness
of rot. Something was definitely wrong in Wessex.

"The land in Mercia is dying, and with it, our Pack. It
is the same everywhere: Anglia and Sussex and Gyrwe."

"*It is not the same here*," interrupted Wulfric, looking
at Seolfer to translate, but Ælfrida waved her off.

"How can you say that? When I was last here, just
fifty years ago." Seolfer stumbled over the word *year*,
and Ælfrida waited for her to translate it into six hundred
moons, a span Wulfric would understand. "The last time
I was here," she started again, "I ran into a tree to avoid a
deer. Now there are neither. The same is true of Mercia,
which is why I have arranged for a boat to take my Pack
to the Colonies. I am asking you to join your bloodlines
with ours. Make a truly great Pack in the New World."

"*Landbuenda*?" Wulfric repeated, missing the larger
point in his fretting about the whereabouts of these
"colonies."

"America," Ælfrida said irritably.

"Omeriga?" Wulfric echoed, still confused.

"Oh, by the Moon, Wessex. *Vinland*." Recognition
dawned on Wessex's face, then he laughed, and Ælfrida
knew that for Wulfric, Vinland was still nothing but a
rumor west of Iceland. "It is real," she snapped. "I have
talked to humans who have been there. It is a great land,
a wild land. There are vast forests that we could buy and
have legal title to and—"

Before Seolfer had even finished translating *we could
buy*, Wulfric interrupted.

"*Why should I travel across the water to* buy *land, when
I have land here. Land that has been ours for centuries*."

"You have *lived* here for centuries, but it *belongs* to Worthing, and the humans will have it."

"*And since when does a wolf care what humans think?*"

"Since they have become stronger than we are, you sodding ass." Seolfer glided without comment over the last bit. Ælfrida'd had a long and depressing fortnight, and her patience for Pack obstinacy was nearly exhausted. "Since they have armed themselves with weapons that will kill us from afar. Since they tear down our woods to build their ships and graze their sheep. Since they rip up the very ground to find rocks to melt into those guns and bullets. It is time for you to face the truth and do the hard thing. Do the right thing. Be an Alpha, and bring Wessex to America with us. Let us start something great and new."

As soon as Seolfer had finished translating. Wulfric signaled impatiently for Ælfrida to follow him toward a stone shed with a sod roof. The tall Alpha of Mercia had to fold herself nearly in half to get inside.

Wulfric looked at her smugly. "*You see, Mercia. I have faced the truth.*"

It took time for the weak eyes of her human form to adjust to the dim light, to see the neat rows of muskets lining the walls. To make out the shelves below loaded with flint and powder and cartridge.

"But…how did he get these?" she asked, turning to Seolfer. "Tell me you didn't help him do this." The girl shook her head firmly. "Then who negotiated with the humans? How—?"

Ælfrida froze as she sensed another presence enter the shed, someone with a new and terrifying stench.

She turned to the man who was only slightly taller than Seolfer and then bent down, sniffing him. Just to be sure. Just to be sure she wasn't mistaken in that lethal combination of steel and carrion. That she wasn't mistaken in that fugitive but equally deadly hint of wild. The man smiled at her, and Ælfrida knew that Wessex had bet the survival of his Pack on a deal with the devil.

"It was my pleasure to help the Great Wessex Pack," said the man with the thinning blond hair who was the size of a large human and human in disposition, but was not human.

He was *Hwerflic*. Changeable and inconstant. A Shifter. More than anything, Packs feared Shifters. Because they could be wolves if they wanted, but they never *had* to be. Unlike Packs, which were ruled by the Iron Moon. For three days out of thirty, when the moon was pregnant and full and her law was Iron, the Packs must be wild.

Shifters mostly lived as humans, but they had much stronger senses and could sniff out Packs. And because all Shifters believed that Packs, like dragons, sat on vast hoards of treasure, they slaughtered them with terrifying regularity.

"The moon is nearly full," Ælfrida said to Wulfric. "The Iron Moon is coming. How will you protect yourself when you have no hands to load the powder and ball? When you have no fingers to pull the trigger?"

"If I may, Alpha," said the Shifter in his polished voice. "I have been able to arrange for a human guard who protect the Pack during those days. Times being what they are, they are glad of the employment and will ask no questions."

Wulfric smiled smugly at Ælfrida.

"Leave us, Shifter," she said. The man hesitated until Wessex nodded. As soon as she was sure he was out of earshot, Ælfrida whipped around to Wulfric. "What are you doing, you old fool? Once they know how vulnerable you are during the change, the Shifter and his humans will kill you. Then they can take as much time as they want to find your gold."

Wulfric didn't wait for Seolfer to finish translating.

"*Wessex does not fear prey!*" he snarled, his lips curling back from dark-yellow teeth set in pale gums. He belched loudly and stalked out of the shed, followed by his Pack and his Shifter, leaving only his *nidling* and a sour fug behind.

"*What do you mean by 'prey,' Wessex?*" Ælfrida yelled from the doorway.

The big male did not stop and did not answer.

"*Wulfric, betelle þu. Tell me*. What have you done?"

Seolfer plucked hard at Ælfrida's loose sleeve. She'd been a tough little thing, outspoken and smart, but now she looked haunted. She shook her head, her finger raised to her lips. Peering around until it was clear that the Pack had followed its Alpha, she moved quietly, her bare heel eliding to bare toe, clearly used to gliding noiseless and unnoticed around the Pack.

The two of them climbed an incline alongside a fast-moving stream. Wessex hadn't offered her anything to eat, a terrible breach of Pack laws of hospitality; still, Ælfrida needed something to drink, at least. But before she could kneel at the water's edge, Seolfer grabbed her arm and pulled her roughly away. For such a tiny thing, she was remarkably strong. Then the *nidling* pointed her

toward a springhouse a short distance away. She pulled
a rag from her waistband. "Cover your mouth, Alpha."

———∿∿∿———

Ælfrida ran as fast and hard as she could. She had left
her clothes with the young woman, as well as the details
of her Pack's departure from Portsmouth on the day after
the Iron Moon. Had she said they'd be sailing on the
Assurance? She couldn't remember anymore, because
all she could remember were the partly eaten humans
cooling in the springhouse. Everything made sense now:
the guns, the fat, the mange, the yellow teeth, and the
stench. The smell of carrion and man-eaters.

The wolves of England were already dead. Running
at night and through streams and in the cover of whatever trees she could find, Ælfrida headed fast for her
own Mercia Pack, praying that they were where she'd
left them, hiding in tight dirt dens in Sussex.

When the Iron Moon passed, Ælfrida led her scrag-
gly group to Portsmouth. She could barely stand to
look back over the thirty thin adults who were all that
remained of the one-time greatness of Mercia. Breeding
had always been difficult for Pack, without adding in
starvation and ferocious hostility to lone wolves and
fresh bloodlines. She had used too much of the treasure
her Pack had accumulated over the centuries for a ship
that was larger than she needed, hoping and praying that
some Alpha had the sense to join her.

What a waste.

A murmur roiled the Pack, alerting Ælfrida to the
faint scent of wolf. Even with her poor human nose, she
recognized it instantly, running it down until she came

to the end of the dock where the *Assurance*'s captain stood yelling at a small woman seated with her legs over the side of the dock, her arms clenched around the harness of a dog cart, piled with three large chests.

Seolfer was weaving slightly, staring at the blood falling from her leg into the water in rapidly dissipating gusts. The little *nidling* looked up with difficulty, her eyes barely focused in her pale face. "The guards shot them during the change. Clubbed them. Cut off their heads and stove them onto the branches of our trees. Bleeding into our earth. They are right now tearing up our land, looking for money. But I have them all, Alpha. I have them all."

Ælfrida breathed in deep and said a silent prayer of thanks to the pale remnants of the daylit waning moon. She yelled for her Delta, the one she'd sent to Glasgow to study medicine.

"This is Seolfer," she said. "Heal her."

Untying the rag around the woman's calf, the doctor frowned. "Alpha, the ball is lodged in her tibia, and she has lost a great deal of blood. It is doubtful she will survive and sure that she will lose her leg." He shook his head sadly.

"Do *not* wag your head at me." Ælfrida bent down, one strong hand clenched around his jaw. "You *will* do what I tell you, and she will live."

"Then what?" Ælfrida's Beta yelled from the back where he'd been serving as rear guard. "Are we to embark on this foolishness saddled by a crippled runt who is not even of Mercia?"

It is not in the nature of a Pack to accept change quietly. Mercia's wolves had not seen what she had. While she had visited the Packs, they had dug holes in the dirt and eaten rats, which had done little to improve their disposition.

Ælfrida bolted through the Pack, straight for the enormous male. She hadn't eaten enough for months, but there was a reason she was Alpha, and every muscle tightened in explosive anticipation. Her lungs expanded as she plowed her struggling Beta to the edge of the dock and then threw him into the disgusting murky water lapping against the quay.

She glared at the rest of her Pack, every tendon and bone wanting to shift. Her shoulders curved high behind her lowered head. Her teeth needed to tear into muzzles; her fingers ached to claw at flanks.

"Your Alpha," she growled, her body heaving, "says that *this* woman and *these* chests are Mercia now."

She might have been weakened by the long, slow hunger, but one by one, her Pack dropped their eyes and submitted.

"You," she barked at the goggle-eyed captain of the *Assurance*, who was staring at her huge Beta flailing in the water. "Fish him out."

She left two wolves to help the captain and two more to help the doctor. Then she commanded the rest of the Pack to carry the chests to the hold. "Gently, gently. Don't jostle them." She sent Halwende, the Pack's single juvenile, for as much water as he could carry.

"Hurry," she whispered as soon as they were in the hold, away from the humans. She couldn't keep the anticipation and dread from her voice. Fastened only with sticks, the chests opened easily, and her heart clenched in her throat. The Pack gathered around the boxes smelling of piss and terror, and one by one they picked up the silent, cringing pups, cradling them against the warmth of their bodies. They gave them water from their cupped hands and stroked their fur and rubbed faces against muzzles to mark them.

And for the first time in many years, Ælfrida, the last Alpha of the Great Pack of Mercia, allowed herself to feel hope.

"Be sure to wash them well," she said, more softly now. She would not have the pups coming to the New World smelling of the corruption and death of the old.

Unfortunately, Ælfrida had one last thing to do to make sure her Pack could leave safely. It was a shitty job, but that's what it meant to be Alpha.

She'd seen the Shifter lingering near the dock and walked until she found his scent and tracked him to a nearby tavern. He seemed no more surprised to see Ælfrida than she was to see him. He was, he said, devastated that the human guards had betrayed Wulfric. Humans, he said, had no sense of honor, of a promise made and kept. But he could not bear life as a lone wolf, he said, and would serve her in whatever way she needed in return for a place in the Pack.

He never mentioned Seolfer or the three great chests that he had tracked to Portsmouth. Nor did he mention the pistol he carried, though the scent of gunpowder was tart in Ælfrida's nose.

Ælfrida watched a young human woman, barely out of girlhood, smile at a customer and saw the customer's body relax. When the girl touched his arm, he leaned forward, his scent becoming suddenly receptive. Ælfrida turned to the Shifter and gave him the same barmaid smile and the same barmaid touch, and his scent became musky. The blandishments that Ælfrida presumed he had used on poor Wulfric he now used on her, along with his fingers and palm. Finally, they went to one of the back rooms. "To formalize things," he said archly.

―⁓―

"If you're going to puke, puke leeward," the captain of the *Assurance* had said, muttering something impertinent.

Ælfrida was beyond caring about impertinence. She leaned over the rail he had pointed to, and as she started to vomit once more, she called upon the moon to witness that as long as she lived, she would never eat Shifter again.

Chapter 1

Upstate New York, 2018

WOLVES WHO DRINK SMELL LIKE BAILEYS AND KIBBLE.

It doesn't matter that Ronan's poison is a 7 and 7 and chimichangas at the casino over at Hogansburg, there's something about our livers that still makes him smell like Baileys and kibble.

He lies slumped partly on his stomach, partly on his side at the edge of the Clearing, the broad expanse of spongy grass and drowned trees that is what remains of an old beaver pond that fell into disrepair when the Pack ate the beavers one lean year. New beavers have established a new pond nearby. Eventually we will eat those too.

And so it goes.

The Clearing is used for ceremonies and rituals because it is open and accommodates larger numbers. Usually the Pack prefers the cool, muffled, fragrant darkness of the forest, treating the Clearing like an anxious Catholic treats the church. We shuffle in on major celebrations and otherwise give it a wide berth.

The *Dæling*, which I suppose translates most conveniently as "Dealing," is one of those celebrations. It marks the transition of our age group, our echelon, from juvenile to adult. Here, we are paired off, not as mates yet, but in practice couplings. We will also have our own Alpha who answers only to the Pack Alpha and is responsible for keeping our echelon in line. The whole hierarchy will be set up. Not that it's permanent or anything, more like the start times assigned before the lengthy competition that is Pack life.

Basically, the *Dæling* is one enormous squabble. There are challenges for the right to pair with a stronger wolf and challenges for a more elevated place in the hierarchy. Our whole youth has been taken up with tussling and posturing, but now it really counts. A wolf who is pinned to the ground in front of the Pack Alpha is the loser. Period. This sorting out of rankings and couples takes a long time, and the others watch it with endless fascination.

Me? Not so much. Born crippled and a runt, I've had to struggle long and hard for my position at the dead bottom of the hierarchy. I've never fought anyone, because there is no honor in making me submit, no rank to be won by beating the runt.

Ronan, on the other hand, is big and was once strong enough to be the presumptive Alpha. But he is, as they say, weak of marrow. With no determination or perseverance, he has become filled with fat and drink and resentful dreams of life as it is lived on Netflix. His nose is cold and wet when he's human and hot and dry when he's not.

"He's not much, our Ronan." That's what Gran Drava said to me. "But he's a male and…"

She gave me one more sniff before leaning back on the sofa in the Meeting House, where the 14th Echelon was gathered for her inspection. Her eyes and back are failing, but her sense of smell and her knowledge of

Pack bloodlines are not. "And he isn't within the pro-hibited degrees of consanguinity."

So because he is weak of marrow and I am weak of body, we find ourselves together at the bottom of the 14th.

When the Pack Alpha eventually turns our way, I nudge Ronan, who doesn't stand until I bite him. Finally, he hobbles up, looking at me mournfully with his greasy eyes. Nobody much pays attention as we approach the Alpha. They're all too busy debriding each other's wounds and sniffing new companions' bodies.

John's paw hangs lazily over the edge of a granite outcropping shot through with mica that shimmers slightly in the moonlight. It seems like a nervous eter-nity, waiting for John's pro forma nod of approval.

It doesn't come. Instead, he pulls himself up, one leg at a time, until he reaches his full height. The paler fur of his belly shimmers as he shakes himself and jumps down to the damp sod.

His nose flares as he approaches us. Anxiously, I push myself closer to Ronan's flank. John presses his muzzle between us, shoving me away. He sniffs the air around Ronan and starts to slap at Ronan, each hit of his head getting harder until Ronan stumbles backward.

John bares his teeth, snarling.

Ronan blinks a few times as though he is just waking. He wavers unsteadily, trying to comprehend the simple gesture that was all it took to exile him from the protec-tion of our law, our land, our Pack. The sentence that forces him into a life wandering from Pack to Pack searching for a place until he dies in a puddle of blood and/or vomit, like most exiles do.

I scuttle to John, my head and stomach scraping the

grass, my tail tucked between my legs, submitting into the earth not because I care about Ronan, but because if he leaves, then I am a lone wolf. There's an old saying that lone wolves are the only ones who always breed, their children being Frustration and Dissent. That's why they are given over to their echelon's Alphas to be their servants, their *nidlings*. A *nidling* has nothing, is nothing. Even at the bottom rank, you're paired with someone who is just as shit a wolf as you are, so at least at home, you don't have to submit. But the *nidling*'s life is one of endless submission.

John snaps at me, then at Ronan. I roll on my back, my eyes averted, whimpering. But since he's made up his mind, no amount of groveling is going to make any difference. John wants Ronan gone. He stands erect, leaning over Ronan's now-shivering body, and a low growl emerges from deep in his chest. Any second now, he will attack.

Ronan backs away, shell-shocked. He stops for a moment, still looking hopefully at John, until the Alpha lunges forward. The exile trips over his own feet as he turns to go.

He doesn't even bother to look at me.

John stays alert, watching until Ronan lurches into the dark forest. He listens a moment more to be sure the exile is truly gone before he howls and signals an end to the *Dæling*. The newly reordered 14th finds their pairs and their places behind John. I'm all the way at the end, where I'm used to being, until our Alpha, Solveig, runs back and, with a growl, reminds me that I am to follow her and her companion, Eudemos, the pairing who now control my life. I take up my place behind them, my tail dragging between my legs.

Stopping suddenly with one paw raised, John focuses on a sharp bark in the night. It is a warning from a perimeter wolf. Probably signaling that a hunter has trespassed on our land. Wolves will be gathering around the interloper now, following the hunter at a silent distance. As there's nothing like an honor guard of seething wolves to scare off prey, hunters usually give up pretty quickly.

John lifts his head, his nose working hard as he looks toward the north woods. I can smell it too. Over the fragrance of fecund grass and swollen water and bog and sphagnum come the subtle scent of a half-dozen Pack and the overwhelming stench of salt and steel and blood and decay.

With a quick snap of his jaws, our Alpha sends our echelon's fastest wolf back to Home Pond for older reinforcements. John runs around to the north flank, closely followed by Solveig and Eudemos and the other newly minted leaders of the 14th. His forefeet are light on the damp grass, his hind legs ready to jump. Hunters don't come this far in. *This* is past the high gates and barbed fences and threatening signs and the trackless tangle of ancient, upended spruce and their young that are the reminders of a violent blowdown ten years ago.

The footsteps are soft and definitely human. Heel, the controlled curve along the outer rim of the foot. The toe barely grazing the grass. It is the footfall of someone used to stealth. I wouldn't have heard it at all, except for the occasional stumble.

Solveig's haunches tighten in front of me.

Finally, a man appears. He blends in with the night, so it is only when he walks into the moonlit clearing that we can see him. Sometimes we say someone has a heart or an ego or an appetite "as big as night."

But this tall, broad-shouldered human is really as big as night.

He pauses for a moment before threading his way through the wolves and lowering his body into the center of the Clearing. He crosses his jeans-clad legs. His feet are bare. Aside from a dark jacket, he has only two things:

A gun and a gaping hole in his stomach.

Chapter 2

"I KNOW WHO YOU ARE, AND I WON'T HURT YOU," the stranger says in a voice that is cool and hard and perfectly calibrated to reach even to the outer ring of the wolves who were following him. "This." His hand caresses the gun. "This is just for protection."

As soon as John gives a nod, I start forward. When I am wild, I am a strong tracker. More importantly, I am expendable. If the man shoots me, then we will know what he's up to. He is armed and will kill many of us. And though he will eventually die, the careful ordering of our Pack will be undone.

His eyes lock on mine, and he slowly moves his hand to his knee so I can see that he's not touching the gun.

I creep close, starting with the wound. He has been clawed and not by one wolf; I can make out at least three different scents. They circled him and came at him from different directions.

For us, only the most heinous crimes warrant a disemboweling. But the *Slitung*, flesh-tearing, is a solemn ritual, not butchery. Every muzzle must be bloodied, so the tragedy of a life that we have failed is borne by all.

This man may not look it, but he is extraordinarily lucky. There is damage to the fascia and muscles, and while there is blood—and a lot of it—there is not the distinctive smell of a gut wound. Those things are hard to repair and go septic quickly.

Lifting my nose to the spot behind his ear, I almost gag at the overwhelming human smell of steel and death. But before I recoil, I catch the scent of something else. Snorting out air to get a clear hit, I try again. It's faint but it's here—crushed bone and evergreen—and it's wild.

There's only one creature in the world that smells both human and wild, and it is the creature we fear most.

Shifters are like us, but not. We can all of us change. But *we* cannot always change back. We are the children of the Iron Moon, and for three days out of thirty, we must be as we are now. It doesn't matter what you're doing—putting coolant in the backup generator, coming back late on the Grand Isle ferry (retrieving the car required some explaining)—Death and the Iron Moon wait for no wolf.

It is our great strength and our great weakness. We depend on one another. We support one another. Without the Pack, we are feral strays, trapped in a human world without words or opposable thumbs.

Shifters can always shift. They are opportunists. They used to change back and forth as it suited them, but now that humans are top predator, it suits them to be human. Like humans, they are narcissistic, self-delusional, and greedy. But they can scent things that humans can't, and they are dangerous hunters.

They know what we are, and in these past centuries, our numbers have been decimated by Shifters coming upon a Pack during the Iron Moon and slaughtering us with their human weapons.

There is something else, though, about this Shifter's deeply buried wild. Something more familiar than simply wolf. Moving close to where the scent is most concentrated, I suck in a deep breath.

"Found something you like?"

Snarling, I back awkwardly away from his crotch, but moving backward at a crouch makes my bad leg turn under, and the pain tears through my hip. Bone grinds against bone, and I stumble.

"A runt *and* a cripple?"

I flash my fangs at him. I may be a runt *and* a cripple, but I am still a wolf, damn it. John and Solveig and Demos sniff at my muzzle and immediately know what I know. Ears flatten, fur bristles, forefeet are planted, haunches bend under, and a menacing rumble spreads through powerful chests.

"Yes, my father is Shifter, but my mother is…was… Pack-born. Mala Imanisdottir."

I knew it. I knew he smelled familiar. John sniffs my muzzle again, scenting for proof of his ancestry.

"I challenged our leader, and I lost. I escaped his first attempt to kill me, but I won't escape another." His mind seems to wander, and then, with a real effort, he focuses again. "My father told me to escape. Find you. You are my last chance."

John looks out across his Pack, now bolstered with the older echelons. He snaps at the air over one shoulder and orders the Pack home. Mala or no Mala, this is the Great North Pack, not a sanctuary. The enormous Shifter will bleed out, eaten by the coyotes who even now are signaling to each other that there is something big and dying. They won't come near us, but as soon as we are gone, they will move in.

Solveig growls softly, calling me to heel. I hadn't

realized how far ahead they had gotten. I stumble after her with my tail between my legs.

"The runt," the man calls between panted breaths. "She's not mated?"

Without turning, John stops.

"My mother said that the Pack would accept a lone wolf if there was another willing lone wolf." A short cough tightens his face in pain. "She told my father," he says. His skin is graying, and the circles beneath his eyes are so dark. "Before she died. She told my father."

There is some truth in what the Shifter says. *Some.* Unfortunately, none of us has the paper, the pencil, the voices, or the hands to sit him down and explain the complexities.

John motions me toward him and rests his head on my shoulders. He's so huge and comforting. His smell is the smell of home, and I can't imagine not being surrounded by him. He represents protection from the outside and order at home.

He butts me lightly with his nose. The stranger doesn't know the complexities, but I certainly do. The choice is mine. If I return with my Pack, the stranger will die and I will be a *nidling.* As low as it is, I will have my place within the Pack.

But if I stay…

Then I am gambling that this Shifter and I are strong enough to fight for—and win—a *full* place in the Pack. It is a gamble, though, because if we can't, both of us are exiled. He will be no worse off, but I will career from bad decision to bad decision, ending up in the same damn puddle of blood and/or vomit as Ronan.

The enormous Shifter weaves in our midst. I run back

and sniff at him. He's lost a lot of blood, but he looks really strong, and with a little help, he should make it. He lifts his head, and for the first time, I see his face. He's darker than John's mate, Evie, but where her eyes are pure black, his are black shot through with shards of gold.

He whispers something that even my sensitive ears must strain to catch.

"Runt?" he murmurs. "I don't want to die." Then he collapses into the grass.

The Pack is already filtering out of the Clearing. Demos gives a curious sniff of the prone body and snarls. He swings his fat head, hitting my backside, telling me to get a move on.

Maybe if he hadn't done that, I'd have crouched down and followed. This is my world, and the Pack is my life, but I haven't put this much work into surviving only to spend the rest of my life obeying every snarky whim of a thuggish half-wit like Eudemos.

I nip at his ear, the universally understood signal—at least among Pack, it's universally understood—to go fuck yourself. I shake out my back and straighten my tail and walk as tall as I can back to the Shifter. I lay my head across his shoulder.

John takes one look along his flank and starts to run. The Pack follows quickly until they are nothing but the occasional flicker of fur among the spruce.

Except for the low, slow plaintive cry of the loon on Clear Pond, it is silent. Then comes the reverberating howl signaling that John is home. The wolves stationed at the perimeter take up the howl.

"We are," they say.

I'd cry if I could, but I can't. I'd howl if I could, just to say *Me too*, but I can't.

All I can do is nudge the huge mound collapsed in a damp hollow of the Clearing. Early fall nights in the Adirondacks are too cold for humans, especially lightly clothed, partially eviscerated ones. It takes a few nips to find a good purchase on his jacket, then I lock it between my jaws. I don't like the plastic taste, but I pull anyway. In fits and starts, I move his inert bulk to a slight rise where it's not so damp, but there's no way that either the jacket or I are going to be able to make it much farther.

After pulling on the jacket to cover as much of his body as possible, I curl around him, giving him the warmth of my body.

The moon shines down on the Clearing. This is a place for a Pack, not for a single wolf on her own, and it feels exposed and huge and empty. Not to mention damp.

A coyote creeps closer, picked out by the moon. I jump up, straddling the body with my shoulders hunched and my fur bristling so I look larger. I growl in the way John would—or Tara or Evie or Solveig or any of dominant wolves would—and hope.

The coyote hesitates and then retreats. I settle back, covering more of this man's big body with my smaller one. As I drop my head to his broad chest, a warm sigh ripples through my fur.

I wish the loon would shut up.

Chapter 3

THE DULL, STEADY PRESSURE AGAINST MY CHEEKS WAKES me at the same time as the yellowthroat's high, insistent call. *Widdiddy, widdiddy, widdiddy, wid*. That pressure is the first sign that the Iron Moon is finished with me. My upper arm stretches and the muscles at my shoulder blades tighten, broadening my chest. As I shake out my hands, the metacarpals shrink and the forearm lengthens and the fur disappears, sucked back in, until nothing is left but a pale, almost-invisible dusting. A few loose silver hairs dance away in the breeze.

The hip with the tendon that is too short pops back into place. It hurts at first, but as I walk the Clearing, the last remnants of pain and numbness subside, and my leg moves freely again.

Despite the pain and the bum leg, no one loves being changed more than I do. I love the freedom and the crush of sounds and smells. I love the close and quiet connection to my Pack. I love the stillness of the cold Adirondack night constrained by nothing but my own fur.

I'd change back to wolf right now, if I wasn't in such desperate need of fingers and a voice. I feel the heat emanating from the Shifter and poke around the wound. Too much of the gash is clotted by the material of his jacket, and peeling it off will reopen the wound. But still, I can't feel new bleeding.

I need saline. And bandages and suture and antibiotic.

Probably lidocaine, because humans are cowards, and Tristan says the bigger they are, the louder they scream when they see a needle. I need blankets and clothes.

"Hey. You," I whisper.

A short breath.

"Hey! Wake up."

One eye opens slightly, then the other.

"Runt?" he croaks and then, "Water."

Of course he would need water. I pat at my naked hips like I might magically find a pocket with water in it. It'll take me at least an hour to make the run to Home Pond and back, and that's too long.

His jacket tasted like plastic and is probably waterproof. I start to pull at a sleeve; since much of the front is shredded, I just need to tear hard at the back. Holding the neck still, I continue the rip along the sleeve.

"Whatyoudoon?" he slurs, trying to move my hand.

"Getting you some water."

He protests weakly.

"I'll be back in a second."

Clear Pond is big and smooth and fed by innumerable springs. Stretching out on the overhanging rock, I fill the sleeve with the clear water away from the weedy edges. It won't hold much, but it's the best I can do. As soon as I siphon the few ounces left into the Shifter's cracked lips, he passes out again.

I know I have to move fast, and moving fast requires reversing the whole process I went through earlier. Taking back the pain that will shoot through my hip and leg, because even a three-legged wolf is faster than a human.

Heading from Clear Pond toward the mountains, away from the low-lying damp, I take the shortcut up through the tangled forests of young spruce and fir and paper birch. The early autumn sun is swept before dark clouds, and one of the frequent short rains starts in with its thick drops that make the bald hardpan slippery. I skitter down until I reach the mix of maple and beech behind Home Pond.

Long time ago, before the Pack was lulled into a false sense of security, an earlier generation dug a long tunnel that led from the basement of the Great Hall into the forest. In case of emergency. Gran Sigeburg told me about it, as she rambled on about a long-ago party thrown by her echelon and how all the juveniles escaped from the Alpha's fury through the tunnel. I think the moral of her story was supposed to be that you can never escape a furious Alpha, but the tunnel was the part that stuck.

I'd found the end of the tunnel in the root cellar, but the other end was blocked. I scratched through the ferns and duff until I found it and came back with hands and an ax and hacked away the spruce root that had grown over it. Like all children, I liked the idea of sneaking and used the tunnel from time to time to get in and out of the Great Hall. Then I got older and more persnickety about spiders, and since nobody really cared where I was or when, I figured I might as well just use the damn door.

There were two spruces: one big one and a small one. If you crouch down low like I am now, the tip of Whiteface is centered between them. I scratch around in the forest litter until I feel the hollow scrape of wood.

I didn't remember the space was so narrow, but I was smaller then and perhaps the taproots that broke through the tunnel roof were a little smaller as well. As soon as I get to the cellar, I squeeze through the light trapdoor and lay myself down, rolling my shoulders and letting the change twist through my body once more.

The doors to the storerooms in the basement are close together in the narrow hallway. As soon as I open the broad wooden door of dry storage, I hear the hum of the dehumidifiers. The open metal shelves are filled with carefully marked bins of clothes. Popping open one of the smallest ones, I find a pair of athletic pants, a Henley, and a hoodie for myself. The Shifter is huge, but so are my people. In one of the several boxes marked *XXXL* (and *Tall*), I find a pair of sweatpants, a Big & Tall flannel shirt, a bright-red sweatshirt, and a bulky anorak. Not stylish and not much, but it'll have to do because the clothes already take up more than half of the big backpack.

Dried apples, ground corn, matches, miso, protein bars, lentils, hazelnuts. Then cooking equipment, a collapsible water carrier, a tarp. I also nab the single bedroll, a sleeping bag, and the pop-up tent the pups use when they play Human.

How do they do it? The humans, I mean. I lasted about five minutes inside the nylon sleeping bag, surrounded by that shell of polyester and silicone, before I bolted out, falling to the grass, my feet already lengthening.

Before I leave the basement, I pull the hoodie tight around my head to hide my telltale hair. I am a silver. Silvers aren't common, but we aren't rare either. It just means a wolf with light underfur and pale gray fur on top. In skin, their hair tends to be dark blond or light brown.

When I'm wild, one tendon stays too tight and cripples me. When I take on skin, my hair stays silver. Just so I never forget who and what I really am.

Gran Tito is up early as usual. His nose has started to fail, but I still steer clear of him as I make my way to the med station behind John's office. Two hospital beds with bedside monitors, ventilators, a freestanding anesthesia system, ultrasound. Mobile storage units are loaded with drugs and first aid necessities. We're strong and resistant to illness and heal quickly, but if we get injured, we can't go to the hospital. Everything about us—our lung function, blood composition, urinalysis, resting heart rate, *everything*—screams alien.

Two big bottles of saline wash, gauze, erythromycin, absorbable suture, lidocaine. Electrolytes.

Someone has started the coffeemaker, which means the Pack will be up soon. Moving carefully out the front door of the Great Hall, I sling the backpack on and make a headlong rush deeper into the trees.

By the time the door closes, Home Pond is behind me.

I've never walked this far in my skin. I'm slow on the path and even slower when I leave it, and at least one of my two feet snags on every bush and root and rock and fallen tree. At Clear Pond, I heave myself into the water, panting like a hunted elk before filling up the water carrier.

The Shifter doesn't wake up easily, even when the saline sluices over his torso and his jacket. I give him water and wait until I'm sure he's awake to give him a tablet the size of a water bug. I add electrolytes to the rest of the water because if he gets the heaves, he'll vomit up the antibiotic.

I cut away at the gore-glued jacket, pouring on more saline and letting it soak, while I wash my hands with chemical cleanser and pull on the gloves.

"You the bitch from last night?" he croaks.

The jacket is still sticking, so I drench it with more saline.

"I said, you the—"

What he says next silences the birds for miles. He curls into a fetal position, his teeth grinding audibly.

The torn and bloody remnants of the jacket hang slack in my hand. *Wow. What happened to you?* Because ripping away the remains of the jacket has exposed not only the explosion of claw marks underneath, but also the vestiges of a whole lot of other savaging. He's got neat slices, like knife cuts, on one forearm. Three small craters at his left shoulder. I'm guessing a "hunting accident" like Sofia's "hunting accident" from twenty moons ago, when a hunter shot her twice. It was no accident, but we continue with the fiction because the pups already have so many nightmares about humans.

But the scariest marks? They're claw-made. Most Pack have scars of some sort, though John has asked that we avoid muzzles during fights, because gouged eyes and clawed cheeks make potential Offland employers nervous.

Still, our scars are not like this. They're not like this tattered collar at the base of his throat. One of the tears stretches all the way through his nipple.

The worst thing is I can tell they are old and he isn't.

"What…what wolf would do that to a child?" It's no more than a voiceless whisper to myself. He shouldn't have heard, but I think he may have.

"Do me the favor of losing the tragic face, runt." His voice isn't angry, just brusque and cold and quiet.

"Turn over," I say and start to pour chemical cleanser into his wound. "I will not answer to 'runt' or 'cur' or 'dog' or 'bitch.' Now, if you feel like playing nice, I can give you a local. If you don't, that's fine too, and I'll stitch you up raw. I'll warn you, though: I've helped doctors do this, but it'll be my first time doing it myself."

He licks his cracked, dry lips and with one hand gestures toward the wrapped lidocaine syringe I hold in my hand. I inject it in a circle around the wound.

"You were really lucky."

"This is lucky?"

"Well, what I mean is, something like this? There's always gut damage. But not here. There was some hemorrhaging, but that's already stopped."

"I heal quickly," he says, craning his neck to watch me cut the flat plastic container holding the suture and the needle. Starting with the muscle, I set the clamp. He lies back down and stares at me. I'm not used to being noticed, and it makes me uncomfortable. It's one of the perks of being a subordinate wolf. As long as you do your work and don't get in the way, nobody pays attention. Not like the dominant ranks, where someone's always watching to see if you're getting sloppy or slack or stupid and it might be the right time to take you down.

Hard to tell what he's thinking. Leonora, who teaches human behavior, says humans rely on words more than "nonverbal cues," but that we should still be careful because what humans say isn't always what they mean. Humans convey disapproval in many ways, she says. Unfortunately, none of them are as clear and expressive as carnassials slicing through your calf.

"Can we start over?" he finally says. "What's your name?"

"Sil," I say, holding the skin up with the clamp for a new anchor knot. "You can call me Sil."

"Sill? Like windowsill?"

"No, Sil like Silver."

His hand moves up to a silver strand that worked its way loose from the messy knot at the back of my head. He has long, strong fingers, smooth dark skin, and kempt nails. Not like my own rough, pale hands crisscrossed with scars from downed hawthorn branches and weasels that didn't want to be eaten.

"It's short for Quicksilver. It was meant as a joke. Irony."

"Well, *Quicksilver*, you can call me Ti."

"Tie? Like tie-dye?"

"No, like Tiberius."

"Pffft. No irony there."

"Nope. None at all," he says, his voice tight and fading. "Are we almost done?"

"Two down. Only four more to go."

"You know, if it's all the same t'you," he slurs, "I was thinking I mi' pass out."

And just like that, he does.

Fever, blood loss, shock, and cold all conspire to keep him passed out through the last stitch and the bandaging. I tape the edges of the dressing. This is going to leave a big scar. Another big scar.

When I smooth out the tape, my fingers stray beyond the edge of the tape. I pull back quickly at the warmth of his skin against mine. Sitting with my arms wrapped around my legs, I prop my cheek on my knees and watch the slow up and down of his chest.

When we first became *schildere*, I'd asked Ronan if

I could touch him when he was in skin, because lots of *schildere* already had and I'd been prey to so many longings. Not for Ronan, but longings nonetheless.

"Remember what Leonora said when we asked her if humans had *schildere*?" he asked when he'd finished laughing.

I did remember. Still do. Leonora had thought for a moment and then told us that the closest thing humans had to *schildere* is buddies. "Buddies," she said, "will hold the bathroom door closed for you if the lock is broken.

That's what we are, Ronan had said, still chortling. *Buddies.*

I didn't like the word. Sounded silly and childish. I like the Old Tongue better. *Schildere*, a shielder.

But supposing the Shifter feels that the only thing a crippled runt is good for is holding the bathroom door closed when the lock is broken? Then what? I will have passed up my chance to touch him.

So, I do. I touch the scarred ring at the base of his neck. Those lines are thick and rough. No one cared for them, and they healed badly.

I touch the sweep of high cheekbones and soft, dark cheek that blends into what was probably once a neatly cropped beard and mustache but is now a little wild. I touch his full lips, leaning down until I catch his warm breath against my own mouth.

This man's body is tough and sinewy, packed hard into his taut skin. My fingers tease across, down to the contours of his chest, crisscrossed with veins that give way under the gentle pressure of my fingers and muscles that don't.

I stop at his waistband. We are always told not to

smell or touch humans here, because that is considered bestial. I touch him, feeling him warm and solid and thickening through his jeans, because what am I if not a beast?

I hold tighter until a growl, like a dreaming wolf, rattles in his chest.

Covering him with the open sleeping bag, I go about shaking the pup fur out of the tent. With a good-size stone, I pound in the stakes, set up the tent, then stretch the bed pad across the top so that it can air out.

Between all the fur and the partly gnawed cheese chew, it smells like childhood.

Chapter 4

IT'S DARK WHEN TIBERIUS WAKES UP. I HAND HIM A BOTTLE of icy spring water laced with more electrolytes and poke the embers of the fire I built close by. I add cornmeal and dried cranberries and ghee and maple sugar to the water in the pot hanging from the green aspen branch I angled into the ground.

He holds the sleeping bag tightly around himself and shivers.

"I brought you some clothes." I toss him the four enormous things that were taking up so much space in my backpack.

He pulls on the flannel shirt and the hoodie, then puts his hand to his blood-crusted jeans and looks at me.

I cock my head.

"Well?" he says.

"Well, what?"

"A little privacy?"

"For what?"

"I was in kind of a hurry when I left."

"Yes?"

"I'm not wearing underwear."

"Yes?"

"I will be naked."

"So? We are all naked when we change."

He stares at the sweatpants in his hands, pulling at the loose ends of the waistband ties.

"Phase? Turn? Shift?" I continue. "What do you call it?"

"*We* call it going to the dogs. It's something we avoid at all costs."

"*What?*"

"*We* are not like you. We don't run around sniffing each other's asses and pissing on trees. We drive and talk and shoot and make money. *We* are human. *I*," he repeats firmly, "*am human*."

Dumbstruck, I turn away, giving him his stupid human privacy.

"But…but…you *can* change, right?"

"Hmm? Can I? Yeah. Probably."

Probably? It never occurred to me that someone who could change wouldn't. Every minute I'm in skin, I can't wait to get out of it. When we are in skin, we are *anfeald*. Single fold: one and singular. Alone. But when we are wild, we exist beyond the limitations of our poor bodies and weak senses. We are ourselves, but we are also part of the land and the Pack. We are *manigfeald*, manifold and complex.

"You really have no idea what you got yourself into, do you?" I say to the fire, listening while his jeans come off in a cloud of dried blood. I can hear him hop from foot to foot.

"My mother died when I was born." He regains his balance quickly, and cotton swishes over skin. "But she'd tried to convince my father to join the Pack. She'd told him that all you needed was to mate a lone wolf and—"

"*Ohmigod*. You have no idea. None. I hardly know where to start."

I really *don't* know where to start. So I start at the

beginning with our first Alpha. She knew that the natural Packish resistance to outsiders would eventually breed weakness. Strength, she said, could only come from fresh bloodlines, which meant taking new wolves from disintegrated packs. Some other Packs do now, but we were the first. And we are still the strongest.

We don't make it easy. A lone wolf can easily disrupt our carefully constructed order, so one of our wolves has to be willing to tie their fate to that of the stranger. To be the stranger's *schildere* during the three months when they are considered table guests. Three Iron Moons. That's how long they—*we*—have to prove ourselves worthy of the Pack.

"What's *schildere*?"

"It's… You don't speak the Old Tongue?"

"Unless by Old Tongue you mean French, no."

"It means…" I start, but I can't spit out the word *buddy*. "'Shielder,'" I say. "It means 'shielder.' But here's the thing… The Pack isn't going to bother even taking you as a table guest unless they're sure you can fight. They won't waste time on the weak or cowardly. And our fights are always wild. Fang and claw. Never in skin. Here."

Ti stabs his spoon into his bowl. "What is this?"

"Cornmeal."

He pokes his spoon into the cornmeal. "Any meat?"

"Are you listening? If we lose that fight, we're out, immediately. No three months, no nothing."

"I am listening. It's just that I figure if I have to dress up like a wolf, I should get some meat."

"Fine. Tomorrow. I'll get you some tomorrow. For now, there's cornmeal."

"Why did you agree to do it, then?" he says after he's taken a few bites. "If you have so much to lose?"

"Because I was going to be a *nidling*. Lone wolves are given to the Alphas as servants. Keeps us busy and out of trouble, but it's as close to being nothing as you can be without actually being dead. There aren't many. Mala was one. That's why she ran away. Do you want this?" I offer my untouched bowl. "I'm not really hungry."

He scrapes the bottom of his own bowl before taking mine.

"I guess I figured that one chance at living was better than a lifetime of being alive."

I think I am going to be sick.

Late into the night, the Shifter struggles with a tent and a sleeping bag that aren't really meant for his big body. His bangs and curses are accompanied by the slithery scraping of nylon against nylon that sets my teeth on edge. No good wolf likes to sleep in a clearing anyway, so I limp off to the edge of the woods and find a nice spot behind the bleached-out cedar stumps. I turn round and round among the dry, fragrant pine needles. Curling my muzzle on my front paws, I fluff my tail across my nose and close my eyes.

Doesn't matter that it's still black as night. It's not the light that tells me to wake up. Honestly, I don't know what does. A bird, maybe. When the temperature reaches dew point. Pull of the moon, whatever. I wake up when I'm supposed to give the Shifter his medication.

I feel the *sproing* in my neck, the pleasant pressure as my shoulders widen, the pain in my hips, and the ticklish rearranging of pastern and forepaw. I need fingers, because the clindamycin comes in a wolf-proof bottle that's in the backpack on John's rock. The same backpack that is currently being rifled through by the biggest mutant coyote I've ever seen.

At least that's what I think until the wind changes and I'm hit with the stink of Baileys and kibble.

John gives exiles money so they can try to find their way to another Pack. Make a fresh start somewhere else. Preferably somewhere far, far away. Somewhere so far away that there's no chance of coming across them scrabbling for food on top of the Alpha's rock. But knowing Ronan, he didn't go far, far away. He probably didn't go any farther than the Akwesasne Casino in Hogansburg.

"What are you doing here?"

He stumbles backward and starts to snarl before he realizes who it is. He turns his back on me and continues rummaging through the backpack.

I jump up and grab the straps. "Get off," I snap, dragging at the bag and Ronan—at least until the bit of fabric he was holding on to tears and he loses his grip. When he grabs at it again, he misses, something he wouldn't have done if he hadn't been drinking.

The big lunk growls and snaps at me, a fang tearing into my forearm. It's just a scrape, but I punch him for being a fool.

He jumps at me, pushing me down, claws and pads rough against my bare skin. I'm not afraid, because while Ronan may be much bigger than I am, he's lazy and a coward. Though now that I think about it, being straddled by a drunk, desperate, lazy coward is a bad time to be in skin.

We wolves have a sick fascination with werewolf

movies. We appreciate the irony that portrays humans morphing into indiscriminate killers. We appreciate the humor of portraying the change in a way that will accommodate human prudishness: wolf men who walk around on two legs with no genitals or genitals *so* tiny and disproportionate that they can be disguised by a wee bit of shadow. Or others who race through forests in shredded form-fitting jeans.

We appreciate the narrative imperative of portraying the change in a way that makes no biological sense—like the guy who starts his jump as a man, and by the time his feet land, he's all wolf. Not a second of transition time, when bones lengthen and hair changes and senses rearrange themselves, leaving you deaf and blind while your gut lurches alarmingly and—if you've recently ingested a lot of beaver fat—very noisily.

There was none of that in-between time when you're half one thing and half another and nothing works together and you're wholly vulnerable.

Just by way of saying that I can't change and have to rely on my poor, fragile human body. I hold Ronan by the neck, to keep his reeking mouth away from me, while I feel the ground behind me with the other, searching for a rock, a stick, a—

Pop.

A crack breaks the silence. Ronan looks down in shock before falling on top of me, a long strand of drool running from the corner of his mouth.

"Oh, for Pete's sake, Ronan!" I jerk my head to the side and push him away. He begins to change, so I know whatever has happened is not mortal.

"As for you..." I jump up and grab the gun from

Tiberius's hand. It twirls through the air in a graceful arc until it lands with a low plop deep in the middle of the bog.

"But—"

"If the Pack finds out that you still have that gun, then you—and me, by the way—are both gone before we've even begun. There are absolutely no guns allowed on the Homelands. No rifles, no handguns, no BB guns. Nothing."

"But..."

"There's a reason we are the oldest and largest pack in the Americas." I check Ronan's chest as the fur retreats and his shoulders pull into a line. There's nothing lower down either as his attenuated feet and legs become pale calves and flabby thighs. Glad to see his cock is as slack and disinterested as ever. "Our first Alpha knew that if we depended on guns when we were in skin, we wouldn't prepare adequately for those days when we weren't. So. No guns. Ever."

"He shot me?" Ronan screams as soon as his voice is back. His hands go to his back. *"He had a gun and shot me!"*

"Oh, calm down. I looked. He missed."

"No he didn't. He shot my tail!" And when he turns around, I see a deep scrape above his coccyx.

"It's nothing, Ronan. You've got to be quiet. John will think it was a hunter, but if he hears you screeching, he's going to send someone to investigate. Did you forget that you're exiled?"

"I did *not* deserve that."

"Yes, you did. You were drunk at your own *Dæling*."

"I was not *drunk*. I had a couple of drinks. John's such a damn prude." Ronan rubs his belly. "Silver, I'm hungry. I need some food. Just a little something until my luck changes."

"And that's your problem, right there. Always waiting for your luck to change." He hiccups and scents the air with 7 and 7 and chimichangas. "Oh, and thank you. That was really foul." I wave my hand desperately in front of my nose. "Why don't you try making your own damn luck?"

Ronan doesn't respond except to convulse with a hacking cough.

"Don't you dare hurl on the Alpha's rock." He looks at me so bleary-eyed and pathetic. "Look, there's a warren in the higher ground above those tamaracks. Some nice, fat coneys—"

"You know hunting's not my thing."

"Maybe you could tell me—because I've never really understood—just what *is* your thing, Ronan?"

"*My thing* isn't here. It's in the real world." He waves in the general direction of south. "I want to be someone who doesn't have to pay attention to the creaky rules and creaky rulers of this tiny shithole kingdom. Elijah does it. Why not me?"

"Elijah?" Elijah Sorensson is the Pack's lawyer *and* the 9th's Alpha. John doesn't like it, because the 9th really needs leadership that isn't Skyped in from New York City between power lunches, but no challenger has been able to unseat him.

"Elijah," I repeat, searching for the protein bars I stashed in the bottom pocket of the backpack, "is dragging the 9th into the mud, *and* he has sex with *humans*."

"That's just a rumor."

"I'm not sure. I've smelled them on him. Here." I hold up two protein bars, which Ronan promptly snatches.

"Maybe sometimes," he says, looking straight at me, "even a human is better than what you can get here." And with that, Ronan lopes toward the woods, blood trickling down his pale, flaccid backside, a protein bar jammed in his mouth.

"Jerk. Fortunately, you only grazed him."

"Unfortunately." Ti slides his hand under his sweatshirt. "If I'd been a halfway decent shot, it'd be me eating those protein bars."

He starts to scratch at his wounded side.

"Don't do that. You're going to open it up again," I say, but his hand emerges from under the shirt with a blood-flecked bandage.

"It itches." He lifts his shirt and looks at the aster-shaped scarring perforated with stitches.

"Jeesh. You really do heal quickly."

"I'd heal faster if I had some real food."

―――⁓―――

I may not be the greatest hunter, but I am patient and observant. I head for that warren of fat coneys in the higher ground beyond the tamaracks. Rubbing my back on the bark of a tree downwind from the warren, I rid myself of a few excess bits of summer fur and then relax upwind.

A wolf with strategy is bad news for bunnies, and I catch two.

Batting at the foot sticking out of the sleeping bag, I wait until he shimmies out. I drop his bunny—the bigger, fatter one, mind you—in front of him before I start gnawing on my own.

"What is that?"

I look up at him under my brow. *Duh.*

"I hope you don't think of that as meat."

Of course it's meat. And not just meat, it's an *autumn* bunny, not one of those stringy early-spring bunnies, always getting stuck between your teeth.

A bone crunches between my jaws. Maybe he thinks it's not fresh?

I nose the other one toward him, so he can see it's still warm.

He backs away, and I wonder. Is this why Shifters have that strange, sick humany smell? Maybe they've become carrion eaters too?

With a dismissive scratch in his direction, I lope off, taking my breakfast with me.

"Don't suppose you could hunt up some bacon?" he calls after me.

Chapter 5

TWO BUNNIES ARE MORE THAN I REALLY WANTED, BUT WHEN you kill something, you have to make that death meaningful. I take the second bunny to the pups, who would much rather fight over a still-warm bunny than a spit-covered cheese chew.

Kayla catches me holding open a small backpack, already half-filled with food.

"John knows you've been stealing," Kayla says, leaning against the entrance to the basement. "They smelled you in the med station."

"Hey, Kayla. I've missed you too. I'm not stealing. I'm giving Pack supplies to a potential Pack member."

"If you'd really thought that way, you would've simply asked rather than sneaking."

There's a reason Kayla was picked to become my echelon's lawyer.

When we first settled here, our Alpha decided that we needed specialists to help us deal with the human world. At first we had doctors and lawyers. Now we have doctors, lawyers, engineers, accountants, fund managers, hackers, and more lawyers. Every echelon has at least one. Lawyer, that is. But they're all here to protect us. They work to make sure that every i is dotted, every t crossed, every p and q minded, so that we are never vulnerable.

Anyone who gets a thirty-page contract for the sale of a used coffeemaker is dealing with a Pack.

Luckily, Kayla likes me. She watches out for me. Slightly older and a lot bigger, she always set aside a rib with a bit of meat still clinging to it from the bigger kills.

"So tell me... What's he like? The Shifter. Do they stink like humans even when they're wild?"

"He's still healing, so I haven't seen him wild." Kayla doesn't need to know that he's healed and all I know is that he can *probably* change. My stomach clenches around my bunny breakfast. "But I think...I think Shifters may have become carrion eaters. I brought him a really nice, fat bunny, and he refused to eat it." I put a bag of pistachios in the bag. "He wanted bacon."

"Gross," she says, her nose wrinkled in a grimace, but she leans in closer, sniffing delicately at the air near my ear. "You're receptive. Do you think maybe he'd cover you?"

I ignore her; she's just being a jerk. "Do you know where those dried, marinated tempeh strips are?"

"No idea. But I'm being serious. They're not like us. Tessa said she heard Shifters will even"—her voice drops—"cover humans." She pulls an elastic tie from her wrist and loops it around her thick auburn hair. "I mean if they'll cover humans, they'll cover *anything*."

Funnily enough, I do consider Kayla to be my *friend*.

I finally find the dried, marinated tempeh strips. The ones we use for bacon and grilled cheese sandwiches.

An otter bites down on a bullhead with a satisfying crunch. The red-edged sugar maple gives way to tamaracks that are in that especially beautiful and especially short phase between summer green and autumn gold.

Even when I'm in skin, a lot of animals either run from me or go silent, because whatever I look like, I smell like something that will hunt them.

My hearing isn't great in skin, but under the endless honking of the geese heading to that other home, I hear an unusual sound. Something big is fumbling around in the distance. I can tell it's not running away. Bears will, when they scent us. Probably moose. We're reintroducing them, but John says we're not to hunt them until the population is truly self-sustaining. They've gotten pretty complacent, which is putting a strain on tempers and appetites across the Pack.

But the longer I listen, the more certain I am it's not moose. I think it's bear—and a badly injured one. Clambering up one outcropping, I take off my clothes and fold them into my backpack, then I hang it over the highest branch I can reach. I start quietly and carefully toward my prey.

If its injuries aren't too bad, I will call the Pack. But if it's as badly wounded as it sounds, I will hunt it myself.

Creeping around the bog mats near Beaver Pond is tricky. Never can be sure when you're going to slip right in, which would alert my bear. Once I get close enough, I realize the wound must be mortal—a bolt maybe. It will be a kindness to put it out of its misery.

What bullshit. All I care about is a chance at the blood-rich chewiness of bear heart. Which I will eat all by myself *before* I call the Pack. If I weren't so full, I'd eat a lung too, just because those choice bits are always long gone by the time I get to any kill.

Under cover of a laurel bush, I finally get a good glimpse of my prey across the inlet. It is the size and

color of a black bear, but with the long muzzle, slim
face, pointed ears, narrow torso, and tail of a wolf. His
teeth shine sharp in enormous jaws. His thighs are coiled
muscle above huge paws. His coat is the color of mid-
night and thickening beautifully, like an autumn coat
should. He smells of wild and steel.

Tiberius is quite simply the most glorious wolf I
have ever seen. Or would be, if he were stuffed with
sawdust on a metal armature and mounted in a pret-
tily painted diorama surrounded by glass and sticky-
fingered children.

Here, he is an abomination. His legs are splayed out
to the sides. His head sticks up high like a horse. His
back is curved the wrong way, and his tail drags along
the ground.

"Hey," I yell. "That's beaver water." He looks at me
with those gold-flecked obsidian eyes. "Who drinks
beaver water?"

He makes some peculiar motions with his mouth
before snapping his jaws shut. Then he tries to walk
toward me.

His back legs move forward one at a time until they
meet with his front paws. Then he hobbles forward with
a kind of old-man shuffle. He stops and rewinds and
begins again.

We are so toast.

The little bones in my feet start to lengthen, and I
fall to the ground, my body contorting, the world fading
from my consciousness, but the moment my change is
over, I race around and snip at his flank to nudge one of
his legs farther under him. He bats me with his head and
falls straight to the ground.

I prod him with my nose until he gets up again. Clearly, the first thing that needs to be fixed is his leg position. He stands like a nursling, with his paws wide apart. Makes me wonder when he last shifted.

This time, I swing my head, bumping against his legs. I pull my own bum leg down as far as I can. It doesn't matter that a tearing pain shoots through my hip; I have to be able to show him what a proper wolf stride is supposed to look like, with his legs nearly lined up straight down the center of his chest.

I walk slowly in front of him. Front right paw forward, rear left paw forward, almost kicking the front left paw forward, then the rear right paw. I bark at him, trying to encourage him to move, but he startles and his hind legs wobble and he sits on his tail, mystified. He holds up his paws, first one, then the other, and opens his mouth, his tongue flapping and his gums slapping, like he expects something to come out.

I slump down on a bed of soft moss, watching my life flash before my eyes, followed in quick succession by a roly-poly and an oblivious shrew. I bat at the shrew. They're not particularly good eating, because their spit tastes bad and numbs the tongue, but I can't help myself and bat at it again. And again. And then I'm up on my paws and running around and herding the angry shrew toward Ti. Maybe all he needs is prey to get him up and moving.

He hasn't had much to eat, and I hear his stomach grumble, but he shows no interest in hunting the shrew. Maybe…I hold its hindquarters under my paw and bite off its head, so Ti can eat it without having to deal with shrew spit.

He just stares at me forlornly and then jerks to the side and stumbles away.

What a crappy wolf.

"You've got mouse blood," he says, rubbing at the corner of his mouth, "here."

Peanut butter. Dried apples. "It was shrew." I rub my chin distractedly. I'm sure I packed the bacon.

"You didn't get it. It's on the other side. And there's more here…" He dampens the cuff of his sleeve with water and wipes hard at my lips. Then he stops. "Are all Pack like you?"

"What do you mean?"

He pulls my lip up, revealing the tips of my canines.

"Ah…no. Just me." When they're in skin, Pack look human, and though their teeth aren't always perfect—orthodontia is not really an option for werewolves—they look human. My canines are perfectly appropriate to a wolf, but they somehow forget to change when I'm in skin and remain too long, too sharp, and too feral ever to be mistaken for human.

"Gran Sigeburg always said my leg and my hair and my teeth don't change the way they're supposed to because I was premature and never cooked properly."

I stare at a bag of acorn flour. Why did I bring acorn flour? "And can I ask you something?"

He picks up the peanut butter.

"When exactly did you last change?"

"I don't know *exactly*. A while."

"But this." I sweep my finger around my neck. "And this." I point to the spot on my own body where he now has the aster scar. "Those come from fights with wolves."

"The men who did this"—he lays his hand on his stomach—"had changed so they could track me. I hadn't changed. It wasn't meant to be a fight; it was meant to be an assassination."

Miso. Dried eggs. He doesn't say anything about his neck. Halloumi.

He looks at all the things I've pulled out of the backpack. "Is it that you just don't like meat?"

"You know that's not true. I brought you a bunny this morning." I scratch at my back and yawn wide. "It was nummy. But that wasn't really what you meant, was it? What you mean is, do you have carrion in that backpack?"

"Carrion sounds disgusting, but something that isn't still breathing would be nice," he says.

"Do you really not hunt?"

"Didn't say that."

"But you don't eat what you kill?"

"No."

"Now you see? That…that's just a sin."

"I think," he says, scooping a finger full of peanut butter, "it depends on your perspective."

He pops the peanut butter into his mouth.

"What a human. You kill without eating, talk without meaning, and turn without changing."

"What do you mean turn without changing? What do you think I was doing crawling around on all fours?"

"You believe what you want, but you're not really a wolf. You're just a man in a wolf suit."

I finally find the dinged aluminum bento box. "Here it is. Bacon."

He opens the box and shakes the broken crumbs of dried marinated tempeh strips into his palm.

They were a lot longer when I put them in.

Chapter 6

THE NEXT MORNING, I HAD TURKEY FOR BREAKFAST AND GOT a feather—one of the tricky little undercarriage ones—caught in my throat. Ti drank his coffee and ate gorp and watched me twisting and turning to try to cough it out.

I really don't understand why humans give thanks for turkeys except that they're stupid and clumsy and easy to catch whether you're a sickly Pilgrim or a crippled wolf.

Finally, I give up and change, because the simple act of changing usually causes the things that plague us in one guise to fall off or go away. As soon as I start, the feather is dislodged, and I cough it out easily. I'm blind still, and deaf, but I can feel a broad hand so warm on my naked hip. I try to struggle away, pulling with contorting front paws on the grass, but a strangled mewl of protest is all I can manage.

He keeps feeling the hip until the joint pops up from its crippled position and falls back into my better human arrangement. His fingers prod and push, the pressure painful and a relief in turns.

As the throbbing waves begin to ebb, he puts his hands on his knees and stands up.

"I think it's nothing but a joint that dislocates when you change."

"That's what our doctors said too."

"Then why don't they just pop it back?" he asks, pouring himself another coffee.

"Because if I was whole during the rest of the month, I would be more vulnerable during the Iron Moon when no one could fix it. I have to be able to function this way."

The spoon hits against the enamel cup—*trink-trunk-trink-trunk*—as he slowly stirs in the sugar.

"When are you going to be ready?"

"Hmmph. I'm not even human until my second cup of coffee," he says and takes another sip.

"*That is the whole point.* The Pack thinks you're still healing, but they'll send someone to check on us soon, and they'll see that you're miraculously cured, and then we'll have to fight the Alphas of my echelon, and if we lose against them, you're no worse off than when you started, but me? I've lost everything. Do you hear me? *Everything.*" My breaths have become shorter, and my voice has moved up an octave, dangerously close to the yipping of a panicked fox. "You need to take this seriously."

"I do take it seriously," he says, taking another sip of coffee. "I happen to be a very good fighter."

"*You also happen to be a very crappy wolf.*" I slap the cup from his hand.

As I fall back to the ground, the last thing I see before the change takes my senses is Tiberius staring sadly into the empty coffeepot. While my ears are filled with static and my eyes with the usual dense veil of floaters, Ti puts his coffee-warmed hand on my hip. At first it feels kind of nice, kind of soothing and sensual and…

I bite him. He yanked my leg free of the joint and turned it, so I bit him. Not because it hurt, but because it unleashed a *frigging avalanche of pain.* Pain that leaves me panting and dragging my leg. He scuttles back as

I chase after, snapping at him. Then I stop, because although it is a little numb, I realize that my leg can actually touch the ground. I stretch it out tentatively at first and then more firmly.

I know I shouldn't indulge in this, but maybe just once. So I can show Ti how a real wolf is supposed to move. Cantering around the Clearing, I run into the woods, jumping over branches and blowdown and bushes that I would have had to skirt before.

Running back, I move faster and faster, and when I hit the Clearing, I bound.

Bounding.

It's what wolves do: pushing off with their back paws and diving up into the opalescent sky before falling back to earth on their front paws, then starting all over again. Bounding propels proper wolves over long grasses and thick snow and each other. It sends them high enough so that when they come down, their weight crashes through the crunchy ice into the subnivean caverns of voles, the buttered popcorn of a wolf's winter diet.

I twist in the air and bound some more until the huge, black wolf blunders after me. I bounce against his flanks and nip at his tail and circle his nose with my jaws. I push his tail up. He always forgets about the tail and just drags it behind him like a thoughtless toddler with a blanket.

He keeps on with his slow, measured walking. I sniff at his foreleg and lick at the spot where I bit him. He noses me away. I squat low in front of him, nipping at his muzzle and jumping away. I do it again and again until he finally gets irritated and tries to nip back, and I leap a yard into the air with my perfect legs. When I hit the grass, I churn it up into his face as I race away.

Now he moves faster, coordinating his legs. It's stuttering at first like a pup, but soon he is scrambling after me. He rounds a copse of tamaracks and loses his footing among the fallen needles and worries the warblers. I run across the edge of the bog, but he comes to a stop, staring first at his muck-covered feet and then at me with dejected eyes. He sneezes and licks his nose at the smell and turns once again to the Clearing.

I refuse to let him. I harry him and tease him and force him to chase me and bring him round until he moves not fast, but not slow and spurtive either. Zigzagging through a throttle of spruce seedlings, I settle into a slow trot, because I want him to follow close behind. I make a break for the high sedges and race through right where the big rock juts over Clear Pond.

I'm flying.

Before I hit the water, I hear the scuttle of claws failing to find purchase on schist.

Another, bigger splash hits the water moments after I do.

I paddle contentedly while he rights himself and splutters. But he's so big that when he does right himself, his paws reach bottom, and he bounds toward me until we are paddling flank to flank.

I clamber up on a submerged rock in the middle and lie on my back, my right leg sagging over the side. It's something I do because there's a spring here and the icy water lapping against my hip is usually a relief.

Something struggles to the shore and flops down. I twist my head and shoulders, watching the huge shadow settle in next to the wooden post that holds the bright-orange ice rescue sled. That's how I lose my purchase on the slick rock, splashing into the water. My front paws churning furiously, I head toward him, my nose barely above water. Ti props his head on his front paws.

When I finally make shore, he rolls his eyes.

Even the littlest pup knows not to annoy a wet wolf. Knows to wait until after the shake-off. Our fur carries a lot of water.

Ti tries to retaliate, but he doesn't understand that it's not just the shaking; it's the torquing. I show him how to do it, slowly shaking my hips one way, my shoulders the other, like I'm wringing myself out. He gives it a try, but the force of his powerful shoulders sends his hind legs flying up, and he falls to his side, taking me down too. Struggling to find his footing, he steps on my tail, pinning me down, and then he trips over me, and we end up tangled together. His breaths are shallow like a man. His heartbeat is slow and human too.

Pretending to be winded, I lay my muzzle across his damp, warm fur and search through the carrion and steel for his wild, for that lovely smell of crushed bone and evergreen.

Nearby, someone gives an ostentatious yawn followed by a snap of jaws. Ti looks into the woods. As soon as I see the big, gray wolf with dark markings, I leap up, my own wolfish heart sinking.

Tara is John's Beta. She sneezes and then licks her nose. Ti raises himself to his full height, his legs no longer splayed but pulled into correct alignment under the line of his body. You don't get to be the Great North's Beta by being a coward, but even Tara steps back, disconcerted by his size.

Since she wasn't at our *Dæling*, this is her first

encounter with Ti in any form. She circles us, scenting and growling. She pushes her nose between Ti's legs, checking for the wound that she knows must be healed if he's shifting and swimming.

He snaps at her, and she snarls, straightening her back, her thighs tight, her ruff bristling. Ti plants his front feet, his rear legs pawing the ground. He refuses to lower his eyes. Instead, he shakes his body, torquing faster than I'd shown him so that he sends spray after deliberate spray toward Tara.

She blinks twice, clearing the water from her eyes, and lays her head next to mine. She howls once, waiting for a response before sprinting to the forest.

Ti bumps at me as I head slowly toward the Clearing. What he doesn't understand—and I can't tell him—is that we have been found out, and tomorrow we will have to go home.

When I look back, Ti is sitting on his haunches, his tail splayed behind him, looking at his raised paw. He turns for me to see. It's nothing, just a burr between the pads. Without a second thought, I nip it out neatly with my teeth.

The man in a wolf suit fumbles up and starts back quickly toward the comforts of camp and the fire and the food in packages. He hesitates, looking over his shoulder to make sure I'm coming.

For all sorts of reasons, I wish we had more time.

Does Tiberius know about fire fairies? Doubt it. Doesn't seem like he had anyone to guide him through the pitfalls and marvels of our dual nature. Sad to think that nobody ever told him stories about the mischievous sprites who lull pups into a trance and then dance their incendiary dance in our fur.

Poking the embers with a green stick makes more fire fairies zip into the air, looking for dry fur. There is none here. Just human skin and damp, musty cotton. Maybe it was spending these hours wild, but Ti is actually warm enough. Too warm, he says and pulls off the sweatshirt. His body twists to the side as he pulls it over his head. For just a moment, I see the curved line that leads down from the top of his hip below his waistband. I poke furiously at the embers.

He starts to unbutton the flannel shirt. He makes short work of it, his fingers flying over the buttons. I stare so hard at the fire that the flames dry out my eyes. He lies back, the muscles moving across his hard chest as he does. His body isn't like the ones I've seen in human underwear ads, where men's muscles divide into compartments like egg cartons. Ti's body is thick and burly and threaded with lines marking muscle and tendon and vessel and vein. The scars that decorate his firelight-burnished skin glow like black runes.

We were always taught that fire fairies loved us best and tormented us most when we were wild, but I think maybe they're just as mischievous when we're in skin, because there's a sharp gnawing burn at the join of my neck, at my breasts, and burrowing deep inside my womb.

Tiberius stretches out on the bed pad, cradling his head on his crossed arms. His eyes closed, his chest expands slowly while his nose flares.

"What are you thinking?" he asks without opening his eyes.

Let's see… That I want to lie on top of you and feel

your belly against mine. That I want to taste your mouth.
That I want to tongue your skin. That I want you to
harden and tear into my…

"Nothing."

When he moves his leg, his ankle brushes against my
calf. It's just the accidental whisper of skin against skin, but
there's a reason we fight wolf and fuck human, and it's skin.

I scratch furiously at my leg with one hand and stir
up more fire fairies with the other, sending them flying
into the sky. I make the mistake of looking toward him.
Now his eyes watch me, all black with shards of gold,
like embers rising in the autumn night.

Standing quickly, my hands fisted under the hem of
my shirt to keep it away from my painfully sensitive
breasts, I mumble vague excuses, bank the fire, and then
start for the woods and the cedar stump where I sleep.

At the entrance of his tent, he stops. He doesn't turn
much, just a little, looking toward the overcast night
sky. In this low light, his eyes glow green. Ours do too,
when we're wild and the lucidum in our eyes concentrates even the feeblest light. But it doesn't happen when
we're in skin. Never in skin.

"You know…when you were stitching me up, I had
a dream," he says.

"Really?" I squeak.

"The moon came down from the sky. She touched
me here," he says, rubbing his hand along his bare chest.
"And she touched me here."

He turns to me with those glowing eyes, his hand
settling at his waistband.

I'm already crashing through the forest cover when
he calls out. "I didn't mind."

Chapter 7

As inefficient as it is, we will walk to Home Pond on two legs.

Me, I need nothing more than water, a good cedar stump, and a bunny. But humans... Ack. Humans need tents against rain and clothes against wind and fire against cold and food against hunger and other stuff against other eventualities—and then they need a backpack to put it in and a back to carry it on.

We—I—pack slowly. A slow breakfast. A leisurely wash in Clear Pond.

A howl rumbles across the woods from Home Pond, telling me to get a move on.

I pull on the backpack, and that's when it hits me with all the force of a bull moose that a crappy wolf and a crippled wolf really have no chance against Solveig and Eudemos, and I will almost certainly be exiled, not in three months' time *but now*.

I will never see our land again.

And all I can do is *see* it. It is beautiful: the dark green of the spruce and the occasional early red of the overeager sugar maples, but it still lacks the depth and dimension it has when I'm wild.

I can hear geese and hawks and woodpeckers. But the under-leaf scrabbling of mice and the under-bark burrowing of beetles and the faraway bolting of a rabbit are gone. I can't smell how the sky will change. I can't smell the fear of the squirrel as it races up the tree. In my skin, the rot of the bog stinks, but when I'm wild, I can smell the heady promise of new life inside the decay.

"Did you lose something?" Ti asks, tightening the straps of his backpack.

Too soon, I hear the sounds of home. Wood chopping, a screen door slamming, voices calling, a car starting. Pups mewling and barking and screeching those high-pitched screeches of a trodden tail or a too-hard bite.

I can't help but slow down, straining against the inevitable, like the future is on a leash that I can control.

Voices drop, and the sound of wood chopping stops. Someone shoos the pups inside.

Varya strides toward us, a heavy ax balanced in her hands. She's the one who's been chopping wood, and her skin is slicked with sweat. She sniffs the air warily. Varya came from a Pack that dissolved into chaos under pressure from hunters. She never speaks about what she saw, but she is a stickler for laws and hierarchies.

Others are gathering behind her. Most are carrying something. A rake, a lacrosse stick, a butcher's knife. Those who aren't simply rest their hands on oiled sheaths at their waists.

My people are a wall of strength, the result of genetics and generations of breeding toward power. Every one of them—every male, every female—towers over me and weighs twice what I do.

Ti's expression barely changes. It helps that he's bigger than any of them. His chest slowly expands as he breathes their scent deep into his lungs. The Pack merely sniffs, reluctant to get too much of that almost-human Shifter smell.

With a small flurry of activity, the Pack makes way for a man who is nearly as tall as Ti. His thick chest strains against the worn flannel shirt. He wears jeans and heavy work boots. He is bare-handed.

"The gun?" John asks.

"Threw it into the bog." I carefully avoid the question of who did the throwing.

"Still smells like steel," our Alpha says, rubbing at his nose. "Solveig and Eudemos?" he asks someone over his shoulder.

"They're on their way," Tara responds, coming up from the back.

John nods before lapsing into the uncomfortable silence of waiting. The intimidating stares of the Pack only make that silence louder and make me more anxious.

"So…when were you thinking?" I ask John.

"We have to wait for Solveig. To coordinate schedules."

I nod, trying to look as though I know what it's like to have a "schedule" that must be "coordinated."

Varya taps the poll of the ax in her palm, her eyes boring so hard into Tiberius that I'm doubly grateful when I hear Solveig's fast tattoo coming toward us.

"Sorry, John. I came as soon as I could." She glances warily at Tiberius.

"I don't think we have to wait for Eudemos to get the formalities out of the way." John turns to me. "Silver?"

I push my shoulders back and stand upright, because our rituals may be ancient and formulaic, but they still deserve all the dignity that a runt in a BU Terriers sweatshirt can give them.

"*Solveig Kerensdottir. By the ancient rites and laws*

of our ancestors and under the watchful eye of our Echelon, our Pack, and our Alpha, we, Quicksilver Nilsdottir and Tiberius—

"Wait… Ti, what's your last name?"

"Leveraux."

"Uh, yeah…so *under the watchful eye of our Echelon, our Pack, and our Alpha, we, Quicksilver Nilsdottir and Tiberius Leveraux, seek to add our strength to the Great North Pack and prove ourselves worthy of a place at your table. With fang and claw, we will attend upon you tomorrow at…* What do you think? 2:00?"

Solveig reaches into her jeans pocket. "Hold on a sec." She swipes the home screen on her phone. "I've got a lunch meeting at 12:30. Can we make it in the morning? Like 10:00? No, better 9:30. You know." She shakes her head. "Road work on Route 9."

"Okay, fine, then add our strength to yours and all that and… *With fang and claw, we will attend upon you tomorrow at 9:30.*"

Solveig squiggles her finger across the touch screen, then slips her phone back into her pocket just as Demos lumbers up behind her.

After a whispered conversation, Demos nods. Solveig takes the long way, walking around Tiberius and watching him carefully. He doesn't move. Finally, Solveig says, "Silver" with a nod. "Shifter." As she walks away, she whispers urgently to Demos.

"John?" I look briefly at John and then down again to the area between chin and chest as is right and appropriate when addressing the Alpha. "Since we'll be here tonight and Tiberius"—my voice drops—"isn't comfortable sleeping wild, I was wondering if—"

"Tara?"

"The Boathouse hasn't been closed up yet."

"Fine, use the Boathouse," he says, turning to leave. "But, Silver? You need to get your things out of the juvenile wing."

As soon as he goes, I start to make my way toward the Great Hall. I am small and familiar, and while my packmates don't get out of the way exactly, I am able to thread through the beefy backs and bulging shoulders. They close behind me, blocking Ti, who stands with his thickly muscled chest pushed hard against the wolfish blockade surrounding him.

"*Oh, for the love of…*" I thread my way back, grabbing Ti with one hand and clearing a path with the other. I love my Pack, but sometimes the only thing they understand is an elbow in the brisket.

It's not far to the outlying buildings of Home Pond. That's what we call the pond and the Great Camp of nearly a hundred buildings scattered through the forests around it. Most of those are cottages for paired wolves. Others are work areas, like the Laundry or the Carpentry, but the heart of the Pack is the Great Hall. It is a huge, rambling two-story building of rough wood with a roof pitched high enough to slough off the thick snow of an Adirondack winter.

This is where we have meals when we're not hunting. This is where we watch movies. This is where the pups live once they're no longer nurslings. This is where the Grans, our elders, live too, because it's warmer and the pups need someone to teach them Pack traditions and stop them from eating the banisters.

Until a few days ago, this was where I lived.

I hold the screen door to the Great Hall open for Ti. The inside smells of Pack, of their shoes and muck boots and cheese chews and damp jackets and fur and slobbery rope bones. When the door closes with a loud pop, my heart clenches.

Soon the screen door that protects the entryway from blackfly in the summer will be replaced by a solid storm door that will protect us from the shattering winds of winter.

The next door leads straight into the Great Hall itself. It's huge, with a high cathedral ceiling, but I've never really thought about how big it is. To me, it's just home. The walls glow warm in the late-afternoon light that streams through mullioned windows and dust motes before making diamond patterns on the log walls' irregular surfaces. And though those logs were peeled more than a century ago, the scent of cedar is still there.

At the far side is the enormous stone fireplace, flanked by huge piles of wood and a big basket of kindling. Its grandeur is offset by the shabby plaid sofas at either side. No point in replacing them because the pups are always scampering across them, picking loops in the upholstery with their untrained claws and shedding uncontrollably in the summer.

Graceful birch trunks support the branch-banistered staircase that leads to the children's quarters and the juvenile wing and where, until a few days ago, I spent my entire life.

Gran Jean stops me.

"Yes?"

Gran Jean's known me since before my eyes opened.

She taught me how to use the library. She was the one who told me that John didn't like books left splayed. "It's bad for the spine," she'd said.

But wolves have little patience for sentiment. The past doesn't matter; what matters is the position you hold in the Pack hierarchy *right now*. It doesn't matter that once upon a time, when I was snug and secure in my mother's womb, I was the much-anticipated offspring of the Great North's Alpha pair.

Within the past few days, I fell from the 14th Echelon's Kappa to *nidling* and then—*pop!*—I dropped right out of the bottom. I am *fremde*—a stranger, an outsider.

"John said I needed to get my things from the juvenile wing."

Gran Jean eyes me like I'm some opportunistic Chihuahua making outrageous claims to kinship.

"*John said*," I repeat.

"Juvenile wing and then out," Gran Jean says, stepping aside to let us pass.

"Can we grab something from the kitch—"

"Are you Pack?"

"No," I whisper.

"Are you guests of the Pack?"

"No."

"Then no," she says. "Juvenile wing, then out. *That's* what John said."

It still smells like the 14th Echelon, even though we cleaned and whitewashed the rooms before our *Dæling* in preparation for the 15th Echelon who now lives here. Most of my echelon have continued their own stumbling steps toward adulthood either Offland or in cabins. Ronan and I probably would have gotten number 98 or one of the other tiny satellite cabins occupied by the wolves nobody much wants to remember.

Ronan's bunk is empty. Mine has been taken over by Avery. I know this because my old desk now has a purple cup with *AVERY* written on it in yellow swirls. Avery is a very strong, beautiful red wolf with dark mahogany markings, and while I remember her scent, I cannot bring to mind a human face. I've probably never seen her in skin.

Did she have to dump all of my stuff on the floor? There wasn't much: some clothes and a couple of books that belong to me that I have, yes, left splayed, even though it's bad for the spine. It all could have fit neatly on her bed. It's not like she's using it. I can tell by the quarter-bouncing neatness of all the beds that the new juveniles are still sleeping wild.

And now some pup has chewed the thumbs from *both* my mittens.

I toss my stuff into the backpack and then rifle through every drawer and every bag of every juvenile until they have all made at least one contribution to Ti's dinner.

For myself, I will eat whatever the wetlands provide, as long as it's muskrat.

Chapter 8

I STILL SLEEP WILD TOO. THE FASCINATION WITH SHEETS doesn't happen until Pack have spent some time Offland. Usually during college. They come home for the summer and start mumbling something about black-fly, but really they've just gotten used to beds and sheets and pillows for their heads. They wear pj's.

And every summer, some of these wolves in sleep's clothing bunk down in the Boathouse.

The Boathouse has three narrow bays. Two at water level shelter a motley collection of boats: a paddleboat and two rowboats, a catamaran that needs some repairing. Kayaks and canoes hang on the rough-planked walls. Between those bays is a narrow room with a high-pitched roof and shallow clerestory windows. Shoehorned into the back is a tiny shower room that never quite airs out and always smells a little musky.

Next to it under a single small window is the kitchen, though *kitchen* seems like a strong word for a hot plate and a sink. The only thing that passes for refrigeration is the hatch in the floor that opens onto a rusted basket where Offlanders keep their stores of Vernors and A&W chilling in the cold waters of Home Pond.

The furnishings are similarly spare: a functional pine desk, a rocking chair, a couple of old lamps with damp-stained shades, two long pullout beds with sun-bleached cushions, and an ancient warped chest that serves as a footrest and coffee table. Every year, the summer wolves leave piles of summer reading wherever they settle, so there are plenty of new books and magazines.

"Where should I put these?" Ti asks, holding up his little stack of clothing.

Putting the books on the floor, I open the chest/coffee table. He drops his clothes to one side, I suppose leaving room for me. "D'you mind if I take a shower?"

I shake my head. And stare at the empty space in the chest.

I'm not sure there is any point in unpacking. This time tomorrow, I'll just pack it all up again. I will go my way, and this man, the root of my misery, will go his way and—

"What's this?" asks the root of my misery, a bottle in his hand.

"Shampoo?"

"It's *dog* shampoo."

"It's what we use. I know humans like to disguise themselves with artificial coconut and fake freesia, but if you do that here, no one will recognize you."

He takes a long look at the label before disappearing into the shower.

What a crappy wolf.

When he comes out, a towel wrapped around his waist, the steam billows out around him.

"Turn around." He circles his finger in the air. "It's too small in there to get dressed."

I look out the french doors that open onto the dock, with its two big Adirondack chairs and the countless claw marks of summer wolves who race across the wood before launching themselves into the pond.

And the reflection of the man standing naked behind me, briskly drying his shaved head.

The paddleboat creaks and jostles whenever the water is disturbed. The first frost will come before long, and then Home Pond will be covered with what looks like crumpled and smoothed foil.

"Tiberius Leveraux, huh? If I Google you," I blurt out, "what will I find?"

"Nothing." He moves on to his well-muscled arms. "If I Google 'Quicksilver' whatever it was…"

"Nilsdottir."

"If I Google 'Quicksilver Nilsdottir,' what will I find?"

"Nothing. Wolves don't leave traces. Humans do. You say you're human, so I should find something."

"No." I can't tell from the reflection if he's actually grimacing or if it's just the way the light shines from the surface of the pond on the other side of the glass. "Like you, we can't go to doctors or hospitals, so there are no birth certificates or medical records or social insurance numbers. But in every other way—all the ways that count—we are human."

He dries his left calf and thigh.

"What is a social insurance number?"

"Canadian. Like social security."

He moves to his right leg.

"How old are you?" I ask.

"Twenty-seven. How old are you?"

He rubs his back.

"Two hundred seventy moons."

"What's that? Like, twenty-two years?"

"A little more. Did you go to school Offland?"

"We don't have a territory like you do, but yes. I went to McGill. You?"

"No. And…"

He dries between his legs.

"And…and what did you do after?"

"I was in human resources management."

"Is that a job you do for your Pack?"

He hangs the towel over the door. I hold my hand to the window, covering his reflected body.

"Sort of. There aren't enough of us to make a Pack"— soft cotton sweats swish against his just-damp skin—"so it's more like a company that employs a lot of humans."

"And you challenged the head of this company?"

"Not the way you think of it. I didn't want to take over. One day I got sick of it. 'Mongrel' whispered one too many times, and I lost my temper."

He picks up his sweatshirt.

"Why do you want to know all of this now? Why not yesterday or the day before or this morning?"

"I don't know. Maybe because it didn't feel real before and I thought there would be more time. But there isn't. And now I'm here seeing everything I've lived with and I'm about to lose."

"What makes you think we're going to lose?"

He pulls his sweatshirt over his head, and I stare for too long, until his head emerges from the collar and those eyes catch mine, and I shake a little, though I'm not cold. "It's a question," he says, "of who needs it most."

"Needs what?" I think I've lost track of the conversation.

"To win. Isn't that what we were talking about? I need it. Otherwise, I'm a hunted man with no home and no country. Is there a bed?" he asks.

I lift the hand-darkened and tooth-chewed rope handles on one of the benches to the storage with bed linens underneath.

"And what would you do," he asks, "if you weren't here?"

One sheet? Is that what they like? I try to remember what my own unused bed in the juvenile wing looked like. I think maybe there were two. I pull out two, and Ti doesn't seem to blink.

Whenever I've been struck by a worst-case scenario, I've always held out hope for the little Pack on Manitoulin that was so desperate for members it would take anyone, or so the gossip went. No challenges or fights or unmated wolves. When I mentioned it a few months ago to Kayla—casually, of course—she said the gene pool of that Pack hadn't been stirred for over two centuries. "Solid *Deliverance* territory," she said.

With one more jerk, the sofa pulls open into a queen-size bed.

"I'm not strong enough to be accepted into another Pack. I think…I think I'd probably go someplace with, like, *no* people, someplace with musk ox. Have you ever had musk ox? It's supposed to be delicious. Anyway, I'd probably go and turn and never turn back."

"Permanently?"

"Hmm. You know, become an *æcewulf*." But I can tell by the look on his face that he doesn't, in fact, *know*. "All the Iron Moon does is makes us wilder. If we are in skin, it makes us wolves. But if we are already wild, it takes us a step further and makes us *æcewulf*. A real wolf. A forever wolf."

"And you can never change back?"

"That's why it's called 'forever.'"

"Jesus." Ti shakes out the bottom sheet. "Wouldn't you miss it? Being human?"

"I'm not human. I'm in skin. Not the same thing. Anyway, not really." I run my hand along the worn softness of the sheets. "Maybe the way things feel against my skin. Wind. Water. This sheet. It *is* different, and I guess I'd miss that." I hold out one end of the top sheet to him, and his hand slides against mine.

Jerking back from the sharp jolt of his touch, I let go of the sheet. It floats down, almost perfectly covering the bed. I hide my burning face deep in the storage chest. "One pillow or two?"

"Two," he says. He moves with more wolflike grace on two legs than he ever could on four and grabs the single knife from the butcher-block stand in the "kitchen."

A second later, the knife hits the floor. I jerk upright. The still-quivering knife has cut through the neck of a long, striped snake.

"You killed a milk snake?"

Ti kneels down beside the poor constrictor.

"Yes, and you're welcome." He pulls the knife out and turns to the sink to wash it.

"It's a *milk snake*, Tiberius. Probably just sleeping in the sheets. Wow. It's a big one, though. Hope you're hungry."

"What do you mean 'hungry'?" he asks, drying the knife.

"Well, you gotta eat it."

He puts the knife back in the butcher-block stand.

"Are you crazy? I'm not going to *eat* that."

"You've *got* to. We're not allowed to kill anything we don't eat. Pack law."

"I'm not eating a snake."

"*You* killed it. *You* eat it."

"*No.*"

"Fine! I'll do it." It's got to be three feet long, and just looking at it is making my stomach hurt. "You do know that I just ate a whole muskrat, and I don't even *like* snake."

Stripping, I toss the decapitated constrictor over my naked shoulder and march to the honey locust at water's edge to change, because I don't want to have to eat this mess of milk snake *and* clean up the floor afterward.

When I finish with the snake, I pull at the door with my teeth. My claws click across the floor, and Ti looks over the edge of the book he's claimed from the pile left by the summer wolves.

"Did you do it?"

I turn over on my back, stretching my three good legs straight above my distended tummy. I flip over again and turn to the book I'd left on the floor. Lying down, with my paws on either side of the book, I stretch my hind legs akimbo, because the pressure of the cool wood against my belly makes the dull weight of muskrat and milk snake feel a little better.

The page crackles as I turn it with my damp nose.

"Well, Toto," Ti says, scratching his eyebrow. "I do believe we're not in Kansas anymore."

Chapter 9

WHEN I OPEN MY EYES AND PEER THROUGH THE SAPLINGS, TI is standing in front of me in his bare feet, a blanket wrapped around his shoulders. "Hunting dream?" he says.

My leg twitches a few more times from the memory of herding the pregnant cow moose. I flick my tail away from my face and hop up, stretching first my forelegs, then my hind leg, and lurch after him back to the Boathouse.

He crumples up the wrappers from the three Snickers bars he had for breakfast and, after a tiny flick of his wrist, sinks them in the distant trash can.

"You've got to stop pacing."

He lies back on the bed, flipping through an old *Vanity Fair* with damp-swollen pages that had fallen behind the bed. Must be nice to be able to just sit there reading out-of-date magazines without a worry in the world. My claws keep up their syncopated *clack-clack, cli-clack* on the hardwood floor.

"Okay. That's it. I can't take it anymore." He drops the magazine and stretches, pushing one elbow to the opposite shoulder, then reverses the process. "Let's just go."

I lead him on a shortcut through the woods, my leg curled tight against my abdomen, steering clear of the sticks and broken trees that might jostle my foot and send those streaks of pain into my hip.

Fighting is a fact of life in any pack. Someone is always watching for that loss of power or respect that signals the time to make a move up the hierarchy. Or to gain *cunnan-riht*, the right to cover a more viable wolf. Aside from the *Dæling*, when an entire echelon is brawling, we hold our fights in a low palisade of logs about the shoulder height of an adult wolf, hammered in to the ground around a big square of scuffed dirt. It is near enough to the Great Hall that it's a short run to the med station. Far enough that blood doesn't splatter on the woodwork.

It looks like a sand box, except that the inside is shredded by claw marks and the dirt is stained with sprays and puddles of brown.

Ti sits at one of the logs that mark the corners and unlaces his boots. A smattering of Pack watch him with undisguised hostility, but he pays no attention, just stuffs his socks into his boots and places them behind the stump.

In his bare feet, he crisscrosses the packed dirt. Heel, slow curve to the ball, toes. His eyes are closed. I stand outside, staring at the low wall, trying to figure out exactly how I'm going to jump with one leg over the enclosure and not make a complete fool of myself.

"Need a leg up, Silver?"

The idiot Demos laughs to himself as he walks off to change. If John wasn't so fussy about paralyzing injuries, I'd be gnawing through Demos's Achilles tendon right now.

After he walks the entire length of the enclosure, back and forth and side to side, Ti picks up his boots and moves to the rough bench carved from an enormous log that the elders use to watch the fights. Folding his hands across his torso, he stretches his legs out and leans his head back, his eyes lightly closed, sucking in the sun. I plop down beside him, staring morosely.

Eventually, Solveig and Eudemos reemerge, the big wolf with light-golden-brown fur and dark-gray markings along her back and down her muzzle and the barrel-chested, broad-shouldered gray. As the two of them spar, my heart sinks lower and lower, because I don't see how we can possibly win. And Ti...I think Ti may have fallen asleep. I jostle his elbow. If it weren't for the single cautioning finger raised slowly from his crossed hands, I might have thought he was dead.

Any challenge brings a few observers. Usually members of the echelon who are just above or below in the hierarchy come to check out the competition. This is *not* a few observers. It's as big an audience as we had for *The Wolfman*, but without the popcorn and cider slushies.

"Silver, I think we should go get changed now," Ti says, suddenly alert.

I look up at him miserably. I *am* changed.

He walks toward the woods and then signals me to come with him. I hop a few times onto my good hind leg and follow. We barely cross into the woods when Ti starts to talk softly and quickly.

"Eudemos," he says, "is very strong, but inflexible. Once he is in his position, you will not be able to move him, but it's hard for him to move as well. He spent the entire time watching me. He doesn't think you're a threat, but even as you are now, you are more agile than he will ever be. Once we pop your leg back, you just need a little strategy to win. Oh, he always swings his head left to right for any attack. I'm not sure how that's helpful, but every tic is good to know."

I stare after him, one paw suspended midstride, frozen by a tone of faith that is totally alien.

"Are you coming?"

We're almost at the old sap house before Ti decides we're far enough in to change. I start the way I always do with the curling back of my shoulder blades; then, it all flows from there. My rib cage becomes shallower and wider, my spine more rigid, my arms and legs longer. Once I'm in skin, I start to shift easily back to wolf—only this time, Ti's hand is on my hip, warm and insistent and then hot and painful. As soon as I'm done, I trot around, working out the kinks.

I sit back on my hind legs and wait for him.

Ti stares at me, then shoos me away. I bend my head to the side.

"Oh, no you don't. *I* don't like to be watched."

Pffft. I don't *like* to be watched either. And it's not as if I don't know what happens. Like I don't know that his cheekbones will push out from his face and his mouth will turn into a long rip with frilled black edges, and that the end of his nose will tilt up and his ears will migrate to the top of his head and he'll still be in skin, except for some reason for his cock, which will emerge completely sheathed in fur.

"*Will you just go!*" he snaps irritably.

Stalking over to a thick bunch of beech suckers, I lie down with my back to him, while behind me, his big body flops and twists to the dull twang of ligaments and the rusty creak of bones and the rubbery distend of skin, until a breeze through fur tells me that the man is once again wearing his wolf suit.

Ti concentrates on walking with his legs centered

under his chest, like a real wolf, but he's still slow. As we approach the edge of the woods, I curl my leg up against my stomach the way I always have. It's an excuse for our deliberate progress, but I'm also hoping that it will give me a slight advantage when I give up the charade. May not be the most honorable thing I've ever done, but a wolf with strategy is bad news for dummies.

The Pack turns to watch as we break through the underbrush. As always, some are wild, others are in skin. John stands at the front, talking to a juvenile whose name is escaping me in my panic but whose scent I recognize as Finn's son.

Solveig and Eudemos lie near the middle of the palisade, their bodies relaxed but their heads alert, watching.

The pups dart between feet and paws, loved by everyone. Belonging to everyone. John is here to make sure the fight is fair and the laws are obeyed. After each *Dæling*, his hair and trim beard seem a little grayer, and now his beard, at least, is peppered with hair the color of his pale-gray eyes. In my life, I've rarely seen our Alpha without a pup nestled against his broad chest. His scent marks us all and binds us together, but I can't imagine how hard it is to watch a pup you've held and cared for grow into weakness, knowing that for the good of the Pack, you will exile him or her into almost certain death.

One little pup tries to jump from the bench to the palisade for a better look. Anna from the 3rd Echelon picks her up, whispering into her fuzzy ear before sending her toward the back.

Solveig stands suddenly, her hackles rising, usually a sign of anger, but now just an instinctual attempt to make herself look bigger. Because in skin, the Pack-Shifter mix has made Ti as big as any male in the Pack. But wild, he is a monster.

The time comes for us to jump over the palisade. I clear it easily, revealing that my hind leg is whole. Ti catches his back paw as he leaps and ends up coming down hard on his shoulder, muzzle in the dirt.

Solveig and Eudemos look at each other. Ti has barely struggled back up on all fours before Tara gives the low warning growl followed by a sharp yip that signals the start.

Trying to stretch out my leg, I stumble a little. It's not for just for show; my thigh is tight from the effort of holding it in the cramped position. But Ti is right. Eudemos is so used to ignoring me that he keeps right on doing it, watching as Solveig circles Ti, until I slink around behind him and bite deep into his hock.

Now he knows I exist.

When he lands back on the ground, he whips around, growling, and paws the dirt, taking his stance. I see immediately what Ti was talking about. Demos is stocky and barrel-chested and just plants his feet into the ground. Fights are about honor and position. Since I never had any position, and there was no honor in beating me, I never paid much attention to them, but I do know that the point is to pin the opponent down until they submit. Since Demos is impossible to down, I'm not sure he can be beaten. I take another run at him, catching his tail.

It's not considered particularly honorable to resort to feints and retreats, but that's another luxury I'll have to do without. I race in, nip him, and run away. He lunges for me, but now that I've got four whole legs, I'm crazy fast and agile, and with a shift of my hips, all he gets is air.

Maybe Ti is right. Maybe all I need is a little strategy. I just have to figure out what it is, but until I do, I keep biting and running, watching Demos get more and more frustrated as he shuffles around the enclosure.

I hear a sharp intake of breath from a juvenile nearby and make the mistake of looking toward Ti and Solveig.

Ti has stumbled again, and Solveig lunges. If she'd been tentative earlier, she's not now. Ti is having trouble turning in the tight space and trips across his front paws. His tail drags in the dirt behind him like a deadweight, instead of the graceful counterbalance it is.

Pain stabs into my shoulder, my momentary distraction having been enough for Demos to sink his teeth there.

I try to pull away, but his powerful jaws clamp tight on a mouthful of skin. One good twist, and he'll have me down.

Then I think what Tristan, our doctor, always says: if it doesn't shatter bone or damage internal organs, it's just a flesh wound.

Curving my spine so tightly that my back nearly folds in two, I anchor my hind leg on Demos's broad chest and push. The skin rips, and icy agonizing shards give way to dull warm spasms. Demos coughs out a bloody gob of fur.

May just be a flesh wound, but it still *really hurts*. I leap away from Eudemos and concentrate on him. I will not be distracted again. Ti was right about that other thing—about the way Demos moves his head. Always left to right, and now I focus on that. On how to use it.

I move as far from Demos as I can to get a running start. He plants his legs firm, his bulk centered, waiting for me to plow into him and try to bowl him over. Which would be just stupid, and I'm not that stupid. As soon as he starts that devastating head sweep, I adjust slightly toward the left and scoot past his jaws and around his immoveable chest and front legs and grab his tenderest bits in my teeth. I don't bite down, but just create a firm cage with my teeth. Teeth that are strong enough to scissor through bone and suck the tender marrow inside. Demos jumps away but yelps when his packaging stretches.

I pull my small body smaller so that I am nothing but an enormous carbuncle hanging from his chassis. Everything Demos tries—biting, scratching at me with his hind leg, everything—starts the painful package pulling. He barks and skitters, my muzzle pressed against his privates, waiting for someone to dig me out from under and make me fight like a wolf.

No one does.

I turn to watch Ti, Demos's fuzzy balls still tight in my teeth, and he has no choice but to turn too. Solveig tears into Ti's haunches and runs around for another pass. Like me, she is going for agility over power, and Ti seems to be losing height, crouching lower and lower, growling with every pass. He looks like he's just centimeters from submission, but his scent hasn't changed. There's no way I could have missed the unmistakable smell of salt and old leather that signals fear.

Solveig coils for the leap that will bring her down on his neck and he will have no choice except to submit. But while her legs tighten for the jump, Ti shoots under her and grabs stiffened legs and twists. She scrabbles in the dirt; Ti contorts once more and grabs her throat. With a wrenching of his head, he forces her back to the ground.

It's not unusual for winners to hold losers down, making sure that there is no doubt submission has been offered. Solveig's ears are flattened, her eyes down, her tail pulled between her legs. John nods his head. The thing is over, but Ti doesn't let go.

There's a strangled whimper.

Letting go of my prize, I hurl myself into the big wolf, jumping around, licking his face, giving him open-jawed kisses, forcing him to let go.

His mouth tastes like blood and Solveig's fear.

Chapter 10

"You really are a crappy wolf."

"And you should have told me I wasn't supposed to kill her."

"Will you keep it down? Supposing someone hears you?" I look nervously around the Great Hall. No one is here, except for a pup peeling the birch bark from the banister supports. "Hey, Leelee! No chewing on the balustrade!" The pup freezes for a minute before scampering back upstairs.

"It was a challenge, Tiberius. You got her submission. In what world would you assume that killing was the point?"

He rubs slow and deliberate circles above the big aster scar on his torso. "The real world."

"Yeah." I put my hand on the door to the med station. "And how's that been working out for you?"

Tristan pulls the curtain shut around one of the beds, though not before I see Solveig's tail limp on the bed.

"How is she?"

"She'll be fine. Tracheal rupture, but I patched it up. The worst part was getting her on the ventilator. You can imagine how happy that made her. Had to knock her out. A little less force next time, eh, Shifter?"

Ti purses his lips and then, before I know what he's doing, pulls up my sleeve, revealing the ripped-up mess at my shoulder. "Maybe you can take a look at this."

"*What are you doing!*" I yelp, pulling my sleeve back down.

"It's huge. He should see—"

"It's nothing." I smile weakly at Tristan.

But it's too late. Tristan, who is the Pack doctor and the 5th's Alpha, shoves his gloved finger painfully into the bloody flesh. "So? It's just a flesh wound," he says. "Something wrong with your tongue, Shifter?"

"*What?*" Ti says, baffled.

"You couldn't just debride it?" Tristan says.

Seeing Ti's continued confusion, I clarify. "Lick it, Ti. He means lick it."

Ti glances at the blood seeping from my upper arm, and his nose curls. "So let me see if I've got this straight. You're a doctor. You have all this." He waves his hand at the med station. "And all you're going to do is to say 'lick it'?"

Tristan's dark eyes roll so far up in his head that they have disappeared. I give him a strained smile.

"Solveig, who has a *tracheal rupture*," Tristan says *with meaning*, "*needs* help. Silver, who has a *flesh wound*, doesn't. She knows she has to tough it out. Otherwise, what happens when she has a flesh wound and all I have are claws? Here," he says, shaking out a pale-green pill from the plastic container he keeps in the pocket of his white coat. "Have a Tic Tac."

I refuse with a frantic shaking of my head, but Ti takes *two* and pops them into his mouth before I can warn him that any wolf scenting wintergreen will know we went to Tristan with a boo-boo.

"When she wakes up, I'll tell your Alpha you stopped by to check on her," Tristan says quietly as we head out the door.

"I thought John was your Alpha," Ti says as soon as the door closes behind us.

His breath is an absolute toxic cloud of Tic Tac. I hear footsteps coming and pull him into the big closet that holds the seeds and tools for the cold frames to wait out the fug of wintergreen.

"John is the Pack Alpha," I explain. "The Pack's been too big for a single Alpha to control for a long time, so it was divided into echelons. They're like age groups, mostly wolves born within sixty moons of each other. Solveig is the 14th Echelon's Alpha. My Alpha for about five seconds before…well, before you arrived."

I put a trowel back on its hook, then fold my arms in front of me, bouncing against the wall.

"What exactly are we doing here?" Ti asks, looking around.

"Waiting until you don't smell like wintergreen."

Now it's his turn to roll his eyes as he stalks out. As soon as he does, I hear Tara's voice telling him that John's waiting for us. I push myself off the wall and head out to Tara's waiting nose and disapproving eyes.

"You went to medical for *that*?" Tara asks, poking her finger into the bloody sleeve of my T-shirt.

I grit my teeth until she goes, then I let out my breath in a sharp *d-owww*.

"I know humans talk just to talk," I say tightly, "but when I talk, it's because I have something that needs saying. And you"—I jab my finger in his chest—"are going to have to listen."

I've always liked John's office. Crammed between the library and the medic station, it is a small space with a high ceiling, one tall window, and a smell like damp manila envelopes. Probably from shelf upon shelf of Pack legal documents that are meticulously copied and filed here. There's even a copy of the original deed from three hundred and gibbety years ago.

Most of what's left of the floor space is given over to John's huge rolltop desk. It is made of cherry and has many drawers, although the bottom four are useless because pups have chewed the drawer pulls to nubbins.

John holds up a finger, then finishes something on his MacBook. Aside from the MacBook and the ancient Rolodex that no one has bothered to digitize, the surface of his desk is crowded with novelty mugs (*Leader of the Pack* or *Alpha Male: Do Not Provoke*) that gather dust and pencils at the back, mostly presents from Offlanders who spend much of the year away from the territory, doing the best they can to pass as human.

The gleaming first-kill skulls are prominently displayed on floating shelves above his desk. They're all small: rabbits, mostly. Beavers. Raccoons. And a single fisher. Mine, a chipmunk taken in my sixty-fifth moon, is on a bottom shelf in the middle, partly because it's small. I think John was also proud, because a chipmunk is fast and lithe, and for a crippled wolf, it's a good kill, if not particularly good eating.

The aged printer hawks out a piece of paper; John swivels toward us, the ancient wooden bank chair creaking loudly. "So, Shifter...you and Silver have won the right to sit at our table. This means that for the next three moons, we will give you food and shelter in exchange for work. Your schedule is there," he says, pointing to the piece of paper on the printer tray.

"During that time, the Pack, *as a whole*, will judge you both to see if you bring strength to the Pack. If you reflect honor and worth upon your mother's blood. Personally, I hope you do, because I don't want to lose Quicksilver. But if you fail, I will implement the consequences of her decision to join her fate to yours." He pulls off the much-washed flannel shirt and hangs it over the back of his chair, revealing a T-shirt with a wolf's head that must be another Offlander offering. *THE NORTH NEVER FORGETS*, it says.

"Let me be clear, Shifter. Do not underestimate Silver. She is strong of marrow and knows the Pack and the land better than anyone. You could not ask for a better shielder."

"John?" I squeak. "His name is Tiberius."

John's hand hovers above the mouse.

"Please?"

One calloused finger hits on the plastic casing (*tick, tick, tick*).

"The Bathhouse should be empty. Tiberius, do us all a favor and *try* to get rid of the stink of steel."

―᚛᚜―

We call aspens the Old Whisperers. For five months of the year, they gossip about us from high up on their pale trunks.

ShiverShiverShiverShiver.

Now, as we make our way to the Bathhouse, I swear the whole Great North Pack has turned into a bunch of Old Whisperers.

ShifterShifterShifterShifter.

"*His name is Tiberius!*" I snap.

"You don't have to keep doing that," Ti says as we make our way to the Bathhouse. "You know, 'Sticks and stones may break my bones…'"

"Yes, they can, though generally I prefer mallets and mauls. At the end of the day, there's less stuff to pick out of the marrow, which makes for better eating."

"That's *not* what I'm talking about. I'm talking about the old human saying. You know: 'Sticks and stones may break my bones, but names will never hurt me'?"

I hold open the door that leads to the screened-in porch, with its long chairs that wolves use to cool off. It may be an old human saying, but I've never heard it, and it doesn't sound right to me. Humans are *always* shooting one another over names. Just ask a Yazidi or a Jew or a communist.

"All I'm saying is that if I'd worried about every name that anyone called me, I'd have had to fight every Shifter in Canada." Ti pushes aside one of the leafy bundles of birch branches hung from the exposed beams. "I don't let it get to me. You shouldn't either."

He takes off his clothes in the changing area and wraps a towel around his hips. I pat the big, slatted teak table in the shower room. He lies down on his stomach and watches me search through the net bag for a brush. "Remember how I told you that I was born premature?" I say once I've found it. I fill a bucket with warm, soapy water. "Like your mother, my mother didn't make it."

"And your father?"

"He passed soon after, but that's not the point. The point is, I was tiny and really weak, and until I was nearly forty-two moons, I thought my name was Fromwart."

"Fromwart? What the hell kind of name is that?"

"It's not a name. I thought it was, but then I real-ized they were calling me *Framweard*, which is Old Tongue for someone going back where they came from. Someone doomed to die. They were so convinced of it that they didn't bother naming me. I was in my sixtieth moon when Gran Sigeburg told John that I needed a name. She was the one who named me Quicksilver."

Gran Sigeburg had told me that story over and over again, and no matter how often she told me, it was always sort of smushed together into one long, run-on sentence. "It was your sixtieth moon, which is a big birthday of course, and I told my son that it was high time you had a name, a real name, and that you should be called Ælfrida to honor our first Alpha, but John said, 'She's got enough problems without being named Ælfrida,' and I was ripe angry about that, but then I remembered that her Deemer was buried right next to her, a spot of honor to be sure, and this Deemer, she ran from Caledonia to Portsmouth with her leg shot clean off"—the way I'd heard it was that she'd come from Wessex to Portsmouth with a bullet wound, but if Gran Sigeburg wanted to heroize my namesake, who was I to gainsay her?—"and she must have been a silver too, because she was named Seolfer, and that's what I told John, that you would be named Seolfer, and he said no but that Silver was fine, and I was ripe angry, because our Pack needed some good, strong Old Tongue names, so I said, 'Quicksilver, then,' because you were anything but quick and I was feeling tart, and he said it was a fine name or maybe he just said 'Fine'?" Gran Sigeburg was already starting to lose her mind by then. She was somewhere around twenty-five hundred moons when she stopped telling the story and asked instead, "Who are you?"

She didn't make it back from the next hunt.

God, Ti has a beautiful back. I start to scrub it with broad circles.

"I know it was only a name, but once they started calling me Quicksilver, the Pack stopped treating me like I was quite so...temporary. I'm just saying that if they focus on *what* you are, they'll never pay attention to *who* you are."

He considers me for a moment and then turns his head, propping his chin back on his wrists. He sucks in a deep breath as I scrub hard at his back and under his arms and his calves and lower thighs, where the sweat stinks of steel.

"Hands."

He lets his arms flop limp at his sides. Scrubbing with soap and a brush does nothing for the smell. I try pumice, but not even that will scrub away the metallic tang.

How long do you have to hold a gun before the stench of steel seeps into your blood?

I'm careful of the wounds Solveig made in his flanks, just letting the water loosen the dried blood. Thin, dark-flecked rivulets run into the drain in the floor, and I can see just how deep Solveig's claws went. Some are nothing, barely more than scratches.

But others are gouges made by claws and filled with dirt. My tongue swirls over the biggest one, gently caressing the caked blood and dried mud, but Ti flinches.

"*Don't do that*," he says, pushing my head away.

"Why? We don't carry diseases, if that's what you're worried about."

"I didn't think you did." He slides his hand under his stomach and lifts his hips for a moment. "It's just, I don't...I don't like being groomed."

"I see. Turn over?"

Holding his towel, he turns onto his back while I squirt a bit of shampoo in my hands, rubbing until it's warm and lathered. I massage it into his scalp, kneading the knotted muscles at the base of his skull, lightly scratching his sideburns.

He grunts softly. "Sorry," I say, stopping immediately. "I forgot. You don't like being groomed."

"You know that's not what I meant."

"I know *exactly* what you meant, even if it's not what you said. It's not grooming that bothers you. It's that we do it in ways that humans don't." I lean over him, my silver hair falling on either side of his face, and I smile wide so that my mouth opens around teeth that are too long, too sharp, and too feral ever to be mistaken for human. "This is what I am, Ti. There are plenty of others here who will play human with you, if that's what you want. But not me."

He brushes my hair away from my face, but it falls back again and lands like a pale wash against the dark mahogany of his chest. He gently thumbs the point of my fang and looks hard into my eyes before turning on his side, exposing the biggest gouge, the one where four claws found deep purchase in his flesh.

I move the towel a little and hold his thigh while the eddy of my tongue gently cleans him. I keep at it, caring and curing until his muscles relax and he exhales, a long, low sound like air seeping out of an inner tube.

Chapter 11

TARA SAID THAT AS GUESTS OF THE PACK, WE COULD HELP ourselves to anything down in dry storage. There are no jeans, because we wear those until the tears in the knees meet up with the holes at the ass, so we find Ti sweatpants from the St. Lawrence Vikings and hoodies from the St. Lawrence Saints.

Upstairs, the screen door opens and closes with a slam. Orders are barked out, and heavy treads stomp back and forth between hall and kitchen. As the Pack passes the stairs to the basement, the complex fragrances of the dishes they're carrying waft down to us. Benches start scraping across floors, and I push Ti's extra clothes into a bag and push the man himself up the stairs.

As soon as we reach the hall, the smile I hadn't even known I was wearing fades. The Alphas of every echelon are standing around the heavy hand-scraped tables, each one of them holding tight onto their seaxes, the sharp daggers that all adult Pack wear at their waist.

There are strict penalties for attacking a table guest, and John will kill anyone who tries, but edgy wolves are edgy wolves and not always in control. I am this man's shielder, and I face them, my thighs coiled low, my shoulders squared, and my lips curled back from my teeth, so these wolves know that I will fight, even in skin.

Tock, tock, tock.

Behind me, Ti is not even facing the right way. He's

looking at the table, opening up casseroles with one hand, while flicking his spoon up and down against his bowl with the thumb of the other (*tock, tock, tock*). As though there weren't a hundred evil-eyed wolves staring holes into his back.

He lifts a hand-thrown lid and sniffs the saag paneer. Another basket with bread. A selection of Corningware casseroles hold cauliflower and lentil stew; sun-dried tomatoes and fresh cheese; corn chowder. Pasta with herbs. Egg salad.

"So…you're vegetarians?" Ti says to no one in particular.

"Not vegetarians," John answers. "But not carrion eaters either. *You are our guest*," he says loudly to remind all the wolves with itchy palms about our very ancient and very strict rules of hospitality, "and free to hunt anywhere on our land, but, Shifter? You must eat what you kill."

"John?" I whisper, pulling at his elbow, and he bends down. "His name?"

John scratches his graying beard for a moment before pointing to one casserole dish in Blue Onion pattern. "Tiberius?" he says. "My personal favorite is the cauliflower and lentils. Be sure to add some toasted hazelnuts."

Someone coughs, but John has broken the spell, and the Alphas reclaim their seats. Though when they do, they seem to have doubled in size, their broad shoulders and thighs now claiming whatever spare space we might have squeezed into.

I bend my head toward one of the empty tables. Those too will be full when the Offlanders come home for the Iron Moon, but for now, we sit there alone, side by side. The Pack starts talking again, bent low over their food because our table manners at home are not all they should be.

Naturally, there is a lot of talk about Ti, and while no one will question John's decision, it is one of the peculiarities of the Old Tongue that the word *giest* means guest and stranger and enemy, so when someone speaks of our new *giest*, everyone understands the double meaning.

Then John says that's enough Old Tongue for now.

A handful of pups scrabble up the stairs from the basement storage. They're chasing something, taking wide frantic turns around the room.

"Mouse," I whisper to Ti. "They don't last long here."

"She didn't take me down," Eudemos complains loudly. "I mean, I was still standing." He hacks at the big loaf of bread with his seax. "Where'sa butter?

"I neber submided," he insists, a pale-yellow crumb flying across the table. He uses his thumb to push the mouthful back in. "If what she did counts as submitting now, I think we should change the laws, thass all I'm sayin'."

"Deemer?" says John.

Victor, our Deemer, our thinker about Pack law, crosses his arms and looks at the ceiling for a moment. "The law does say an opponent must be pinned down," he says. "But while Eudemos was not down, he was very definitely pinned, and that is the more important part of the law."

"Your Alpha agrees. The spirit of the law was upheld."

And with that, Eudemos will not say another word about the matter.

The mouse finally caught, Golan trots up to John,

followed by a roiling mass of fur. He lays his tiny prey at the Alpha's feet. John looks at it, making sure the kill was clean and the mouse didn't suffer, then he scratches Golan's ear and wishes him good eating.

Suddenly, Ti jumps and lowers his hand to fend off a juvenile, who has her damp nose in his crotch.

"Rainy!" shouts Gran Moira. "Come here!"

Rainy cocks her head to the side and stares up at Ti before running off.

"Why do you have so many dogs?" Ti asks, his legs now tightly crossed.

"*Nooo*," I hiss. "*They're not…*"

It's too late. He didn't say it loudly, but our hearing is very good, and one set of very good ears is all that's needed. One by one, the Pack falls silent, appalled by what Ti has called our children.

Four fuzzy snouts peek over the arm of one of the fireplace sofas. Other pups glower down from the curved stairs that lead up to the children's quarters.

The only sound is the brittle crunch of Golan's sharp, white teeth.

"Excuse me, Shifter?" pipes a small voice. A ten-year-old girl with long, pale-brown curls, wearing shorts and a much-washed blue T-shirt with a picture of a pickle on it, scratches the back of her calf with a bare foot. "I am sorry I smelled your crutch?" she says, glancing back at Gran Moira, who mouths the word *crotch* with an encouraging smile. "But that's what I said. 'Crutch.'"

"It's 'crotch,'" corrects Gran Moira.

"Oh," Rainy says, turning back to Ti. "I am sorry I smelled your crotch? I didn't mean to be offensive. I am just in the Year of First Shoes?"

The Year of First Shoes is the first twelve moons in the juvenile wing, when you're too old to scamper around and be fed tidbits from the table, and you're too young to see even the remotest advantage to being human. It's when we first wear shoes and clothes. It is a terrible, terrible time.

"Good girl, Rainy," says Gran Moira, with a gentle pat on the girl's cheek. "Now go get yourself something to eat."

John carefully picks up a pup and uses his napkin to clean the little muzzle and its row of tiny needle-sharp teeth. He gives the pup's ear a big, openmouthed kiss.

"Oh," Ti says. "I see."

"That's right. 'Oh.'"

Tristan appears at John's shoulder, whispering something to him. Our Alpha's hand slips to his chest, his forefinger rubbing the narrow leather braid around his neck. It is the only ornament we ever wear, the symbol of a mated wolf.

John's mate, Evie, is not here. She hates Shifters and makes no secret of it. There is no doubt that her absence is a none-too-subtle slap at Ti.

John stands quickly, grabs an apple from the huge, old wooden bowl, and heads out, rubbing the apple's skin against his shirt. He takes a big bite and another, and by the time he reaches the foyer, the apple is gone.

He slides one foot into his boot and then hesitates. He slides his foot out again and lifts the boot. Picking up the other, he opens the door.

"Adrian!" he barks out into the night. "What did I say about marking my boots? You *know* what that does to the leather."

Chapter 12

WE WILL BE WORKING WITH STEN, THE MONOSYLLABIC WOLF who oversees Carpentry. Few in the Pack like to work with him, because he has a reputation for being surly. I don't mind him. He just really wants his wolves to pay attention the first time, so he doesn't have to talk to them again and can listen to the things going on inside his head.

Getting to Carpentry involves picking our way through the little groupings of pups and juveniles and the adult wolves who teach them.

One group of juveniles squirms in a semicircle around the bench John uses. A chalkboard propped against it reads:

> Thy body permanent,
> The body lurking there within thy body,
> The only purport of the form thou art,
>   the real I myself,
> An image, an eidolón.

The quote is one of John's favorites from *Leaves of Grass*, and he teaches it every year, so that even when we are wearing clothes and standing upright, we will always remember the importance of that other self inside us.

We are a well-read Pack. Of course, we pay attention to the other wolves who teach us history and math and politics and law and science. But we really have to know our Shakespeare, because John is our Alpha and he bites.

Right now, he is talking to Leonora, the wolf who teaches us why humans do the things they do and how to blend into this world they now own. Her wardrobe is one long, painful teaching opportunity. Today it consists of a pale-beige bouclé skirt that binds tightly around her thighs all the way to her knees. The matching jacket has black piping and large gold buttons and bunches uncomfortably over her broad shoulders. She's constantly pulling at the hem. When she glances at Ti, I grab his sleeve, trying to drag him into the safety of the woods, but it's too late.

"Silll-*ver*." Leonora terrifies me, and my spine tightens at the drawn-out first syllable and the barked second. She starts toward us with an uncomfortable staccato stride in a pair of stiff brown brogues. Draped awkwardly over her wrist is a matching handbag with a gnawed corner.

"Shifter, I am Leonora Jeansdottir, and I am the Great North's HumBe instructor."

"Human behaviors. And his name," I growl, "is Tiberius."

She flicks her eyes to me. "There is no growling in skin, Quicksilver. You know better." She turns back to Tiberius, shaking her head. "You see what I have to deal with? As I was saying, since you are for all intents and purposes human, I thought—and John agreed—that you might be able to help me with today's lesson."

"I'm not sure what I could—"

"My classes are generally held inside the Meeting House"—charging on as she always does—"but I've found that for the First Shoes, it's best to stay outside until they have mastered certain basics."

Like chair sitting. When we come to the spot Leonora has staked out for her class, we find eight chairs and eight children, studiously ignoring each other. These First Shoes are in clothes, but they are awkward and lumpy: bulky sweatshirts under backward T-shirts, pockets bulging with puzzling garments, mostly underpants.

"Perhaps we could start by having the class scent you."

"Absolutely not!" I snap. "He's Mala's son, not one of those stupid poisonous bushes Gran Ferenc always made us scent and mark."

"And thanks to Ferenc's efforts, many hazardous plants have succumbed to nitrogen burn."

Leonora looks through her handbag and pulls out a stick of fake blood. She pats her lips with it, then sucks on them before loosening them with a pop. It smells like wax and makes her mouth look like she ate weasel. She told me once why humans do this, but I forgot.

"Good morning, children."

"Good morning, Mr. Jeansdottir."

"*Ms*. Jeansdottir. Remember, females are *Ms*." She pulls again at her jacket. "We have a special guest today. I'm hoping most of you have scented him already?"

I cough loudly.

"In any case. This is a Shifter. Can anyone tell me what a Shifter is?"

"Someone who can phase, but doesn't has to?"

"*Have* to, but yes, Toby. And this means that they are almost exactly like humans except they know what you are, whether you are wild or in skin, so"—Leonora

suddenly starts talking very fast—"if you scent one
Offland, you must lead them as far from the Pack as—"

I start coughing again, hacking and hacking until
Toby looks at me in alarm and asks, "What's wrong
with her?"

"Turkey feather." Pounding at my chest, I look mean-
ingfully at Leonora.

"So, if you have any questions about life Offland that
you'd like to ask the Shifter—"

"And his name is Tiberius," I say *again*.

The class goes quiet. Catha has dug a hole, and several of the children gather around with their noses tight
to the ground.

"Children?"

"There's a mole," Catha explains.

"You can get the mole later. Now is the time to ask
questions of our guest. You could ask him about games
he plays, school, jobs, food, anything. Just phrase it as
a proper question."

"What jobs do you have, Mr. Shif—"

A quick glower, and Harald corrects himself.

"What jobs do you have, Mr. Tiberius?"

"Before coming here, my job—it's generally singular, by the way—was in human resources management,"
Ti says.

Catha looks up from digging for moles, her nose and
right cheek covered with dirt. "What's that?"

Ti hesitates a moment, then says, "It's basically figur-
ing out how to get people to do what you want them to."

There's a long silence. Jillian scratches her ear. "Why
don't you just bite them?"

"Jillian has brought up an important point.

Remember, even small humans are punished for biting without appropriate cause." I remember Leonora drilling this into our heads every time I took Basics of Human Behavior, but I don't think she ever clarified what "appropriate cause" was. Maybe that was covered in Intermediate Human Behaviors.

"It just occurs to me… Tiberius, perhaps you could help us review this week's dialogue?"

He shrugs. "I'll do my best."

"Aaand…Xander. Xander, you will initiate communication with our guest, and he will respond. Xander?"

Xander scrabbles forward.

"What happened to your shoe?"

He lifts a shod foot up high for her to see.

"The other one?" she asks.

Xander looks shocked at the single filthy bare foot and shakes his head sadly. If the missing shoe hasn't been chewed beyond recognition, someone will put it in the box on the stairs leading up to the juvenile wing. We go through a lot of footwear.

"Good morning, Mr. Tiberius," pipes Xander's childish voice. "How are you?"

"I'm fine, Xander. And you?" Tiberius replies with exaggerated courtesy.

"Better, because I had a tick right here?" He lifts his leg and points to a spot between his legs. "Next to my left ball? But when I turned yesterday? It fell off. It was like this big." He holds his hands to indicate a monster tick the size of a hockey puck. "I pinned it on the wall next to my desk." He hesitates, looking at Leonora, and adds a quick "Thank you for asking" before sitting back on the ground.

Leonora turns to the rest of the juveniles. "That was a good first try, but what would have made it better?"

Long silence.

"Anyone?"

Toby ventures a guess. "Xander said he turned, and we must never mention turning?"

"Yes, absolutely. We never mention turning or fur or muzzles or claws or hunting. The wild must always be protected. But there was something even bigger than that."

"He talked about his balls? Humans don't like genitals?"

"I wouldn't say they don't like genitals; they are just very squeamish. Fair point, but I'm looking for something else."

"Parasites? They don't like talking about parasites?"

"These are all good suggestions, but there is one critical point missing. Anyone?"

No one says anything. There's a lot of scratching and broad jaw-popping yawns, and Catha lies flat, her nose to the ground, scenting for moles. Leonora gently reminds Harald that there is no changing until after lunch.

"Tiberius? Can you tell us what Xander did wrong?"

"He made the mistake of assuming that I actually wanted to know how he was."

"Exactly! When humans ask how you are doing, it is meaningless. Tiberius, would you care to help me show the class how it's done?"

"My pleasure," he says and stands facing Leonora in front of the class. Leonora clears her throat.

"Good morning, Tiberius. How are you?"

"Fine, thanks. And you?"

"Just fine."

"Now," says Leonora, looking over her class. "See how simple it is?"

And Jillian bites Harald.

Chapter 13

THE DAY OF THE FIRST WAXING CRESCENT OF FALL IS WHEN all of the wolves who live on the Homelands traditionally run the perimeter and make sure that our land is properly marked before the ground freezes and damaged posts become hard to replace.

The entire Pack is wild. Barking and wagging tails, they lick each other and jump around each other, their ferocious jaws open and gentle. They chase mice through windrows, their hind legs scratching leaves into a brightly colored explosion high in the air, so that the pups can twist and turn and catch them in snapping teeth as they spiral down.

Not me. *I* have to pull on heavy muck boots over thick socks with jeans shoved inside. And I won't mark our territory the way wolves are supposed to. I will mark it on an iPhone 6 Plus, crammed into the big pocket of a thick orange vest. All because Ti refuses to phase and John doesn't like it.

"He tells himself he's human," John says. "But if he lies to himself, what makes you think he's not going to lie to us?"

So because I am Ti's *schildere*, I have to stay in skin too. Keep an eye on him.

"I mean, what were you thinking?" I ask as Ti fits the Outlast cap over his clipped skull. "When you came to a bunch of wolves asking for protection. That you'd just keep on being a human? Was that your grand plan?"

"I didn't have a *grand plan*. What I *had* was a hole in my stomach, a vague set of directions to my mother's pack, and a need to survive. I changed long enough to fight; I never thought you'd be asking me to give up my humanity."

"No one's asking you to give up your humanity, but if you refuse to admit what you are, it is going to rise up and bite you in the ass."

"Well, how about you?"

"*Me?* I *love* changing. I—"

"I know you *love* changing. You do it all the time. The second Sten doesn't need your thumbs, you evaporate, and there's nothing left but clothes hanging from a branch. I may be a crappy wolf. But *you*... You're a crappy human."

I cringe, because he's right. I've never been happy in skin, but then those stupid fire fairies burrowed into my body all those days ago, and that spark has caught fire and burns so fierce that now when I walk beside him and hear his quiet, low voice or look into those gold-flecked black eyes, my tendons strain and my muscles coil and my lungs open up and my blood beats hot and fast. The only way I know how to deal with need is to run hard and far until I collapse, unable to feel anything at all.

A brindle pup barks worriedly at my feet. All of the other wolves have disappeared, fading like a whisper in the woods.

"I know, Leelee. We're coming."

"She's going with us?" Ti asks.

"We're supposed to take her along. Help her learn the farther reaches of the Homelands." Leelee scampers on ahead, leaping awkwardly over a huge downed log and sliding down the other side, her fur covered in the sooty brown decay.

Ti clears it in one stride and stands close, not helping me exactly, but I know if I falter, his big shoulder is there for me to grab on to. I make it by myself, but I appreciate his silent gesture.

Leelee watches, her head cocked to the side, as I take a running jump over one of the numerous small, mucky streams that crisscross our land. I slip down the other side, my foot sinking into a soft bruise in the moss. She yips and worries, waiting for me to pull my boot out with a dull sucking sound.

I lift her up and give her an open-jawed kiss on her ear, but she sees a squirrel and won't stop squirming until I set her down.

"No farther than the Stones, Leelee."

When we finally catch up, she's clambering over the variously sized rocks that form rough circles around the ancient central stones. Over the years, the circle has encroached farther and farther into the forest, surrounding the trees.

Leelee marks one of the stones.

"What is this?" Ti asks.

"It's, um…the *Gemyndstow*? The memory place? But we just call it the Stones."

"Like a graveyard?"

"Graveyards are for bodies, aren't they?"

"Yes."

"So, no. Coyotes eat our dead. That's why we call them *wulfbyrgenna*. Wolf tombs. The stones are only for wolf names and the date of their last hunt so that we can remember."

When Ti crouches down and looks at one near the front, Leelee runs up to him and looks too, trying to figure out why it is so interesting.

As soon as he stands, she marks that one too.

An ill-advised squirrel runs across the outer rim of the Stones, and Leelee turns quickly to run after it, the wind tickling her fur and the scent in her nose. I know that feeling of taking it all in—moldering pine needles, owl pellets, borer beetle, tree sap, two-year-old porcupine den, sassafras bush—until the scent of prey hits you right in the back of the throat and everything tenses and you chase, even if your tummy's little and full and all you really want is for the thing, whatever it is, to escape so you don't have to eat it, but still you can't help but hunt.

She peels off after her squirrel, looking behind to make sure we're watching.

The squirrel chitters at her from the safety of a maple. Ti stares, his hands fisted by his sides, as Leelee scampers and bounds and falls on her back and twists her little legs in the air, her belly dotted with leaf litter. A tiny furrow cuts through his usually impassive brow, and his mouth, while still tightly closed, turns down a little at the corners. His wild—that seductive scent of crushed bone and evergreen—radiates thicker now, and when I touch his arm, he jolts as if from a waking dream and blinks down at me, looking in this moment like a lost boy.

But then he turns and walks on.

At the perimeter, we check the barbed wire that serves as our boundary fence, making sure that it's secure and continuous. We check that the posts are firm in their foundations and don't smell of termites or dry rot. Leelee races around, chasing another fat autumn squirrel.

We check that the signs are 660 feet apart, that we mark those that have been defaced by shot or spray paint. In short, we do all the things our lawyers say that we need to do to protect what the law calls "unimproved" land.

"Leelee?" I realize that I can no longer hear her claws skittering across the forest floor. "Leelee?" There is no response.

"*Leelee!*"

I veer off the path, racing to where I saw her last, but Ti signals for me to stop. "Call her again," he whispers.

As soon as I do, he turns abruptly, back the way we came. My hearing as a human is not what it is as a wolf, but I hear migrating geese passing over the high pines. I hear a mouse shuffling through the matted leaves. I hear the water tumble in the stream a hundred yards away, I hear a hickory nut drop to the ground, I hear a bird searching for a worm in the bark. I do not hear a pup.

I follow Ti's silent tread, keeping as quiet as I can. We've gone nearly fifty yards when I finally hear scrabbling and whimpering, and I run toward the sound, shouting to Leelee that we're coming.

We stop short at a sign that reads:

TRESPASSERS

WILL BE SHOT

The Pack never goes in, not because the sign would hold up in any court, but because beyond it is a dump. Over the past centuries, the Pack has bought parcel after parcel of land, but not this one. At first it was owned by a stubborn homesteader with a vegetable garden. Then a stubborn farmer with twenty acres. Now by a stubborn landlord with a junkyard and an access road. We bought fifteen acres from the current owner's older brother, but these five acres have eluded us every time.

The owner claims it's a thriving business, hauling people's broken-down refrigerators and air conditioners and car parts and dumping them in this spot. He claims it makes more than what we've offered him, but I know that John sees this as a wound in our land and would pay almost anything to get it.

John says it's not about the money. It's about four generations of spite. "Leonora always says humans are motivated by either love or greed," he said once, "but I think she underestimates what they are willing to do just for spite."

With my boot and gloved hands, I hold the barbed wire open for Ti.

"Leelee?"

The whimpering is close at hand. Ti points to a busted-up car chassis with a broken Frialator thrown precariously on top. I lie on the ground, looking under the chassis. Leelee is trapped in a hole, her paws and chest wedged tight, so her head is bent backward, her snout high in the air. She can't do more than whimper.

"Leeeeleee." I croon to the terrified pup. "It's okay. Everything's going to be okay." I try to reach her, but she's too far under. Even when I lie on my back and shimmy my shoulder under the busted chassis, she's still out of reach.

Ti's body is too thick to fit under the chassis, but he

crouches down anyway, breathing deeply. He stills for a moment, a distracted look in his eyes, before standing again and pulling me to the side. "We can't get to her without moving the fryer, but we have to be careful not to move the chassis," he whispers quickly. "If it falls or shifts, it will break her neck."

"Any idea how much that thing weighs?"

"Four hundred pounds? A little more?"

He doesn't ask *Do you think you can handle it?* He doesn't pretend that he can do it on his own. He just says that we have to move it, end of discussion. And we will, because I'll be damned if any pup of ours is going to be crushed by a trashed fish fryer.

Gingerly we step over the side rails of the chassis, trying to find spots that give us the best leverage we can, but even so, Ti will have to lift with his arms nearly straight out.

My hands are sweating inside my work gloves, but Ti's already gotten hold on his side. "Make sure that you're not holding something that will open or fall off. At the count of three, throw it. Then grab Leelee. I want to be ready if the thing shifts."

"Which way?"

"What?"

"Which way do we throw it?"

"Yeah, of course, to the back."

I feel around, grasping the front wall and a rear corner, and plant my feet firm, making sure that the dirt won't shift under me.

"Are you ready?"

"Yes."

"Okay, count of three."

And he counts to three. Four hundred pounds isn't that much, but it's a lot when you have to stand with your legs in an awkward position and a pup's life depends on it. And when your glove tears and the fryer starts to fall and you know that it will break her back. Ti grunts from the effort of not losing his grip, his legs straining to stabilize his big body. I catch it just before it hits the chassis.

"Are you okay?"

"Yes. Sorry."

"Count of three, to the back."

This time he counts to three, and we heave it a little—not far, but far enough. Reaching through the skeletal chassis, I grab Leelee by snout and tail. It's horribly undignified and probably more than a little painful.

With her out of the way, Ti steps on the chassis and pushes hard with his shoulder until the fryer tumbles over the back of a washing machine.

I cuddle Leelee close to me, whispering that we love her, but her ass is grass once John finds out that she went into the junkyard. She knows it's true and whimpers, pulling closer under my hair, already trying to hide from John's fury. Only then does it register that her chest and forelegs smell like oil.

"Hold her for a second?"

Ti takes her and holds her tight. "What are you doing?"

"I want to see what this is." I lift the surprisingly light chassis.

"Sil, no. She's shivering. We need to go."

Leelee's struggling scraped the top edges of the hole, but farther on in, I can see that it is perfectly circular and very deep. Water glistens in the bottom, but beyond the fetid water is a clear smell like a million tiny deaths that have not gone into making new life.

"*Sil!* It's a long walk back. Will you just leave it alone?"

When I scrabble out, Ti has wrapped Leelee in his T-shirt next to his bare skin. "I'll keep her. She's cold, and you don't know from cold."

We move quickly toward home, taking Leelee immediately to the medic's station. Someone must have gotten John, because he was running toward the back before Ti had even finished extracting the pup from the impromptu sling of his T-shirt.

As soon as Tristan determines that she's just bruised and shaken, I tell John everything. He calls for Tara—who is not only his Beta, but also an engineer—and makes me repeat the story to her.

"Describe the hole exactly."

"This wide." I hold my hands to circumscribe a hole about four inches wide. "I couldn't tell how deep it was because there was water in the bottom but had to be over ten feet."

"And it smelled like oil?"

"Yes. If you check Leelee, you can't help but smell it."

As John sniffs the air around Leelee, she wakes up. She looks at him and begins to shiver once more. He puts his big hand on her tiny head, sweeping his thumb across her muzzle until her eyes drift closed again.

This is the time for love. Discipline will come later.

"Tiberius?"

"It's a dump, and the whole place smells of antifreeze and Freon and diesel. I didn't see the hole. Probably from some old fence post."

"Yes, there were other smells around, but this wasn't Freon or diesel," I maintain steadily. "And it wasn't a fence post either. It was a perfectly round hole. Perfectly. Like it was drilled."

"Tara, I think we better take a look at this and also find the original of the DEC report from—" Ti and I are at the door when John stops.

"Tiberius," he says. "Every child is a *wuscbearn*, a wish child, beloved and adopted by the Pack. A symbol of its future strength. The Pack will appreciate that you take that future seriously too."

Ti stands facing the open door, his hand on the knob. "Just so we're clear here. I don't give a shit about symbols, but I didn't want Leelee to die."

As we head back to the Boathouse, Ti stops, looking at the sky. Then he turns, pulling at my arm. "There are blueberry muffins at the Meeting House," he says.

Later, as I lick blueberry and butter from my fingers, I wonder how it is that a man who can smell blueberry muffins in an enclosed structure one hundred yards away couldn't distinguish the stench of oil at his feet.

Chapter 14

"Over there."

"Where?"

"On the sofa." I nod toward the fireplace and the despondent four-year-old with the rich caramel skin, a shock of tight black curls, and SpongeBob pj's. "Leelee," I whisper. "Except for Iron Moons, she has to be in skin until November."

She curls up, her knees against her chest, picking at the loose upholstery. I bring her a bowl of fried rice fragrant with cumin and onions and set it on the low table in front of the fire.

"You should really eat something, Leelee."

"Don wan wice," she says with that slurred diction our littlest children all have on the rare occasions they are in skin. "I wan squido. I awmos caughded it."

"It doesn't matter. You have to obey Pack law. That junkyard is well marked."

I smooth her hair back from her forehead. "You know something, though? I don't think I've ever seen such a perfect midrun turn, and I've watched Kayla chase down a healthy adult weasel. You are going to be a *great* hunter one day. When you fell your first bear, will you give me a place at the kill?"

Leelee perks up a little, justifiably proud. "Lugs o' hawd?"

"You kidding? Bit of heart and a couple of ribs, and I'm in heaven."

"Me too. Bud I mosly lig lugs. Or libber." Her lips smack together. Just the thought of bear liver makes her hungry, and she reaches for the bowl. I pull it away from her eager grasp. She's too young to have eaten in skin, so I hand it to Ti for a moment while I snap a big napkin open and tie it around her neck, making sure to spread it over her entire chest. As soon as Ti passes the bowl back, she sticks her mouth straight in, snapping up the top bit with her teeth before digging at it with her hands.

I put the spoon in her fist and try to motion how it works. She looks at me skeptically, and then she pulls it to her mouth, using the spoon as a shovel until the rice is gone.

She wipes at her mouth with the back of her hand, licking it in turn.

Pups come up to her and nuzzle her and whine. Some lick at her, but when she doesn't change, they give up and trundle out. When the little door that we put in the big doors swings shut behind the last pup, Leelee lies back against my thighs and stares forlornly at her hands.

"It's not so bad, you know," Ti says, holding her tiny hand in his big one. Though they soaked her thoroughly to get rid of the oil, there are still dirty spaces between her fingers. "There are tons of fun things you can do with your hands."

"Lig whad?" she asks groggily. I stroke her dark curls as her head falls more heavily into my lap. Her feet squiggle against Ti's leg.

Ti's face is blank as he tries to imagine what hands can do that will make up for being a lonely little wolf. Then he looks at me.

Like I would know. I have no idea what children do except watch television.

"Poker," he finally says. "Poker is fun."

But Leelee is past hearing. Her breath has slowed and her leg shakes, like pups' legs do. Ti volunteers to carry her upstairs to the children's quarters. Since none of the beds are ever slept in, I choose one by a window facing Home Pond and yank the sheet and blanket off with a jerk before settling them loosely over her body.

It doesn't matter. The moment her little body sinks into the softness of the mattress and she feels the unaccustomed weight of the blankets, she begins to flail.

We creep out as quickly as we can, heading past the pups curled together in their puddle of fur.

"Didn't work." Ti nods toward the Great Hall and the little girl staring through the window. "She's awake."

"It takes a while," I say. "Learning how to sleep with walls and blankets and sheets and pajamas. It feels like a cage. But she'll learn. And then she won't be able to sleep without the cage."

The caged wolf man stares long and hard at the caged wolf girl. She presses her hand to the window.

"Ti?"

He doesn't move. I touch his hand.

"Ti? Do me a favor, will you?" He looks down blankly. "Run with me. Be wild and run with me. Please." I throw my hoodie over a branch and then my shirt.

He starts to pick up my discarded clothes.

"Leave them." I grab his arm and try to pull him toward the trees, but he's too big and too strong and too stubborn.

"I already told you, Silver. *No*."

I kick off my boots and leggings and stumble behind

a yew, arching my spine, the knobs of my vertebrae extending and my shoulders bending forward and the thin dusting of hair thickening to fur.

There's a hollow roar in my ears, a swirling blindness in my eyes, the nocking of the bones in my jaw. When it's all over, Ti is standing on the Boathouse dock, looking distractedly over the streaky moonlight on Home Pond.

I grab his shirtsleeve in my teeth and pull.

"No."

I grab the back of his sweatshirt and pull again.

"*No!*"

I smelled the longing of his wild when he watched Leelee in the forest. That was real. This isn't. These are just more meaningless human words. Tiberius is meant to be a wolf. I know it. He has to know it too.

I grab the ankle of his sweats and pull hard. He starts to topple over, catching himself on the arm of the chair. When he falls to the dock, I drag at his pants.

"*Cut it out!*"

I chuff in annoyance and shift up, putting my head on his chest, trying to think how I can get him moving. He tilts his head back, staring once more at the moon on the water. So I open my jaws as wide as they will go and gently set them on either side of his neck. It's what we do, and it means *trust me*. It means *I see you at your most vulnerable and will not hurt you.*

But he's not Pack, and he doesn't understand, and he shoves me away so hard that I fly off the dock and skid into the honey locust at the water's edge.

Now he's done it. My ribs are bruised, and one of those nasty thorns from the locust is sticking out of my hind leg right above the stifle.

"*D'ooowww*."

"Sil," he calls, running down from the dock. "Sil! I'm sorry… I just… I didn't mean to…"

I try to pull at the thick end with my teeth, but the angle's all wrong, and damn it hurts. When I look up, Ti is squatting down beside me.

"Shit, Sil. I really am sorry."

I hobble away, hiding behind a hazelnut thicket, but he keeps following me.

"Let me see, will you? Let me help." He holds out his hand toward me, and I nip him.

"Okay." He shakes his hand. "I may have deserved that. But obviously we need to talk. And I can't do it if you're like this."

I can't change. There's a thorn the size of a pencil in my leg, and until I get it out, I can't change. I move further around the hazelnut.

"Are you really going to make me talk to a bush?"

It's not a bush; it's a thicket. And since I have every intention of keeping said thicket between us while I pull at the stick and seethe, *The answer is yes. Talk to the thicket.*

He sits down and doesn't say anything at first, but Leonora says that the same way nature abhors a vacuum, humans abhor a silence.

"It's just… Well, I don't like anything at my throat." He clears his throat. "Sil?"

What does he think I'm going to say? The thorn finally comes out, and I lick my wounded leg, but bending that way hurts my bruised ribs.

"You once asked what wolf would do this?"

I stop licking and peer at Ti through the little forest of twigs. He is sitting with one arm tight around his knees and the other absently tracing the ragged scarring at his neck.

"It was me," he says. "I did it."

I shift forward until I can see him more clearly, then drop my head on my front paws.

Ti stares at Home Pond for a while and then starts talking again. "Shifters say that changing is all about self-control. Either you have it or you don't. We—well, *they*—have it. It's what sets them apart from the Packs, makes them better.

"Better than humans too, by the way, because humans just are. They never have to fight to stay that way."

When he extends his hand toward the thicket, I stiffen, but he only plucks at a tangle of my fur caught on the branches when he threw me. He brings it to his nose, then rubs it between his fingers, releasing the strands into the cool autumn wind.

"But...I never saw a Shifter struggle like I did. I mean, sometimes one of them would pick a fight for no reason, and that usually meant the itch to change was there, but an extra drink, an extra round with a punching bag, an extra woman, and it was gone. For me, it wasn't an itch. It was something inside that clawed at my skin. Something that threw itself against my skull until I thought I would explode."

He holds up his fingers and, with a single breath, blows the last bit of silver fur into the night.

"Sometimes I think I remember shifting when I was very young, though maybe it was a dream. Anyway, in that dream, I changed and felt..." He takes off his Outlast cap and scratches the short hair on his scalp. "I felt almost holy. I don't know how to explain it. I remember my body dissolving. Every breath I took brought the world into me, and every breath I let out sent me into the world. Everything around me was so clear and so…so *present*, and I just wanted to run and feel… And *feel*."

As he remembers, the scent of his wild seeps from his skin. I smell it, sharp and urgent and real.

"But then it happened again, and this time, I know it wasn't a dream, because they caught me. You've seen me. I was young and didn't really know how to move on four legs, and the other Shifters hunted me easily and dragged me back home. They thought it was funny, but my father was furious. From then on, before every Iron Moon, he locked me into a prong collar and chained me to the fence. Like a dog."

Without even really noticing what I am doing, I leave the thicket and sit next to him, so close that when I breathe, my chest brushes against him.

Ti pulls a leaf from my fur. "I did this"—he lays his hand against the ruined skin at his neck—"trying to get that stupid collar off. For the next three years, I spent my Iron Moons chained to a tiny patch of dirt, until I finally understood that there was nothing holy about a necklace of beveled steel pushing into your throat. That there was nothing holy about being surrounded by the stink of your own shit. That there was nothing holy about a waterlogged column of canned offal in a dirt-encrusted food dish. That there is nothing fucking holy about loneliness and humiliation. You cannot begin to understand how much I wanted this thing inside me to die. I hated it. *I hate it*."

I catch the glint of his glowing eyes. There is no wild

in him now, only anger. His jaw is so tight that I hear the joint grind.

John once described the way humans divided their stories into three types: Man against man. Man against nature. Man against himself.

It's so alien to us. After all, we are nothing without our Pack, our land, and our other sacred selves. But listening to Ti, I am struck by the unspeakable, lonely againstness of humans.

It took years to chain his wild and will take patience to unchain it. I lie down on my side and start to change, and the world disappears except for the tumult of my body until I am aware of the cold ground against my naked skin. Ti must have gone back into the Boathouse while I was changing, because he stands near me with dry clothes and my boots. As soon as I finish tying the frayed laces with the DIY duct-tape aglets, I turn to him.

"If you won't run with me," I say, "then walk."

"Where?"

"Through the trees, into the mountains. Somewhere. Doesn't matter. But remember, I'm not like you. In skin, I'm barely better than a human. You will have to be my senses. You"—I lay my hand on his chest—"will have to be my wolf."

I have no plan, just my own wolf telling me that if Ti feels the wild *outside*, really feels it, that may open a window for the wild that is dying day by day inside him.

We walk silently. Ti reads the world around us, and I read Ti. *He* sees the root stick up under the rock. *He* hears the snake through the leaf litter. *He* smells the algae that will make the newly exposed hardpan of a drying riverbed slick.

Two wolves running together are synchronous. Partly because we are attuned to each other, but mostly because we are attuned to the world in the same way. We both catch the scent of Pack, the sound of water, the sudden flash of prey, and our bodies move as one toward it.

This is different. My human senses are more likely to mislead me in the dark of the night woods, so I have to let Ti lead me.

He started holding my elbow, steering me like a wheelbarrow, which I really don't like. I shook him off and slipped my hand lightly in his. With his skin against mine, I can feel the slightest tightening of his muscles, the change in his heart's rhythms. When he breathes longer, scenting something, I can hear it. I read him so clearly: his pauses, his sparked attention, the caution or sureness of his steps.

We emerge from the woods at a granite promontory that looks over the stillness of our land. The dark stretch of balsam below smells like heaven. When the clouds shift, I see the thin waxing crescent that means I have twelve more days before I can no longer hold this form.

I feel Ti watching me, and I make the mistake of looking into gold-flecked black eyes, more beautiful than night.

I have never been so profoundly aware of someone in my life.

Chapter 15

THOSE EYES, THE MOON SHIMMER ON HIS SKIN, THE BODY I'VE watched so often from the corner of my eye and enjoyed so thoroughly in my waking dreams. It's all right here, and I clutch tighter at myself, my breath hitched permanently in my lungs.

Then…he touches me, just pulls something from the hair near my face, but his fingers skim my cheek and I…

Run.

Ti leaps after me. Something sends me running crazy fast and just plain crazy, because I can't see what I'm doing, so I trip over logs and slip into streams, and Ti—who does know where he's going—is busy doing whatever he can to keep me from killing myself long enough to get to the Boathouse.

Throwing my clothes in the hamper, my boots into the corner, I blurt out a quick "Thanksforthewalkseeyoutomorrow," but with one long step, Ti is at the door.

He holds my wrist. "You're bleeding."

"It's nothing. Just a flesh wound." I try to sidestep him, but he won't let go. When he touches my naked thigh, the lighter skin of his palm is stained dark. Stupid thing must have opened again during my headlong rush into disaster.

The muscles in my leg quiver against his hand, tensed and ready for escape. Maybe Ti feels it, because he doesn't let go of my wrist as he heads to the kitchen for a damp, clean towel. He doesn't let go as he leads me to the bed. He doesn't let go as he dabs at the edges of the puncture. He doesn't let go when he throws the towel to the side and leans over my thigh, his iron arms holding me down.

I feel the tentative sweep of the tip of his tongue on my skin. The strokes grow stronger and more insistent, cleaning away the blood. He sucks out a bit of branch or bark that hasn't bled out.

"I have to leave," I whisper, pulling away. "*Now. Please.*" My voice sounds high and panicky. He still doesn't let go.

"You do know," he says, "that I can smell you." He breathes in deeply, and a little eddy of air runs against the damp skin at my thigh.

"And?" I choke out. "And what do I smell like?"

"You smell like clove," he says and exhales in a long, warm sigh that I feel all the way to my womb. "You smell like sprouting earth. Like charcoal and moss. You, Quicksilver, smell like lust."

Of course, he would know what desire smells like. Man like this must smell it all the time. I freeze, waiting for him to laugh like Ronan did at the pathetic longings of a crippled runt.

Ti doesn't. He just slides up along my body, the soft, well-washed cotton suddenly feeling like thistles against my bare skin. He turns his head, exposing the spot between jaw and ear where scent is strong. "Now… what do *I* smell like?"

Like angelica and green corn and the air before a thunderstorm and rutting buck. My expanding lungs crowd my chest, sucking in more of the heady scent.

"So?" he asks.

"You smell really…really nice."

"*Nice?*" He turns on his side, propping his head on one hand. With his other, he takes my fingers and slides them down his hard body to the long bulge at the front of his sweats.

"And is that *nice*, Silver?"

I jerk my hand away, that warmth in my womb almost agonizing.

He slides his hand under my breasts, lightly brushing the lower fullness.

"And is that *nice*?" he whispers, his hand sliding down over my belly where the skin is stretched far too tight.

As he moves further down, my back arches, and my knees bend until he reaches the silvery vee at my apex and slips his hand between my legs. I squeeze my thighs closed, pressing hard against his hand.

"And is this—" He slides one finger in and then stops, pulling his hand away.

"You're a virgin?"

I freeze. My mind is a blank, and I've totally forgotten what Leonora said a virgin is. "That's… Is that what humans call someone who's not a viable mate?"

He scowls slightly. "Viable? What do you mean by 'viable'?"

"Same as any Pack. Big. Strong. Fast. *Whole*. A fighter with good reflexes and a hunter with good strategy. You know. *Viable*."

He turns on his back, silent for a moment, and then grabs the hem of his sweatshirt. He pulls it over his head and throws it toward the chair. It slides to the floor.

"The thing is, Silver, for better and worse, I am *not*

Pack. I am a man. And god help me, but as a man, I really want to lay you down."

Lay me down?

"And is that"—I clear my throat—"is that something humans do?"

"Humans do many things," he says. "Shifters too. Why don't you tell me what Pack do?"

"The female presents," I whisper, "and the male covers. Everyone hopes for the best?"

"I see." He moves in very close, so that something hard and cotton-covered just touches me. "And is that what you want?"

He's so close that even though I can't feel his skin, I feel his heat calling to me. I move closer, sliding my hand around his head, and touch his mouth with mine, but he shakes his head and pulls away, his fingers gentle against my lips. And with that, I've failed at the only thing I thought I knew about human coupling. That it starts with the tasting of each other's mouth.

Ti lifts my tightly fisted hand and unfurls my fingers. I'm not sure what I'm supposed to do. Hands don't really come into play in Pack couplings. I stare at our palms, mine small and rough against his large, smooth one. I slide my hand hesitantly against his until the inside of my wrist rests against the inside of his.

His skin here is silky as water but warm as blood, and I feel the lapping of his pulse. Like the sound of his heart when I lean my forehead against his chest. Like the subtle expand and contract of the ropy veins over the thick, sinewed muscle of his chest. Hesitantly, in case he doesn't want my mouth anywhere on him, my tongue traces the long tear he plowed from his neck to his nipple. I run over the dark tip with my fang and then sheath it in the soft warmth of my lips. It tightens under my lips, and Ti weaves his fingers into my hair, gently pulling my head closer.

Some scrapings and tonguings and touchings make his sex jerk. Make dark sounds rumble through his chest. Make his own explorations of my naked body rougher and more urgent until every move abrades my nerves. Now, gliding over his tight muscles feels like a bruise. Now, the sweep of my hair against my hypersensitive skin feels like a lash.

The washed cotton of his pants chafes the inside of my thighs. It's unfair. He should be naked like I am, with nothing to block my access to his body.

I slide my hands under his waistband and feel the taut, hard ass. The waistband catches on something.

"So free me, Wildfire."

Running my hands slowly around the front, I feel the obstruction and free him. Like a conjurer doing the tablecloth trick, I pull away his sweats. With a sigh, they fall to the floor, and I kick them away.

I freeze, looking at his body. It is everything I could have wanted. Not smooth and civilized like I've seen in humans' magazines. It is hard and fierce and wild and makes my soul ache.

"Your teeth are showing."

Every desperate desire I've had to run from now forces its way out, and I want to touch everything. Everything from the high, taut arch to the curve of his calves to the carved line around his knee to the thick strength of his thighs. I push them apart and bury myself in the tight curls at the base of his sex, absorbing the smell of crumbling wood and musk, the loamy smell of old death and new life that is almost enough to send me over the precipice. I know enough to be gentle with the twinned weights below, tightening just enough so that the skin is taut and I can see the shapes underneath, and the skin is smooth under my tongue. I pull him into my mouth with a gentle scrape along my fangs, and his breath comes out in short gasps.

I move my hand to his sex, feeling the skin slide like silk over steel. Feeling the pulse of it now as I curl my hand around it. Tracing the vein with my tongue, swirling the thick—

"Stop," he grunts. "Silver, stop." He pulls me away. "Or I'm going to be finished before I've even started."

"Started what?"

"I want this to be good for you, or you won't want to do it again. And I..." He runs his hand slowly up from my hip, his fingers separating as he does. "Want to do it over." When he reaches my breast, the soft swell feels almost painfully heavy. "And over." His fingers drift and separate until they reach across my pale breast like a dark vine, my nipple trapped in the vee of his fingers.

"And over..."

He squeezes gently, and with one hot, rushed breath, my lungs cave in.

"Again."

A boat bangs against the moorings and then floats out again, the rope taut and straining. He looks back down at me with those glowing eyes and bends low over my breast, each little pull with his lips sending a new shock along a separate path until my skin burns.

His fingers slide along one of those paths down my

belly, across my womb, to the soft, straight silver hair at the join of my legs.

He circles his fingers through the soft strands, moving wider and farther, and when his hand cups between my legs, my thighs clutch at him, begging him to come into me. His finger scrapes lightly over the almost electric part of me and then slides easily inside.

This time, he stays, his finger like a tongue of fire, sweeping against places inside me and making them burn. And when he pulls out, I hiss. He uses that same finger to circle my nipple. In that cool damp, it tightens even harder. He follows the path with his tongue, skirting around the sensitive tip until my breast and body ache for his mouth, and he finally laps at it and his tongue feels like cool suede against the searing heat.

The air is saturated with clove and moss and green corn and rutting buck. It's a fog of combined lust, and I can hardly breathe. His thigh shoves my legs apart, and I shake my hair out of the way, stretching my head to the side, so he'll anchor me with his teeth. Hold me tight for that first tearing blow.

Instead, he nuzzles against me with the tight beard on his cheek. His hips move slowly, and with each pass, he intrudes a little farther in toward my core. His muscles quiver, straining to hold back.

"Are you ready, Wildfire?"

I'm just barely holding on to my veneer and growl in response. And when his hips make their next teasing pass, I grab the cord of *his* neck in my strong jaws and anchor *him*. My legs reach around his hips, and I pull up, impaling myself on the full length between my thighs.

Ti sucks in a sudden breath, his lips curling back from his clenched teeth, and in that one second, I see strong, white canines that are too long, too sharp, and too feral ever to be mistaken for human.

He releases that breath and shifts slowly until he is buried bone deep inside me, then he starts to move for real. Each thrust in brings diminishing pain. Each drag out brings growing pleasure. As it builds, muscles I didn't know I had set up their own rhythm, pulling at him, and he sweeps against the mouth of my womb. With every plunge, his chest brushes against mine, and then he bends his finger against my entrance to my sex, so that with each pass, I feel the press of him inside me and out. I chase that feeling like it is prey, moving faster and faster until finally, with one last crash of blood and adrenaline, I catch it. My back arches tight, my deep snarl vibrates loud against Ti's chest, and I immolate.

Ti grabs my thighs hard and thrusts into me one, two, three more times, and then stops, the beat of his life pulsing into me thick and steady, like the first blood of a felled hart, his body jerking hard, like the hart's final throes.

In the end, death and sex look the same.

He collapses, panting into my hair, his hand pressed firmly on my belly, feeling the throbs of my body as it continues to clench hard around him.

He stays inside me for a long time, but when he finally pulls out, I feel shattered. If it weren't for Ti's heavy body weighing me down, I think any passing breeze could just pick up my pulverized remains and blow me away.

I lay my head on his shoulder, one of his scars under

my cheek. I press each finger of my hand to the lines radiating from his neck. He tenses but doesn't move.

"Tiberius?"

"Quicksilver?"

"What I did to you before? When I put my teeth on your throat? Did it hurt?"

"No," he says after a moment's hesitation. "No, it didn't."

"You know we can't always talk, but it doesn't mean we don't communicate. What I did means 'trust me.' It means 'I see you at your most vulnerable, and I will not hurt you.'"

He turns toward me, his eyes glowing the way they do, and covers my hand with his big one, pressing it tighter over the ravages of his throat. I smile softly at him, just the tips of my canines poking out. I see his tongue run over the points of his own, but he keeps them hidden behind his tightly closed lips.

I lay my head back down on his shoulder.

I make sure Ti is asleep before I creep out naked toward the trees. I tried, I really did. But I can't sleep like Ti does, with his vulnerable underside exposed. I can't sleep on my stomach, because I sink into the soft mattress like a boulder in a bog and can't breathe.

The blankets weigh on me like chain mail.

I really am a crappy human.

Chapter 16

BECAUSE SOME PERSNICKETY WOLVES COMPLAINED, TARA sent us to the Bathhouse to sweat out the tiny lingering scents from the junkyard.

Ti couldn't be happier, stretched out on the top bench of the sauna where the heat is most concentrated. He exhales slowly, an almost noiseless sigh of contentment. He stretches out his hand, feeling for me, but I've crept down to the floor, a dampened washcloth over my face. I don't care what Tara says; I'm not going to last more than five minutes. Offlanders use the sauna most. All that time spent with clothes and HVAC have left them in need of frequent defrosting.

Four minutes later, I race for the door and the icy waters of Home Pond, and when I return, a new pair of shoes is lined up beside the Bathhouse door. A quick sniff identifies them as belonging Caitlin, the 8th's Beta. Solid flank strength. A real endurance runner.

I knock gently on the door.

"Oh, for fuck's sake," Ti yells. "*Just come in.*"

At first, all I see through the crack in the door is Ti, pressed into the corner of the upper bench, his hands folded tightly atop a towel draped across his lap. Another towel is wrapped around his neck. He stares resolutely at the bucket of steaming river rocks. Caitlin is a foot to his right, resting on her knees and elbows, her ass in the air, presenting.

"Hey, Silver."

"Hey, Caitlin. Been here long?"

She pushes her lank dark-blond hair back from her pinched, sallow face. "Long enough to wonder if he actually knows what to do."

Ti looks up at me with a bleak expression and frantically pats the spot next to him.

I shake my head. "No, thanks. Too hot."

He glares at me and pounds the seat again, slowly and deliberately. With meaning. I'm not sure what's up, but I take the seat, shielding him from Caitlin's pockmarked ass. It's not really pockmarked, but her body bears the remnants of not one, but *three* run-ins with porcupines. She wears the scars proudly, emblems of her perseverance and tolerance for pain in her quest to eat porcupine. I have always thought that even *one* encounter with a porcupine is an emblem of congenital idiocy and have simply settled for raccoon.

Then again, she's a Beta and I'm not.

With an exaggerated sigh, she swings around, sitting next to me, and dries her armpits with her towel. "You're his *schildere*. Explain things, will you? Because now look," she says, pointing to the clock with her sharp chin as she towels off between her legs. "I've got to get to work, and I don't have time.

"Silver," she says, taking her leave, her hand already on the door. "Shifter."

He creeps toward the door, his finger to his lips, his ear pressed to the cedar until he is satisfied that she is well and truly gone.

"Okay," he hisses. "What the hell was that?"

"She was presenting, Ti. You were supposed to cover

her. The Pack knows what you did for Leelee, so now Caitlin sees you as a potential bedfellow, and I bet she won't be the last. She's a good herder; you should be flattered."

"I'm not *flattered*. I'm fucking queasy." He rubs his chest. "And what about you? Why aren't you my 'bedfellow'?"

"Me? It is *way* too hot in here. I don't know how you can stand it." I move back down to the floor as close to the slightly cooler bit of air by the door as I can. "I don't have anything to do with it." I start to pour ladles of water over my head. "I'm not your bedfellow. I'm just your shielder."

"You're not just my shielder. If sex doesn't make you a bedfellow, what does?"

"But it's not just about sex. Shielders have sex all the time. Being bedfellows is more like a trial mating."

"Like being engaged?"

"I don't remember. When you're engaged, do you have to fight others who might want to cover your engagee?"

"That'd be fiancée. And generally, no."

"Look, it was only a matter of time before you were approached by a viable female." I catch Ti's hand before he pours more water on the rocks. "Don't do that. I can't take any more."

"Quit it with the 'viable female,' will you? Supposing I don't *want* to screw the herder with the strongest thighs?"

"What you *want* has nothing to do with anything." I pull myself up and grab the door handle. "We are not human. It is not about we want. It's about the strongest wolves breeding still stronger ones. You are powerful and smart and have these...these weirdly amazing senses, and if you don't mate with your equal, we would consider it a waste of seed."

The door closes behind me, and the cool air cushions me. I don't really want to have this conversation. And I certainly don't want to have it while my blood boils to vapor in my veins.

I bend forward, my forehead and hand on the chilly tile, the shower's cold water carrying the heat from my head down the shallow canal of my spine.

Then through the blasts of cool water, I feel new heat. The heat of Ti's body. The heat of Ti's hand as it covers mine, his fingers sliding between mine. The heat of his chest pressed to my back. The heat of that solid length that makes my hips buck against him. "Is that what you want? For me to screw Katherine?"

"Caitlin. I told you it doesn't matter what I want. It—"

"Bullshit," he whispers, his rough chin chafing the skin between neck and ear. "You took on a complete stranger, *a Shifter*, no less, because you didn't *want* to be a cog in the Pack. What was it you said? One chance at living was better than a lifetime of simply being alive? That's what you *wanted*."

When he tilts his hips, I feel him more insistent against my ass.

"So I'm asking you now, Wildfire, a simple yes-or-no question."

He moves gently against me like he knows the torture of these tiny brushes. Like he knows how to use every part of his body—the soft scrape of the ridged scar; the jab of the tight nipple; the tingle of those few, very few, tightly curled hairs; the soft caress of his sloping navel—to sharpen my senses and make me feel him more intensely.

"Do you *want* me?"

The voices of generations of Pack echo around my skull, yelling incoherently about Tradition and Law and Survival and Strength and Will and Sacrifice. But there is another voice too. It is small and hesitant, but it is clear and it is *mine*, and that voice says:

"Yes."

"So take what you want." He bends his legs on either side of mine, and his erection slips between my thighs. "Just make sure it's me, because I sure as hell want you."

He hisses as my hips punch against him. I feel him growing harder and thicker still between my clenched thighs. My hand reaches back toward him, but he turns me around, the cold water now running down our fronts, and he lifts me up, his big body between my legs. In two steps, he props my ass on the teak table and pushes me back against the slats. "Relax," he says, holding me down with one firm hand on my chest. He bends over me, his mouth finding the promontory of my hip bone and swirling it with his tongue before angling feather-light kisses down my pelvis.

He buries his nose between my thighs and breathes in deeply, the roughness of his trim beard pricking my thighs. The bristling of the rough fringe above his lip chafes my sex—followed by the long, firm, silky strokes of his tongue—and the rich combination of being abraded and soothed takes me higher and higher. My body shudders, and I don't remember the last time I breathed. Ti stretches my legs wider and makes a seal with his lips, pulling insistently until my body contracts.

When his tongue pushes in, I fall apart with a million little screams that only I can hear.

"Open for me," he says, his voice raw and his hands hard on my still-rigid legs. "Let me in."

And I do. Lying on my back, I let him in because that's what I *want*.

I was right that Caitlin wasn't going to be the only one to set her sights on Ti. Hilda flagged him as we walked toward the Great Hall. He seemed oblivious to her invitation, though. I don't bother to point it out to him, because if he doesn't understand what it means when a female moves her tail to the side and shoots him a come-hither look along her flank, it's not my job to tell him.

He understands Selena's intent perfectly well, because she wiggles her Lycra-covered ass against him as he picks up his plate and utensils. He looks to me for help, but I just shrug.

We have an old saying: a strong wolf with a weak bedfellow is as good as single. As shielders, we are free to cover whomever we want. But if I were his bedfellow, I'd be expected to fight off challengers for rights to Ti's body. I mean, he'd be expected to fight off challengers for rights to my body too, but let's be realistic.

And Selena? She's a mean fighter who took out Gideon's left eye two years back. Seeing as she has no fuzzy balls, I don't like my chances.

Then just as he's straddling the bench, holding his loaded plate and glass, Tecia reaches across to put her hand firmly on his crotch.

Ti starts, sending the water in his glass flying.

"*That does it*," he says, dropping his plate onto the table and stomping over to John.

I watch nervously as Ti whispers close to John. John signals first to Victor, our Deemer, then calls for one of the juveniles to fetch Leonora. I get up, because whatever else happens, I am still Ti's shielder.

John shakes his head as I walk toward them. Ti pats the air softly with one hand. *Wait*.

"He washed up pretty nice," says Tecia as I take my place again.

I stick my fork halfheartedly into a plate of pickled something with feta.

"I mean that carrion stench when he first showed up"—she sticks out her tongue and makes a soft gagging noise—"it was almost human."

My stomach has tightened and my throat has too, and the food simply will not go down.

"The steel, though… Is it noticeable when he covers?"

Maybe it's because my heart feels big and painfully hard.

"I'm thinking maybe if I spray him with a good coat of Skunk-Off and leave him in the sun for a—"

"*Will you just shut up?*"

Ever the teacher, Leonora teeters up to John on high heels that make her almost as tall as our Alpha. She drops her blood stick back into her handbag, closing it with a snap as she smacks her lips.

I can't hear what's going on. Ti says something to the three of them. There's some gesticulating and nodding. Ti cradles his zipper. Everyone looks at Tecia. There's some more talking, more gesticulating, and more sage nodding. Everyone looks at me. I wave.

Leonora says something and touches the braid around her neck. John nods. But Victor strokes his beard and says something that makes Ti's control slip a little, because his voice grows louder as he says "…not be put out to stud."

John signals, and Tecia swings her legs free of the bench. "No," says John, shaking his head. "Quicksilver."

"Because viable females have started presenting themselves," John says, "Tiberius has asked to be formally declared your bedfellow."

"But you know what they say: 'A strong wolf—'"

"'With a weak bedfellow is as good as single,'" interrupts John. "Yes, we all know that bit of old wisdom. It is true that under normal circumstances, you would not be able to defend your *cunnan-riht*, but Tiberius is asking that you be released from any obligation to defend your rights to his services."

At the phrase *rights to his services*, Ti scratches his eyebrow, a gesture that I've come to believe means he has found something amusing.

"Is that even legal?" I ask.

"Turns out it's custom, not law." Victor gives a reluctant nod. "We've never had a guest who was not raised Pack, but Victor agrees that while we can expect Tiberius to follow Pack laws, we cannot withhold Pack rights and expect him to follow our *customs*."

John turns to the Pack. He has barely finished announcing that Ti and I will be bedfellows when Selena pushes away from the table, using her current bedfellow's shoulder. She stalks toward me, her eyes narrowed, ready for a fight.

"Selena," John says. "I wasn't finished."

Then Victor details the "special circumstances" that preclude challenges and Selena returns to the now tight-faced Maximilian.

Finally, Victor straightens his back and pulls himself up to his full height. With a stern gaze, he looks over the assembled wolves, and in the portentous voice he uses for all pronouncements in the Old Tongue, he delivers the traditional blessing:

Eadig hæmed.

Happy fucking.

Chapter 17

ALL I NEED IS A QUICK CHECK OF THE SKY TO TELL ME I HAVE only five days before the Iron Moon. Though there is, of course, an app for it.

In five days, Pack members who work or study in Vermont, New Hampshire, Downstate, or Canada will all come home, because no one is allowed to change Offland.

Everything that requires hands and voices must be done before sundown on Thursday. John rotates through a long list of plausible excuses he leaves on the outgoing message explaining why he is "unable to take your call at this time," without saying anything about the difficulty of picking up a phone with claws and the impossibility of speaking.

Supplies are inventoried, and lists are made for the Iron Moon Table, when the moon is finished with us and the whole Pack is together and in skin and we are able to converse and conduct Pack business. Ti and I are repairing the roof on one of the dormitories for Offlanders who might need a night at home in their skins before or after the Iron Moon.

Since Ti doesn't truly understand what it means to have a Pack or a territory, which I still find just so sad, I try to explain exactly what an Offlander is.

"Some Packs still rely on isolation to protect them. The Nunavut Pack does. Of course, the Siberian Taiga Pack, but who knows how much longer they'll be able to do that? Ready for the lathing?" Ti holds out his hand as I pass along the thin strip of wood. "Our first Alpha insisted that we learn and adapt to human ways, so nearly half of our wolves live Offland at any given time."

"Doing what?"

"Students. Others work to protect the Pack's interests as fund managers. We have a whole bunch of lawyers."

"I thought Victor was your lawyer," Ti says through the nail clenched tight in the corner of his mouth.

"Victor's our Deemer. He deals only with Pack law. The others work within the human legal system. They're the ones who maintain the Trust that protects us. Well, mostly Elijah Sorensson, the 9th's Alpha. He's been in charge of it ever since I can remember. Can I have some nails?

"Ti?" He is crouched on one knee, staring into the forest. "Are you okay?"

"Fine. I'm fine. Here." He passes me a box of nails. "How about you?"

"Me?"

"Yeah, I mean, have you ever lived Offland?"

"No." I set the lathing carefully in place.

I know he's looking at me.

"Have you ever *been* Offland?"

I hammer a little too hard, and the lathing splits.

"Silver. Have you ever been Offland?"

"The Homelands are big," I say a little defensively. "And there's lots to do…"

He jumps down from the roof before I can even get to the ladder.

"…here."

I run after him, skipping every third step, trying to keep up. "Where do you think you're going?"

He doesn't say anything, just grips his stupid hammer tighter. He steps over the little stream that separates the dormitories, heading straight to Cabin One.

"Ti!" I hiss. "This is his home and Evie's… Evie is *very nervous* around Shifters, and you can't just walk in—and certainly not carrying this." I grab the hammer, but Ti keeps going. My heels scrape long tracks in the cold, damp ground.

He doesn't let go until he starts rapping on the door of the Alpha cabin. I let fly the hammer, and it hits the shallow water with a dull splash, just as Evie peers through the crack of the door. I lower my eyes.

"What do you want, Shifter?" asks Evie, lengthening the consonant blend so it sounds positively venomous. *Shhhifter*.

"I need to talk to John."

Her mouth tightens. "Get away from my house," she snaps and slams the door.

But before it closes, Ti pushes his work boot against the frame and keeps it open a tiny chink. "Can I ask… What have I ever done to you?"

"It's not what you have done," she spits out, a single hate-filled eye visible through the crack. "It's what you *will* do. The others, they know *about* Shifters. But I've actually known them. Shifters are a lie from the moment they draw their first breath. And you… You're worse than any of them. Pretending you're human when it's convenient. Pretending you're Pack when it's not. You can lie to the world. But the second I know you're lying to us, *I will tear your goddamn throat out*."

Maybe I shouldn't have said that Evie's nervous around Shifters. Maybe I should've been honest and told him she hates them.

"Evie?" John comes running. He walks up to his mate and whispers for a moment; she whispers back angrily. He shakes his head and then comes out, pulling the door closed behind him.

Maybe he saw us approach the cabin or heard Evie's voice from the Great Hall. Whatever happened, John hadn't bothered to put on his boots before he ran over. He sits heavily on the steps.

"You wanted something?"

"She's never been Offland?" Ti asks.

"I told him not to come," I blurt out.

"How about we try one at a time," John says, peeling off muddy, gray ragg socks with burgundy heels.

"Silver has never been Offland?"

John looks at me, and I shrug. He shrugs and hangs his socks over the low railing. "Don't think so. Pack go Offland when they're needed."

"So she hasn't gone because she's not needed?"

"*Ti!*" I whisper urgently and pull at his waistband. That is no way to talk to your Alpha.

John puts his hands on his knees and then stands, descending a single step so that he is face-to-face with Ti, their noses almost touching. "Before you judge us, *Tiberius*, let me put this in terms a human would understand. Silver is my brother's child. My brother's only child. I *loved* my brother. He lived a great Alpha. And he *died* a great Alpha, dragging this"—here he points to me—"tiny, deformed, frozen thing halfway across the Great North with a hole in his chest.

"I brought her home so she could be marked by her Pack and die on her land. But she wouldn't do it. *She wouldn't die*. And in defiance of every law and tradition,

I kept that broken-up pup in my pocket. I fed her with a dropper until her eyes opened. Three wolves fought me, because they took it as a sign of weakness in a new Alpha. And we cannot coddle weakness."

"But if she's your brother's only child, don't you owe her something more than this?"

"You really are a human, aren't you? That's all they ever think about: What they're owed. Their *rights*. Never about what *they* owe. Never their *responsibilities*."

Lana, a tiny nursling who lives next door, has heard the commotion and stumbles toward John, looking for comfort. He scoops her up, and she rolls over onto her back, her head twisted to the side, staring at us from the protection of the Alpha's arms. Next year, she will leave her family's cabin and go to the children's quarters so she can be with her echelon. Pack ties must always take precedence over family.

"Silver is as good a wolf as any in this Pack," John says, scratching behind Lana's ear. "But going Offland requires her to be a convincing human."

"I can do it, John. Ti's been very helpful, and I'll even do that online human behaviors course Leonora's always—"

"A man notices a wolf sitting next to him at the movie theater," John interrupts.

"Ouu. I love this one."

"I know you do, Silver. But maybe Tiberius doesn't know it? So…a man sees a wolf sitting next to him at the movie theater. And the guy says to the wolf, 'What are you doing here?' The wolf shrugs and says, 'Well, I liked the book.'"

And I laugh and laugh and laugh.

John looks at Ti before gently pushing my upper lip down to cover my teeth, the ones that are too long and too sharp and too feral ever to be mistaken for human.

The screen door bangs in the cabin next door, and Paula calls for her daughter. John waves to her, pointing to Lana.

"I wish I could hold on to them all," he says, stroking the pup nestled in his arms. "But you're right, I can't. Silver, tell Tara that you two will be making the town run on Wednesday. She'll get you an ID and give you the list. Then, Silver, come see me in my office. There are some things I need to go over. And, Tiberius, this is on you. If something happens to her, know that we will hunt you down."

Lana squirms as John passes her to Paula. The retreating pup stares at him over her mother's shoulder.

"Don't worry," says Ti. "If something happens to her, you won't have to hunt me down, because I will already be dead."

I tell Tara that I'm going into the City, and she says Plattsburgh isn't the City. I tell Gran Tito that I'm going into the City, and he says Plattsburgh isn't the City. Even Leelee has the gall to tell me that Plattsburgh isn't the City.

"Can you drive a stick?" Tara asks Ti, her hand floating over a shallow box of keys.

He motions with one hand, one eyebrow up, which must mean something to Tara, because she throws him a key. "The red Wrangler."

John and Leonora both gave me careful instructions about dealing with humans, trying to explain the balance between interacting with the community and keeping it at arm's length.

I check three times to make sure I have the list and the cash and the prepaid card and the map of Plattsburgh. I plot out the places we need to go: the post office, the Corner-Stone bookstore, the True Value, Hannaford. We also have to go to Tails of the Adirondacks, because the pups have hidden all the cheese chews and we need more peanut butter toothpaste. Last minute, Tara tells me to get another gallon of Skunk-Off. "I don't know what the pups are up to, but we're going through it like water, and the skunks won't be dormant for two more moons."

Tara says if we need lunch, we should go to Himalaya, because the other restaurants serve mostly carrion.

In the Wrangler, Ti puts on a leash. This is a man who tore his throat raw trying to get out of a collar, but he voluntarily puts on a leash.

"You have to put yours on too," he says.

As if.

"It's the law, Sil."

"I don't care what any stupid leash law says, I'm not wearing it."

"It's not a leash; it's a seat belt. Protects you from accidents, and if you don't wear it, we will be stopped."

"Oh."

"That's right, 'oh.'" He starts jostling down the rough road leading from the Great Hall. At the gate, I tell Gabriel that we're going to the City.

"So I've heard. Yay, Plattsburgh," he says and gives me a fist bump.

It's a slow trip down our rough access road. We wobble and bump, and stones spit against the bottom of the car.

"Why didn't you tell me you were John's niece?"

"It's not like it means anything. All that matters is Pack."

At the end of the road, we make a right-hand turn and we're on the human road, made entirely of crushed stone glued tightly together. It's very smooth and Ti starts going faster and when I push the button, the window comes down and a thousand scents flood my nose and the wind whips my hair every which way.

"How did your parents die, exactly?"

"No one knows *exactly*," I say to the wind. "They stopped on the road, probably something to do with the pregnancy because they had changed. Someone with a gun saw them. My mother was shot in the head and died instantly. My father was shot in the chest. He managed to rip me and my two brothers out and then ran. He was dead when the hunters caught up with him, and by the time the Pack tracked us, my brothers were dead too."

We turn onto another road that has space for two cars going in opposite directions, and Ti goes even faster.

"You told me your parents passed. *That* is not passing."

"It is if you're a wolf."

I love the wind on my face and the smells that keep coming faster and faster. Mink and bog and granite and cedar and roadkillandbalsamandporcupineand-honeyfungusand—

"Wildfire," he says, reaching across to my hand, "keep your head in the car."

And I wrap my fingers in his and smile because my lungs are full, my heart is full, and the wind is beating against my skin, and I'm going so much faster than I could ever run.

Chapter 18

ONE OF THE THINGS THAT LEONORA FAILED TO TELL US about Offland is that movies add like a solid foot to humans. It turns out that among the humans of Plattsburgh, at least, five foot nine isn't all that runty.

At Hannaford, Ti leaves me in the checkitout line with our cart so that he can run back and get the coffee that I didn't pick up. I was moving down the aisle, looking for the right brand, when I was absolutely socked by the overwhelming smell of carrion. By the time Ti found me staring terrified at the cases filled with watery pink slabs of rotting flesh, I'd completely forgotten about the coffee.

"Stay here, Sil," he says. "I'll be right back. Just keep moving the cart in the line and don't do"—he looks around briefly before adding—"anything." He draws two fingers down my upper lip to remind me about my teeth.

But then a woman tries to maneuver a cart filled with three children and food down the aisle behind me, and because it has a balky wheel, it gets jammed behind a display of hand sanitizer. No matter how much she pushes and pulls, the cart won't move. She doesn't seem to understand that it needs to be lifted. There is a man behind me in a Patriots sweatshirt who is mumbling something about Bill Belichick. I tell him I'll be right back.

"What? No, hold on, Frank. What did you say?"

"Frank? My name's Silver, actually. And this is my cart. I'll be right back."

He rolls his eyes.

"You need to lift it," I say to the woman, but she doesn't seem to understand, so I just do it myself, hoping that she won't be angry and think I meant to expose her weakness.

She opens her mouth and closes it, but no sound comes out. Humans are always talking, so this naturally worries me. I make conversation, like Leonora told me I should to put humans at ease. I ask if the three children in the cart are all hers. She nods slowly, and I congratulate her on her fertility and on surviving so many live births.

The littlest kid who is seated up front starts to cry, and the mother takes him out and glowers at me. One of the kids in the back says I'm very strong for a grandma. He is small, so I explain to him that I am 270 moons and it will be many, many moons before I breed. If ever. A lot of people stare, and it's not friendly, and I suddenly feel very self-conscious about my hair. I tuck it under my hoodie and suck my lips tighter over my teeth.

Someone pushed our cart out of line. The man in the Patriots sweatshirt is now almost at the front.

I'd told the man in the Patriots sweatshirt that I'd be right back, I explain when Ti tumbles his armload of vacuum-packed coffee bricks into the cart that is at the back of the checkitout line again. "He probably figured he could move our cart, what with me being a subordinate and all."

The man, who has already put his groceries on the counter, keeps talking and laughing, though his laughter fades as his eyes wander from me to Ti, whose massive arms are folded in front of his chest. The man grabs at his groceries and stumbles away, oranges dropping to the floor. Not that Ti has done anything. Just stared through him with those hard eyes.

I put a box on the conveyor belt that moves it from point A to point A plus two feet. The lady rubs it over a window until it chirps. I put another box on the conveyor belt and watch it proceed on its strange little pilgrimage. The lady's eyebrows shoot up.

Someone behind us coughs irritably, and Ti starts cramming things willy-nilly on the conveyor belt, and they all crowd to the lady, who no longer has time to do anything with her eyebrows. A boy at the end tries to put things into plastic bags, but I open up the old firewood bags we use instead. We get enough of other people's plastic bags flying around, and it makes John angry when they get stuck in our trees. A few years back, one got tangled around Tilly's neck, and she ran terrified through the woods with this white bag that said…

Thank you

Thank you

Thank you

Thank you

…flapping around her head until a posse of Pack finally corralled her and got it off. I worried for nearly a moon about why someone would demonstrate gratitude in such a blatantly cruel way until one of the older wolves explained.

I toss one bag over each shoulder, take one in each hand. Ti slides a plastic card back into his pocket and then takes the other four.

I'm starting to feel less and less comfortable, feeling like for all the reading I've done, I don't really understand this world, and at Tails of the Adirondacks, I forget myself and suggest that twelve dollars is a lot to pay for a guinea pig that seems to have a lot of fur and very little meat. I stumble over the answer to why we need a gross of cheese chews and twenty-four tubes of peanut butter toothpaste. "Because the chicken toothpaste tastes disgusting."

"What she means is that the dogs prefer the peanut butter. We breed dogs," Ti says. "Huskies and Northern Inuits."

I know it's what John wants us to say, but I can't get my mouth to form the sounds. Our pups don't like carrion toothpaste. *Our children like peanut butter.*

I'm not hungry; I just want to go home, but we have one last stop. We get stuck waiting while huge machines tear up the earth with massive claws that rip through the roots of trees. New Mun✳pal ✳arking Lot Openi✳g Soon, says the bullet-riddled sign.

At our final stop, Ti pumps gas while I take my list into the station. The boss is a tall, lanky young man with lots of pimples, straight-cut bangs, and a blue polo shirt. He wears a red and white hat with a grease-stained bill that says Utica Club on it.

He seems nicer than most and helps me find the remaining things on our list. I've got two cans of oil, a compressor belt, an air filter, and a sealed beam headlight.

"Never seen a girl color up her hair all white 'n' gray."

"Didn't color it. It just comes this way."

"Can I touch it?" he says, his hand raised.

Now, honestly, if he wants to cover me, he should just say so. Though he's got Omega written all over him. I wish Ti would hurry up.

The boss puts his hand in my hair. "You're real pretty," he says quietly.

"I see that you have an erection," I say, trying to sound sympathetic. "But I feel I should tell you that you would probably have to fight him"—I point out the window—"if you want to cover me."

Ti sees me and mouths, *You okay?* I wave back.

The boss looks at me and then at Ti and, with his mouth still gaping, lurches toward the back office. I'm guessing he hadn't anticipated that a runt like me would have a bedfellow like Ti.

Not a minute later, a man in a red button-down shirt, camouflage jacket, and blue jeans belted high around his waist comes out of the same office.

"That your car?"

"The red one? Uhh, yes?"

"You up there with John Torrance?"

"Yes, I'm John's niece," I say, remembering what John told me about blood being more important to humans than Pack.

"And him?" He points to where Ti just hung up the gas nozzle. "He with you?"

"He's my bedfellow." John told me that if anyone asks, Ti is my boyfriend. Not bedfellow. *Boyfriend.* But I can't do it. It's like the thing about dogs. Some words feel wrong on my tongue. Ti is no boy, and he's not a friend either. A friend doesn't make me feel like climbing him, my legs tied around his hips, until he thickens and swells into my mazy spaces.

The man in the camouflage jacket sucks on his back teeth with a sharp *sluck*.

"What the hell goes on up there?"

"We are a group of like-minded individuals"—this time, except for one little fumble, I recite John's instructions exactly—"who seek to live in harmony with nature and our fellow Pack…man." There was another word he told me, but I've forgotten what it was. I leave out the dog part.

"Hippies?"

"Hippies. That's it."

"Where'd your 'bedfellow' go?"

I look toward the deserted car. "I'm guessing the bathroom."

There are a lot of irritating noises here. The flickering lights overhead. The refrigerators. The countertop oven with wrinkled carrion sticks circling endlessly on metal rods.

"I don't much like hippies."

And everything smells like death: the gas, this man, and those wrinkled carrion sticks. HOT DOGS, the sign says, 2 FOR $1.50.

The dog in me is getting panicky. She doesn't like the overheated air buffeting my skin or the slick plastic smell everywhere.

And she wants to claw out that man's disapproving eyes.

The bell rings, and those disapproving eyes narrow, watching Ti carefully. "Where'd you go?"

"Bathroom," Ti says in that quiet, dark voice that feels like night air on my soul right about now. "If that's okay by you."

"No, it's not okay. I don't like you people. I don't like that you buy up all that land and don't do a damn thing with it. I don't like that when I try to do something with *my* land, land that has been in my family *for generations*, Torrance calls in the government with some crap about polluting the aquifer."

Ah. So *this* is the Junkyard Man.

"You know, one of our pups fell—" I start, but Ti interrupts me.

"Why don't I just pay, and then we'll be on our way." He hands the man another one of the prepaid cards the Pack keeps in a box in the office.

"I'll take a receipt," Ti says when the man hands the card back.

"You'll take yourself out of here is what you'll do." And the man pulls back his camouflage jacket. I see the handle of a big gun stuck in a holster.

In that second, my breath comes fast and my heart beats hard and a growl rumbles through my chest, but Ti just shakes his head at me.

How is it that he is never afraid? How is it that I never scent that cocktail of salt and old leather, the potent combination of sweat and adrenaline, the smell of fear? In one step, he pulls the receipt out of the cash register and hovers above the man so that the Junkyard Man can feel the many inches Ti has on him. Feel that this man, my *bedfellow*, has the BMI of a jackhammer.

The bell rings at the door, and the man lets his jacket fall, covering the gun. It's no one, just a thin older man with a yellowed mustache and yellow fingers.

The man looks for a moment at Ti, and then his eyes slide back to the Junkyard Man. "Marlboro Red, Anderson. Soft pack."

Ti's mouth tightens, his nose flares under his furrowed brow, and my unflappable bedfellow suddenly smells like a crushed cottonmouth.

"Time to go," he snaps, putting his hand around my arm.

The door to the back office is opened slightly. The boss watches through the crack.

"I can't believe you let him treat us that way." Bafflement flits across the boss's pimply face as I point to Anderson. "I don't know how you got to be in charge, because you've got the balls of an Omega."

Ti jerks hard on my arm, and I stumble across the threshold of the body shop.

"What would make you say that?" he says, clambering into the car beside me. "He's not in charge; he's just some high-school kid."

"Didn't you see? It said, right here…" I jab my finger at a spot high on my left breast. "It said 'BOSS' in big letters."

"Oh Jesus, Sil."

Ti starts the car, and the engine roars on. I sniff hard, trying to get rid of the smell of the carrion sticks, but all I get is the smell of petroleum. The faces of the angry junkyard man and the frightened boy who was not the boss and the man with the yellowed mustache tapping his red-and-white package against the heel of his palm stare through the window until we are out of sight.

At a stop sign, Ti reaches across me to pull on the seat belt.

But I'm feeling angry and like I need to run, and I push him away.

"You have to wear it."

"*I can't.*"

A car behind us beeps, and I leap out of my seat.

"Listen to me," Ti says. "Let me just get you out of town, then we'll undo it."

Whoever it is leans on their horn, and my breathing comes faster, and I kick off my shoes.

"Shit," Ti hisses, then steps on the gas, one hand holding the wheel, the other pushing me back against the seat.

Unzipping my jeans, I wriggle my hips until my bottom half is bare.

"*Not now. Just try to hold on for me.*"

But it's too late. My face starts to push forward before I've even stripped off my shirt. Ti floors it, taking the curves at a squeal. At a dirt road, he peels off down what will probably be a snowmobile track soon.

He hits the brakes and then comes around to my side and opens the door. He lifts my grotesque half-changed body from the seat. My eyes can't focus and my ears can't distinguish, but as I lean against his chest, I feel the rumble of his voice.

As soon as he lays me on the moldering pine needles beside the path, I start to stumble off, ricocheting against a willow.

I'm already far away when I can finally hear him, his usually soft voice raised in a yell.

"*Run, Wildfire. Don't let anyone see you.*"

I'm careful to keep low and to the trees as I race for our territory. Once I cross the marked and posted boundary, though, I don't head straight back to the Home Pond. Instead, I run wild, reveling in the crunch of frost-covered leaves under my paws. At the peaks, I breathe deeply the ice-cold air and watch the subtle shifts of soft gray over the lower peaks and valleys all around me, each damp caress washing away the heat and death.

John howls, telling me that's enough already and it's time to come home.

The sun is almost gone by the time I stumble awkwardly up to the Boathouse dock. Both big wooden chairs are occupied. John nods to Ti and puts his hand in my ruff.

"Tomorrow," John says. "Early," he says. He doesn't say that I'm in deep trouble, that there will be hell to pay, but as I lay myself down and roll my shoulders back, starting the change, I know there will be.

No law is more strictly enforced than the law against changing Offland. It is the only way to protect our sacred wild. The humans already slaughter the *æcewulfs*. Hunt them with rifles and bolts from the ground and from the air. If they found out about us...

Shit.

As soon as I'm in skin, Ti opens the big red-and-gray-striped blanket wide. I curl naked into his lap, and he props his head on mine.

I lay my hand on his chest. "Why were you so angry about that man in the gas station? Not the man with the gun. The other one. The man with the dying lungs?"

"I wasn't. You were getting upset. I was worried about you."

I frown, my finger beating with the speeding rhythm of his heart. I know there's something going on inside here. A man as much as threatened him with a gun. But Ti stayed stone-faced and quiet voiced. That changed, though—I know it, I smelled it—when he saw the man with the yellow-stained fingers and breath like coal and rot.

"Ti?" I shift up so I can whisper in his ear. "You

know we're not allowed to kill without eating. But if you need me to, I will eat him for you."

He doesn't say anything, but his thick arms pull tight around me. We listen for a while to the coyote shrieks in the distance.

"You know," he finally says, "you're the only person who has ever wanted to protect me."

When the sun is gone and the clouds cover the waxing gibbous moon, he says, "I don't think he would taste very good."

"No. I didn't think he would."

"Kyle," I call softly to the young man coming from the kitchen with an enormous hunk of corn bread. "Kyle!"

Kyle is the 12th's very sweet, slightly anxious Theta. We didn't know each other well, what with him being in the 12th, but then his bedfellow left for an internship at some office in Albany last year, and we started running together from time to time.

"Do me a favor, please?" I look back into the office where John and Victor are still hunched in conversation. "If you see Ti coming this way, can you stop him?"

Kyle stoops suddenly and loses several inches.

"M'ou wan *me* to thtop *Tibewius*?" he asks, crumbs spewing.

"Just *stall* him. You know, talk to him. Engage him in conversation? Pleeease."

"Silver?" John calls out. "A decision has been made."

At the sound of John's voice, Kyle disappears.

"*Kyle!*" I hiss into the hall. "*Pleeease.*"

I duck quickly back into John's office. I knew there

would be a punishment, and I was pretty certain I knew what it would be. John and Victor have offered me a choice that is no kind of choice at all.

"Right," I say. "So let's get this over with."

"There have to be witnesses," Victor says. "And you are not wearing *that*"—he points to my jeans and long-sleeved T-shirt (*Geek Mountain State: Geeking Out in the Green Mountains*)—"are you?"

"John? Tiberius wasn't raised Pack, and I'm not sure he's going to understand—"

"I agree. Get Tristan and gather your witnesses, Deemer. We will not be standing on ceremony." Victor starts to object, but before he can get a word out, John says that his Alpha wants him to make it snappy. Victor slinks out, huffing and chuffing about respect for the Old Ways. I know that Taking the Stone like this is not in keeping with the dignity of the Old Ways, but if Ti tracks me down, I think we will discover that he doesn't give a rat's ass about the Old Ways.

Luckily, the fire is already going in the Great Hall. Victor starts to object to the ritual being performed inside, away from the view of the moon, in front of an unhappy batch of witnesses who keep looking at their watches, but drops it as soon as John catches his eye.

"Is it ready yet?" I ask.

"No, it's not ready yet," Victor snaps. "Right hand or left?"

"Right," I say immediately, and Victor nods. *That*, at least, is as it should be.

Kyle's screeching yelp in the distance makes us all turn.

"Shit," I observe.

"Quite," John agrees and signals for Tara to lock the door.

Something breaks through the undergrowth. "*Silver!*"

"Deemer?" says John, as the sound gets closer. "Any time now."

"We need to bind her hand to keep it open," Victor says.

"No time," I say. "Just do it. I'll manage."

When the searing-hot stone settles onto my hand, every breath I have ever taken explodes from my lungs. My hand stays open, though.

Ti crashes through the storm doors into the foyer and starts throwing himself at the main doors of the Great Hall, screaming my name. Built to withstand the carelessness of the Pack and the aggression of the Adirondack winter, the doors are solid oak, but even they start to groan.

"Ach," says Sten disgustedly. In that one sound, he compacts a world of complaint about replacing the storm doors and possibly the frames and even the main doors and how no wolf who values his pelt had better grouse about their dinner getting cold. *Ach.*

"Are we almost done, Deemer?" John asks. "I'd like to open the door before the hinges give."

Victor nods. I hiss a little as he pulls the branding stone off my hand with a pair of fireplace tongs, then skitters away, leaving Tristan to treat my hand with cool water and bear grease.

On John's signal, Tara turns the lock and steps back.

"*What the fuck is going on?*" Ti looks around at John and the witnesses, his eyes unflinching and his nose flared. "And why does it smell like barbecue?"

"Hey, Ti. I think there's some corn bread in the kitchen, if you're hungry."

"Do *not* change the subject."

"I think perhaps we should leave Silver to explain," says John, and with a nod, Victor, Tristan, Tara, and all of the other witnesses stream out after him.

Ti bends over me, honing in immediately on my throbbing hand, slathered in bear grease. His jaw twitches as he looks at the swollen, red skin of my palm and the clear arrow there.

↑

"Just what the hell is that?" he asks furiously.

"Ti, please, you've got to stop fracking out."

"It's freaking out. I'm *freaking* out!"

"Listen to me. The most sacred thing we have is our wild. By changing Offland, I endangered that. It is *fela-synnig*, most wicked. I had to be punished."

"*So they branded you?*" He jumps up and turns quickly toward the back. Victor's head pops back into the safety of John's office, and the door locks.

"This was *my* decision," I snap. "It's just a flesh wound. Besides, I am proud to wear Tiw's mark."

"Do *not* say that's my mark," he says. "I had nothing to do with it."

"Not Ti's mark, *Tiw*'s mark." He looks bewildered. "Tell me you don't know the story of Fenrir and Tiw?" But of course, he doesn't. How could he? His mother dead, his father hostile to his wild, it's up to me to make sure he knows our stories. Not the version humans tell themselves, but the one that wolves tell. The real one.

"So." And I start to tell him about Loki's son, the huge and terrifying wolf, Fenrir. I tell him how even the gods were afraid of his ferocious wildness and wanted him bound.

"The humans say Tiw volunteered to put his right hand in Fenrir's mouth as surety that the fine ribbon the gods meant to wrap around him would do Fenrir no harm, but as usual, the gods could not be trusted. The ribbon being made of bird spit or something was actually magic so powerful that it was able to chain Fenrir. Furious at this betrayal, Fenrir bit off Tiw's hand.

"We wolves have a different story. We say that Tiw did bind Fenrir, but he bound the wolf *inside* himself, having fed Fenrir his right hand, the hand that gods and humans use as warranty for their lies, so he would never make a false promise again. We say that once the wolf was bound within him, Tiw stopped being the god of war, as he had been, and instead became the god of law, because he understood in a way no one else could that law is the balance of freedom and restraint.

"It's the mark of a real wolf," I say urgently, my good hand against his cheek. "Someone who was more human would have taken the other option and stayed in skin for two moons."

He cradles my swollen, greased palm.

"And you, of course, couldn't do that, could you, Wildfire?"

"Never."

Later in the medic station, while waiting for Tristan to bandage my hand, I ask Ti what happened with Kyle.

"Mmmph," he says, taking a bite of apple. "When a Yankee says, 'Wow, so you're from Canada. How interesting,' you know you're being swindled."

Chapter 19

THE FIRST SUNNY DAY AFTER TWO WEEKS OF UNRELENTING gray, and Sten rushes us to put in the last storm windows and doors for the tempest just around the corner. I look at trees that are almost neon yellow and orange and red under the searingly blue sky, I sniff the air, listen to the unperturbed sounds of the animals, and ask him what makes him think it's going to rain.

Sten looks at me from under one bushy, reddish eyebrow and makes a little cough-rumble deep in his chest and hands me a rubber mallet.

Two hours later, as we are pounding the last of the tight-fitting second windows into their casings, black clouds skirt the mountains to the northwest and rain tumbles down in torrents.

A wolf runs through a puddle, heading fast toward the woods to the north. Then another heads to the woods to the west. More wolves come, their noses close to the damp ground.

Something's not right.

Ti stops hammering, his eyes unfocused, listening. "Who is Golan?" he asks.

Another wolf runs past.

"A pup. He's in Leelee's echelon. He was the one who caught the mouse that—"

"He's disappeared."

Rains are coming even thicker now and the cracks of

thunder faster, but outside, I can hear the voices calling Golan's name and the howls across the Homelands telling him to come home.

At the Great Hall, Pack in fur and skin wait for directions from John. Golan was last seen in the basement, hunting mice.

Wolves have circled the woods nearby and found no hint of Golan, but no hint of coyote either. Usually coyotes won't come near Home Pond because it's too well marked, but sick coyotes are unpredictable, and a pup is an easy meal.

"He's afraid of thunder," his father retorts when someone suggested again that he was probably outside.

We head to the empty basement, even though I tried to tell Ti that it was pointless. Every member of the Pack has already been here, and I can scent them all, but Ti just stands in the narrow hallway and opens his lungs long and slow, drawing the air through his nose.

"Ti, it's—"

But he holds up his hand and inhales again, moving slowly toward the door to dry storage. He leans down to a spot on the doorframe and looks at me. I sniff at it once, smelling first the traces of a dozen wolves. Then newly administered Skunk-Off. And finally, the oh-so-slight but unmistakable scent of Baileys and kibble.

I yell for John.

His heavy tread is already racing downstairs. I point to the spot Ti found without saying anything, hoping that we're both wrong.

"Did anyone see Ronan?"

"Ronan? He's probably dead or with the Nunavut Pack by now," Tara says.

"He's not. He's here," John snaps before raising his voice and asking why the hell no one stopped Ronan from coming into the Great Hall, doesn't exile mean anything to—

"John?" I say, looking only briefly into his eyes before settling on his chin. "Maybe he used the tunnel?"

"What tunnel?"

I head toward the root cellar, sensing John's fury behind me. The trapdoor is camouflaged with the same packed earth as the rest of the floor, so it blends in, but it isn't hidden exactly. I assumed that if I knew about it, John did as well.

But when he traces the scuff marks and finds the spot near the wall wide enough for fingers or claws, I know he's never seen it before.

John opens it and breathes in.

"Where does this go?"

"Pretty deep into the woods." I start up the stairs. "It was supposed to be for emergencies. To escape. That's what Gran Sigeburg said."

"And Ronan knew about this?"

I nod. "I honestly didn't know it was a secret."

At the top of the steps, John bellows for Golan's parents. "And Charlie too."

My stomach tightens. I like Ronan's father. Charlie's always been very sweet to me. He pretended to be pleased when it was announced that I would be Ronan's *schildere*, even though it had to be a disappointment.

Charlie lost his mate and Ronan's two littermates during childbirth and poured all his sad dreams and affections into the sole survivor. Now, if we're right and Ronan is on the Homelands and did something, anything, with Golan, then the Pack will hunt the last member of Charlie's family. And they will kill him.

Water collects in the forest canopy, weighing down the weakening leaves until they tumble down in thick clots.

The rain made it impossible for Ronan to disguise the mouth of the tunnel. Oscar and Livia, Golan's parents, scratch at the door with their claws at the damp pile of mulch over the hatch. When John pulls it open, they drop their heads in, smelling with their keener wild senses. It doesn't take long for them to confirm that Golan had been there and Ronan, but the downpour wreaks havoc on the scent above ground.

"Your Alpha," John says, using the commanding voice and the formulation that brooks no dissent, "will have you find Golan Liviasson and Ronan Eardwrecca."

Ronan has no rights anymore. Not to Pack land, or Pack law, or even a Pack name. He is Ronan Eardwrecca. Ronan Banished.

Whenever John speaks, the Pack listens, but when he speaks as Alpha, the Pack obeys. Those of us who are still in skin shrug out of our clothing and fall to the ground, changing.

What started with the shivering of my naked human body under cold autumn rain becomes a ripple and then an undulation and then a violent thrashing as tendons twang, muscles slide, bones shift, spine lengthens into tail, lungs expand, and my heart strengthens. My nose itches, but I'm helpless to scratch it. Ti yanks on my leg, and the pain makes me forget the itch in my nose.

The bigger the wolf, the longer the change, so they are still roiling and gurgling and stretching when I am done.

Ti has put on some wolf's discarded parka and stands

utterly still as the rain pours over his face. He moves his head a little, angling it to the side, his chest expanding on long, slow breaths.

As a wolf, I can see the silvered movement of water on the black bark of a distant cherry. I hear the scrabble of salamanders and the creak of branches. I smell woody fungus on the roots of a downed tree that I can't see. But aside from that tiny hit of Baileys and kibble at the entrance to the tunnel, I can't smell Ronan. This explains how we've been running through so much Skunk-Off.

"This way," Ti says and starts to jog through the woods.

Ronan never cared much about the Homelands, preferring the promises of the world beyond. So my guess is if he's anywhere, it's in one of my hiding places. As Ti picks up speed through the High Pines, I know where Ronan has gone.

The Pack doesn't like the Krummholz, "the Crooked Woods," that tormented nowhere land between the High Pines and the wind-scoured peaks. Here, nature is stretched thin to breaking: there are no forests, just scattered treelike deformities clinging to the mountaintops. Some creep near the ground like penitents. Some stand like flags, scrubbed bare on the windward side.

It haunts our tales as the place between places:

> Winter-blasted, wind-twisted,
> The world's last sentinel.
> Forsworn, forsaken
> By all but the forever
> Wolf.

Sounded better in the Old Tongue, but I've forgotten the original.

I brought Ronan here because while I love the whole of the Homelands, I have a special warmth for the Krummholz. Maybe it shouldn't have come as any surprise that where I saw something noble in the small and crippled trees clinging fiercely to their precarious existence, Ronan saw only pathos and failure.

Ronan had once been the presumptive Alpha of our echelon. It was years ago, so it's hard for me to remember, but I think that was very important to him. He'd been born with a lucky genetic mix that made him biggest and most powerful almost without trying.

Because he didn't have to work at it, he was eventually surpassed by those who did. Like Solveig, who'd spent grim hours shifting big rocks. After a few months of rock shifting, she challenged Ronan and, in the fight, tore into him over and over again until John told her to put an end to it. She didn't want Ronan as her Beta, so she not only made him submit, she made him weak, vulnerable. Challenge by challenge, he started his slide down until he landed at the very bottom with me.

The only thing his big size got him was alcohol when he was nineteen. He'd come home usually drunk and sometimes with money. He hid his winnings under my mattress. "It's not like you're ever going to use it."

I kept his secrets, because without him, I would be a lone wolf. And I shared my own, hoping he would see that while I might be a crippled runt, I had cool stuff in my arsenal too.

Ti follows me toward the eye-shaped break in the layered rock that would be tough for him to squeeze through, but I slip easily over the lip and under the lid. As a wolf, my eyes adjust to the dim light. As a wolf, though, I am almost undone by the smells. Sickly sweet spilled liquor. Rotting meat. Ammonia and excrement. My nose is overwhelmed and useless for scenting out Golan.

"Is that you, Silver?" asks a tatty sleeping bag at the back of the cave.

I sneeze as I push aside some old boxes.

"Not looking for me, then, *schildere*? He's in the bag. Stupid thing. Would not shut up. Couldn't very well have the Pack knowing the exile had returned, could I?"

My heart pounding against my ribs, I gently scrape at the cord of the backpack near Ronan's feet until I hear a tiny muffled whimper. With my paw, I nudge Golan out. His little eyes look terrified over a crumpled muzzle of duct tape. Though he stinks of fresh piss, I pick him up gently between my teeth—the pup goes limp as they always do—and hurry him away from all this dirt and misery to the mouth of the cave.

As soon as he feels the fresh air, Golan's little legs churn up the dried wort that serves as ground cover up here, but I don't let him go. Pulling a Swiss Army knife from his pocket, Ti clamps one hand tight around the struggling pup's jaw and carefully cuts through the tape so Golan can at least open his mouth.

I let him go, and the terrified fur ball runs, with Ti hot on his trail.

"I don' suppose you can just take the kid," Ronan slurs behind me. "Forget you foun' me?"

I suck in a deep breath of cold, wet Krummholz air and howl.

John responds almost immediately.

"Of course not." Ronan turns in his sleeping bag and stares at the roof of the cave. "You know I went to John before the *Dæling*. After I'd had those two disastrous challenges. It wasn't fair; the ground had been so slick during that first fight that I'd slipped. My leg was still messed up two days later when I had my second challenge, but John refused to let me have another chance."

I don't know why he's telling me this. What has this got to do with kidnapping a tiny pup, taping his muzzle, and shoving him in a backpack?

"Anyway, we got to talking about how I was born to be an Alpha, and once my luck changed and I got back on my feet, I would be again, but—and I don't mean this as an insult or anything, you understand, it's just true—you were never going to be anything but a Kappa *at best*. So while I might be your *schildere*, I would never mate you."

I peer over my shoulder.

"You know what John said?"

Ti comes back with the struggling pup held tight against him. He strokes Golan's head and sits on the rock outside the cave's entrance. The rain has soaked the cupped hood of his borrowed parka.

"John said you were twice the wolf I would ever be, and he'd be damned if he'd ever let you be mated with me. With *me*."

I hear Ronan struggle with the zipper of his sleeping bag.

"What a waste," he says. I look toward the back of the cave. Ronan is sitting now on top of the sleeping bag, a once-white dress shirt falling open, revealing soft, pale thighs and a limp, dark cock. "I mean him. The Shifter. Yeah, you. I'm talking about you."

Ti turns his head to the side, not far enough to see Ronan but far enough to make clear he's heard him.

"I told you my luck would change, Sil, and it did. I got back all the money John gave me and more, and I was free. I rented a car, and you know where I drove it? East of no-fucking-where. I had no place I *had* to be. Nothing I *had* to do. I bought shirts that weren't easy to care for. And guess what? I screwed human women who were never going to breed more Pack. I was free to do what I wanted.

"I was *free*," he murmurs once more. "But then my luck changed again, and I was right back where I started."

Golan has settled a little and allows his head to fall against Ti's broad chest.

"Silver?" Ti says quietly. "Any water in there?"

Ronan leans back and, grabbing something from behind him, throws it toward me. I nose the bottle toward Ti, who pours it into his cupped hand.

With a sharp bark, John announces himself. Ronan turns his face to the wall. He doesn't have any fight left in him, but that doesn't mean he's going to walk to his death. They're going to have to drag him out.

Chapter 20

THE CIRCLE OF WOLVES IN THE CLEARING TIGHTENS AROUND Ronan, and for the first time since my *Dæling*, I am deeply grateful that I am not Pack. I am just a guest and don't have to be part of this.

But when I start to lope away, Ti doesn't move. He doesn't understand what is happening, so I nip at his pant leg. The Alphas of each echelon are taking up their positions at the front of the circle. Everyone wants this over with quickly.

Opening a passage for Charlie, John nudges Ronan's father toward his son. In its mercy, Pack law allows First Blood to Ronan's family, so that when the Pack eviscerates him, Ronan won't feel anything. I plant my front paws and pull Ti harder, because I really don't want to watch Charlie rip out his son's throat.

Ti doesn't move.

John nudges Charlie again, but Charlie just stares at Ronan, his head cocked, his mouth open. His eyes roll around the circle searching for help he won't find, because to be on Pack land as an exile is bad enough, but the only response to an attack on a pup is a *Slitung*, a flesh-tearing, and every wolf shows teeth. Charlie throws himself on the ground in front of John, his feet up in the air, his hips shimmying back and forth in a clownish show of submission.

John snaps at him.

Charlie follows our Alpha around, one ear up, the other down, his mouth open in a rabid leer, until with a quick look over his shoulder, John signals Tara to drag the broken wolf away the Pack. Tara grabs his muzzle tight in her powerful jaws and drags him off mewling. I run beside him whimpering too, begging Charlie to come to his senses long enough to do this last kindness. He seems not to even see me, more interested in the furry thing following behind him. As soon as Tara lets him go, he starts to chase his tail, barking.

Tara turns her back on him with a growl and a dismissive kick of rain-sodden soil. She heads back to the Pack, which clears a path for her. As John's Beta, Tara has a place of honor, but she also has a place of responsibility and is expected to be right up front for the *Slitung*. I stick to her slipstream and push through to the whimpering Ronan.

Rubbing my muzzle against his, I turn to John, my body down, my head between my paws. I'm not sure he will accept my claim to First Blood, but I have a better chance if I at least smell like the wolf who had been my *schildere* but who never wanted to be my mate.

John's nose bumps against mine, telling me to get up. With a quick snap of his jaws, the Pack retreats, giving us room. John is a good wolf and a great Alpha and, if given a choice, will always choose mercy.

First Blood allows for one bite only, and if Ronan decides to fight me, I doubt I'll be able to make the kill. But after everything that has happened, the once-upon-a-time Alpha of the 14th Echelon seems to understand that his luck is not going to change again.

He lies back with his chin stretched high, staring

at the mountains and the pinpoints of stars and the real world, the world of men, that he so wanted to be a part of.

Opening my jaws wide, I gently take his throat between them. It's what we do, and it means *trust me*. It means *I see you at your most vulnerable*.

I bite down fast and hard on the cartilage tube, giving it the same fatal break I would for a deer. Ronan struggles a little, and blood spurts into my mouth. I curl my tongue against the back of my throat, because I don't want to swallow this blood. I don't want to be nourished by this death.

The pulse of his blood slows, but I don't lift my head until it stops.

Before I even stumble out of the way, the Pack surges forward, eager to be done with this particular bit of ritual butchery.

I race for Clear Pond, my paws sinking through the cold, thick mud and dying sedges. Pushing the air out of my lungs, I sink into the water and stay down until my own throat is on the verge of collapse, and the blood that had already started to stiffen on my muzzle and chest and legs begins to melt away from my fur. Maybe there was so much that all of Clear Pond is tainted, but no matter how many gulps of water I take, my mouth still has the sharp, metallic tang of blood, and there's something stuck in my teeth.

I start to change, and as soon as I'm finished, I pick at the thing with my fingers until it comes loose. I don't look at it before throwing it into the weeds. I think the change was a mistake, though, because in skin, I feel the intense cold of the schist on my naked body and the icy water running from my hair down my back and the taste of death in my mouth. I can't stop shivering. I try to get wild again, but my muscles are spasming so hard that I can't. I lurch up on all fours and then to my legs and stumble only a few steps before collapsing again, my head on my knees.

A warm coat that smells like angelica and green corn and the earth before a storm settles around my shoulders. "Put it on," says that quiet voice, and Ti lifts me, guiding my arms into the sleeves, and then pulls me close to his even-warmer body. He says nothing, just holds me tight, letting me shiver against him.

"I killed him," I finally stutter.

He lifts my sodden hair out from under the collar of the coat.

"Yes, you did. And if you hadn't, he would have died in pain, and the whole Pack would have had the burden of it. Now only you do."

Ti doesn't say that I wasn't responsible or that I shouldn't feel guilty, but rather that it's a burden worth carrying and one that I'm strong enough to bear. His faith calms me in a way that no amount of coddling ever could.

It's one of the things I love about him.

"I can't get the taste of blood out of my mouth."

He doesn't respond. I guess he didn't hear, or knowing him, he did hear but doesn't think there's any point in responding. It doesn't matter. I settle my head back on his chest and listen to his heartbeat.

Did I say love?

He frees one arm and lifts my chin. It's dark for my poor human senses, but he's not like me, and the nearly full moon lights up the green glow of the lucidum in his eyes.

He hesitates, his lips hovering above mine, like a boy nervously contemplating his first kiss. But I know what he's hiding, and I stretch up as high as I can and wrap my arm around his neck, feeling the shape of his skull under the roughness of his cropped hair. I feel his mouth against mine, firm and ripe and warm and still closed.

Nuzzling the seam of his mouth. I catch his lower lip gently between my fangs, pulling him closer. *I know you, Tiberius. I know the wildness that you've always hidden there, but I am not human, and I want the untamed, inhuman sharpness of your mouth.*

I let go and lick my lip before gently circling his, my breath feathering his sensitive skin.

Finally, his lips open softly, and I seal my mouth around his, because this is his first kiss and mine too, and I am his shielder in all things. My tongue reaches into the warm, damp velvet of his mouth, gliding against his tongue, entangling it, and I sweep against the sharp tips of his canines. They are *just* like mine. Long and sharp and too feral, no matter how human he wants to pretend to be. His tongue flicks against mine, growing more insistent, raiding my mouth, taking and leaving me burning with the taste of bittersweet and tannin.

He picks me up, and my legs wrap around his waist, feeling the enveloping warmth of his coat swinging big and loose against my back and the hard denim-covered cock pushing fierce and tight against my front.

"Tiberius," I whisper against his mouth. "Make me warm again."

He walks slowly, making sure that with every step, his

hard length rocks deeper against me. Bracing me against an old pine, he lets go and pushes his jeans down, until I feel him press against me, and then he presses into me, into my mouth and into my sex.

This is what I need. This is raw and visceral and primal and wild. My thighs wrap around Ti's thrusting hips, the rough tree bark pushing up the anorak and chafing at my back, my killer's mouth tight against his.

With all the fierce grinding and sharp teeth, one of us bleeds—maybe both—and the new blood that seeps into my mouth washes away the taste of First Blood.

Pulling away, I sweep my damp, knotted hair to the side, and Ti breathes in deeply before biting down hard enough to ensure that when he slams into me, I stay anchored and ready for him. My legs clench around his thighs, as wave after shattering wave crests through me. And when his life pulses hot and deep inside, I am finally warm again.

Chapter 21

I THINK TI BELIEVES THE PACK HAS AN INNATE PASSION FOR hierarchies and laws and traditions. That's not it at all. It's that the complicated logistics of dealing with those three dumb, thumbless days *force* us to have all those hierarchies and laws and traditions. If it weren't for the Iron Moon, our orbits would have tightened long ago, shedding the Pack in favor of family until eventually we whirled in a tight circle of just ourselves alone.

Then we would have become like Shifters: human except with grumpy lunar dispositions.

"You know John's still going to be watching you."

"I figured as much."

"Are you really sure this is what you want to do?"

"I just can't, Silver. I think if I spent three days as a wolf, I'd never be able to turn back."

"Well, you better learn how, because I'm not doing this for you again."

"Just do it, will you? Wait, not yet. The gag."

I give Ti the thick, folded strap of clean T-shirt. As soon as he grips it between his teeth, he nods, and I bring the maul down hard on his leg.

Not sure the gag was even necessary. He doesn't scream at all, just gives a cracked groan. A light sheen of sweat covers his face.

"I heard a snap. Do you think it worked?"

He nods, the gag still clenched tight in his jaws.

"Good. Like I said, not doing that again."

It takes a bit of maneuvering, but I finally get Ti up. He drapes his arm over my shoulder. The sweat under his arm soaks into my shirt.

"How did you say this happened?" Tristan asks.

I explain how Ti slipped while jumping over that little gully.

"The one near the bayberry?"

"No. The one where the moose was sick and we herded him to the edge, and we thought we might be able to have moose, but John made us wait to see if it got better and then it got better?"

"That was a terrible day," Tristan says, nodding sadly. "Tragic."

"I know." I sigh. "Do you think we'll ever have moose?"

"Excuse me," Ti hisses. "My leg?"

"Oh, yes. Oblique fracture of the tibia. For anyone else, I wouldn't set it this close to the Iron Moon, and they'd just have to deal with the pain of changing. Since you don't have to change, I will set it. But be sure you tell John what happened."

When I tell John, I can see in his expression that our Alpha isn't happy about Ti spending the Iron Moon in skin when all the rest of us are wild. Tara sets up a rotation to watch him. She will also turn off the Wi-Fi, I guess so my bedfellow won't be tempted to buy a gun on Amazon.

Windows are closed, anything that might spoil over the next three days is composted, and the propane to the stove is switched off. The start batteries and fuel levels for the emergency generators are checked, because if something happens when we're changed, there's not a thing we can do about it, and nobody wants the pipes to freeze.

John's answering machine now says that he has gone to Florida to visit an ailing relative and please leave a message. *Meeep*.

Marco must have drawn gate duty, because he comes trotting up the path from the access road with his iPad and Elijah, whose hectic life Offland means he's always late to Homelands. With everyone checked in, the tall barbed gate is chained. Most of the Homelands is just posted, but the mile near the access road has been fenced with a six-foot-high, razor-wire-topped chain-link. Humans will happily buck the law and hunt on our land, but we have found that forcing them to carry a two-hundred-pound carcass over a mile to their illegally parked cars has significantly reduced their numbers.

At six o'clock, we all gather at the Great Hall. Friends who haven't seen one another for a month exchange greetings and bits of news while we strip down, putting our clothes in neat little stacks on sofas and benches and chairs.

We head out into the blue-gray gloaming. John is the last out, as always, and pulls the door closed behind him. I'm surprised to find Ti sitting on a log in his single work boot and sweatpants. One leg is cut high over the purple-wrapped cast. He has a thick anorak and a crutch.

Everyone takes a seat, watching. The sun is no longer visible beyond the peaks, but its rays color the clouds on the horizon a golden peach. A light dusting of mist rises from Home Pond into the newly frigid air. The grass is already a little crunchy under my bare feet, and I know tomorrow it will be covered with hoarfrost.

"What're you doing here?"

"Wanted to help you with your leg. You helped with mine, so it's the least I can do."

I probably shouldn't let him fix my leg, but maybe just this one time. To have one Iron Moon when I can keep up with everyone else, when I can maybe even squeeze my way in and get something better than bones and hide at one of the bigger kills. I sit, leaning against his good leg, because if the Iron Moon takes you when you're standing, you will topple over like a rotten beech in a gale.

The sun has almost set, and there are a few final murmurs of *Eadig wáþ*, which is still always said in the Old Tongue, because "Happy Hunting" doesn't begin to capture the full sense of *wáþ*, of wandering and journeying and, yes, hunting.

The inevitable reply, "And be yourself not hunted," has just one meaning.

The only other noises are from the pups, who run everywhere barking and yipping and scrabbling over the adults who will join in the running and leaping and hunting. John always brings a lung back from one of the bigger hunts for the pups to fight over.

"Don't they have to be in skin before the Iron Moon?" Ti asks, pointing with his chin toward the yipping tangle of fluff.

"The Iron Moon makes us wilder, but since there is nothing wilder than a wolf pup, they're kind of immune. It's only when they start taming that they are in danger. After the Year of First Shoes."

John and Evie sit near the front, watching the gold being sucked out of the sky.

He lays her down gently and curls his body around hers.

"What happened to John?" Ti points at the Alpha's shredded skin.

But it's too late. The gold is gone, and my heart is already beating faster, my blood is running hotter, my face is distorting, and as the roof of my mouth lengthens and narrows, I have said my last word of the Iron Moon.

Maybe Ti said something else, but I can't tell through the ocean rumble in my changing ears. I feel his hands on my hip and my leg.

Through one unfocused eye, I see his achingly handsome face bent over me. I try to turn away, because I love him now, and as much as I hate myself for this petty vanity, I don't want him to see this horrifying midway point.

Of course I love him. Only a wolf who loved him would break his leg with a maul so he could stay human.

He pulls hard, and I yelp, my leg twisting, the tendon being pushed back, and he lets go, and my leg goes numb. When I've finished phasing, I stand and shake it out.

I finish first and run around the writhing Pack, showing off the speed and agility that they have always had but still feels new to me. A pup jumps on me, because I'm a competent adult, damn it, and it's time to get this hunt cracking. I tear around the Great Hall, a whole covey of fur balls following me.

When John finishes his change, he shakes his magnificent coat of tan and dark gray, then throws back his head. The whole pack howls to the world, announcing the untamed joy of being us.

On his two legs, Ti towers among the roiling mass of

giant wolves. He turns to go, but before he does, I jump up, my front paws on his chest. I lean my head against him, then twirl around and bound after the Pack.

Kayla noses my hip and cocks her head to the side. I leap into the air. *See?* I show her. *See?*

Mostly we range wide in small groups or in pairs of mates or bedfellows or shielders, returning only occasionally to Home Pond. When the pups tire out and can't keep up, someone has to guide them back home so the coyotes won't pick them off. Since it's my turn to watch Ti, I drag the deer lung back to the Great Hall, and the pups come trundling after.

That night when I take up my position by the Boathouse, Ti is reading in bed, looking so human and lonely. I watch him intently from the deep black of the overcast Adirondack night. Sitting absolutely still on the dock, I follow the shape of his thighs under the warm fleece blankets up to his hard, ropy stomach and the folds of dark skin leading to his thick, naked chest. His long, strong fingers swipe across the touch screen.

Finally, he puts down the tablet but doesn't turn off the light. Instead, he kicks off the covers with his good leg. Did I imagine he wore pajamas just because I'm not there? Did I imagine he wouldn't have an erection, just because I'm not there? He slides his hand slowly across his chest. He pinches his nipple between his thumb and forefinger. Not hard, but firmly and slowly and deliberately. The other hand slides further down. He lifts his good knee. I can see everything as his hand gently cups the twinned weights. He knows how much I like to feel them heavy in my hand. He tightens his fingers, tugging until the skin is smooth and taut around them and his erection leaps slightly from his torso. He makes a fist in front and pushes in until he crowns.

Somehow, without me noticing, my front legs straightened, and I shuffled closer to the glass, every muscle tight.

Slowly, he pulls back out. He doesn't move his hand much. It's all in the hips, in the languorous rocking of those perfect thighs and that fighter's torso, pushing into and pulling out of that hand, which simply cannot appreciate the honor done to it.

He props his other arm under his head, his obsidian-and-gold eyes focused straight into mine. His mouth opens, his eyes grow hazy, and great pale streaks slash across his chest.

I stumble back, whining, and Ti smiles.

Drawing far back into the dark, I wait for my replacement.

It starts to snow. Not heavily, just the light, small flakes that gild leaves for a day or two before melting. It does nothing to mute the light *scritching* of claws. I lay my muzzle to the new wolf, handing over responsibility, then I break into a run.

Higher up, the snow churns around me and the downed leaves swirl behind me and I run with my whole legs, faster than snow or wind.

Past the High Pines and the Krummholz, I keep going until I hit the incised rock of the peaks. Up here, the wind cuts through even the thickening undercoat, but the chill feels so good on my skin.

Exposed and without much prey, the Pack doesn't bother much with the peaks, but from here, the Homelands spread out soft and muted. Leaves look cottony; needles are frilled. In the overcast night, the dusky clouds of tomorrow's snow settle in the valleys like gray ribbons.

I throw back my head and howl.

"I am."

From scattered hills and deep forests, wolves answer.

"We are."

On the final day of the Iron Moon, we gather back near the Great Hall. Except for the occasional bunny snack, no one is hunting much now, though Tara came across a beaver who was too slow and too stupid to get out of her way. She wasn't hungry, but she did her duty to the beaver gene pool and brought the still-warm body back for the pups.

Mostly, now that everyone's eaten their fill, they fight. This is the most boring part of the Iron Moon. Challenges are mounted and met. Echelons are rearranged. Fucking rights are gained and lost. Ti finds me at the palisade and puts his hand in my ruff. He's no longer using his crutch.

I butt him irritably and stalk off. I can't masturbate thankyouverymuch and am in an extremely pissy mood.

He tries to keep up but then steps in something. "Oh hell," he says, jumping back on one foot. "What *is* that?"

When the sunlight finally emerges on the third day, we go through the whole process in reverse. There are always a few stragglers out in the woods, but when it starts to get cold, nobody wants to be too far from home in their bare skin.

I pull my clothes back on and brush my teeth quickly but don't even bother to comb the burrs out of my hair before I rush to find Ti, who is already running across the lawn. "I heal quickly," he says before I splutter out anything about his missing cast. He scoops me up, wrapping his arms around me, and twirls back toward the Boathouse.

"Three things," I whisper to him. "About John's back—it's an Alpha thing. What you stepped in was beaver intestine. And what the hell were you reading?"

"*The New Yorker*," he says and kicks open the door.

Chapter 22

EVIE'S BEEN IN JOHN'S OFFICE FOR A LONG TIME. I SAW her, her rigid back toward the doorway, when I brought out one of the wood trenchers filled with breads for the Iron Moon Table. When I squeeze my way past my Packmates bringing out jams and butter and cream and cheeses and muffins and fruits and eggs, she's still in there. John catches my eye and closes the door.

"Eat up," I tell Ti. "Once John starts in with Pack business, we'll have to leave."

It seems like only a few minutes have passed when John stands. That's enough to bring all the extraneous clattering and chatting to an end.

"In our laws are we protected," he says solemnly.

"And in lawlessness are we destroyed," I murmur. I grab one more cranberry pecan roll and signal Ti that it's time for us to leave.

"Silver? Tiberius? Not quite yet." John turns to the rest of the Pack. "Let's deal with the status of our table guests first. Are there any for-speakers?"

In the Old Tongue, a *fore-spreca*, a for-speaker, is an advocate. There's a lot of curious looking around, but no one is willing to speak on our behalf. John nods at me, signaling that we should leave. We have two more Iron Moons to go, so I'm not surprised that no one jumps right in.

Ti is still straddling the bench, trying to extricate his legs.

"I'm not sure I have the right to address the Pack as for-speaker?" says a reedy, uncertain voice.

Tara's eyes turn quickly to John, who gives an almost imperceptible nod.

"The Pack acknowledges Charles Bjorksson," she says.

I hadn't seen Charlie since the *Slitung*. I don't spend much time in the Clearing during any Iron Moon, but this time, I avoided it altogether. I didn't want to see the coyotes eating Ronan's remains, and I dreaded finding Charlie there, still chasing his tail.

This Iron Moon took a lot out of him, and when he stands, he supports himself against the table.

"I am ashamed to come before you. I can only imagine what you think of me. I failed to do what needed to be done once. I can't fail again. Everyone knows Quicksilver Nilsdottir. Most of us remember her parents as great Alphas. Most, but not all. The younger echelons don't. My son didn't. I was honored when I learned that their daughter would be my son's *schildere*, but he felt she was… He felt her… He resented her.

"I'm not a very good speaker, so I think I may be making a mess of this, but what I mean is that Quicksilver didn't owe Ronan anything, not as a mate, not as a bed-fellow. Not even as Pack. But when I… When I *failed* to take First Blood, to do this final service for my son, she took that on herself as a kindness to him, to me, and to the Pack. It was an act of worth. At least, I think it was."

He lowers himself to the bench and then stands back up. "That's it," he adds lamely. "That's all I wanted to say." Then he sits.

John leans back and whispers something to Tara, who strides quickly toward his office.

A few moments later, Evie comes out. Okay, now *this* is why we've seen so little of John's mate in the past few weeks. She's pregnant, and the entire room erupts in cheers.

Evie and John have been mates for what must be 360 moons, but there is something about our genetics, our chromosomes constantly in transition between our two selves, that makes it very hard for us to get pregnant and even harder for us to *stay* pregnant. Because so much can go wrong and usually does, pregnancy is hidden as long as possible, but Evie can't anymore. She is entering the last and hardest moon of her pregnancy and will need the help of the entire Pack.

Everyone shouts "*Anhydig hama!*" the Old Tongue blessing meaning something between Resolute Birthing! and Stalwart Lying-In!

Evie pulls out the chair next to John, but before she sits, her mate whispers to her. She remains standing, her body tense.

With a sigh, John asks if there are any *wiper-spreca*. Against-speakers.

Evie asks leave to speak and then tells the pups to go. "Juveniles too," she says when a few of the older ones stop, unsure if this means them.

Tara signals to Marco, who opens the ties on two small cloth bags and starts to walk between the tables distributing the pebbles—one dark, one light—for each wolf. These are what the Pack will use to indicate which of the two speakers was most convincing. This is how the Pack will vote on our application to join the Pack.

"Quicksilver," Evie says in her still slightly accented voice, "if I could, I would treat your Pack claim separately. But by law, I cannot, and my objections to the Shifter"—she stares at him, her fingers splayed on the table—"are simply too strong."

As Marco comes to our table, Ti watches Gran Jean receive a smooth pebble from each bag. He glances at my tightly folded hands and does nothing.

"I wanted this to be a time for focusing on the future," Evie continues, "not for dwelling on the past, but I am the only one here who knows what you really are."

Her hard eyes bore into Ti.

"It is amazing…all these years later…what that smell means. It was two oceans and nearly six hundred moons ago, but I still recognize it. And you *still* smell like steel, Shifter. Just like the Shifters who overran my poor pack in my eightieth moon, looking for treasure we didn't have. Steel was in the guns they used to shoot every male and female and pup, except for the little one whose scent they missed because she was cowering in the cesspit.

"It was in the knives they used to skin them. It was in their laughter when they poked at my Pack's flayed bodies and joked because they were not human underneath, just naked dogs." Her voice breaks, and the last words come out in a hoarse whisper. "It was in the shillings they made selling the skins of my Pack. The only treasure they ever found."

She stares out the window, her jaw clamped so tightly that I think her teeth must shatter. John waves to Tara, who collects the Thing from the mantelpiece. The Thing is what we call the deep box with a hole in the top big enough to accommodate even the largest fist, so that when the stone is dropped, no one can see whether it is dark or light.

Evie's story has been whispered among the Pack, but this was the first time I have heard it directly from her mouth. This is not going to go well for us.

But we have two more moons to prove ourselves.

The bench bends a little under Ti as he sits back and pulls himself upright. He doesn't say anything at first, just stares at the floor. Then he strides over to the Thing in Tara's hands.

"I know I am only a guest here and that this vote is for Pack, but I must say something." One hand is tightly fisted by his side. "Until I was old enough to live on my own, I spent every day listening to the whispers of my father's people. The Shifters who hated me, who called me a dog and son of a bitch because I was half Pack.

"Then I came here and became half Shifter."

He holds up a dark pebble, the one that Gran Jean didn't know she was missing, and shows it between thumb and forefinger for the entire Pack to see. "I don't want to go through that here. Silver, you don't deserve to have your fate tied to mine. But I would rather be alone than live with that loneliness again."

He drops the pebble into the empty wooden box, and with that dull knock, Tiberius votes against himself.

⌇⌇⌇

As soon as the Iron Moon Table is over, Pack crisscross the three short stairs that lead to the Meeting House, carrying things in and carrying things out. Each time snow is tracked in on boots or paws, shovels scrape and brooms sweep, so that the wood is clean and no one will slip and the slush is kept outside.

Except for two tables and a few chairs, all the usual furniture of the Meeting House has been piled into the tiny room in the back. Everything is being scrubbed, from the top of the rough-hewn beams to the hearth of the stone fireplace under the wood-burning stove.

Ti carries the heavy canvas bag loaded with blackout curtains we will hang.

Once everything else is done, the floors are scrubbed and a thick, muffling carpet put down that was cleaned and stored after the last lying-in. Four strong Pack move a big bed under the middle beam. Hooks there support the lights that Evie will control from her bed.

On one side is a chair and a bed for her mate. On the other, every conceivable piece of medical equipment.

Food and drink flow in until the pantry and the little refrigerator are stocked with everything Evie likes best.

The backup generators are double-checked.

Sara flies down the few steps, car keys in hand. "I'm getting bagels from Myer's. Anything else you can think she might need from Burlington?"

"Seems kind of over the top," Ti says, watching Sara's retreating back.

"Well, what do Shifters do for a lying-in?"

A chair is brought in for Evie's attending physician.

"Ti? What do Shifters do?"

"I wouldn't know," he mumbles. "I was the last live birth."

A new pillow top is brought in to make sure she will be comfortable.

"Don't say anything," he says.

"Did I say anything?"

Finally, Evie herself is escorted in by the Alphas of every echelon. Each one lays their head beside hers. She tries to smile, but she still looks apprehensive.

The Alphas make ready to move her into the bed. They pull back the blankets, fluff the pillows, smooth the sheets. When the six most senior Alphas, her mate included, lift her gently onto the bed, I can't help feeling that they look like pallbearers. Evie is stiff and awkward, but she knows that this is the tradition for every female at her lying-in. She knows it is an important symbol of the Alphas' responsibility to the future of the Pack.

Gabi, the obstetrician, helps Evie into the holster that will keep the ultrasound transducer against her pregnant stomach. She adjusts it, laughing and trying to put Evie at ease. Alex, who is a radiologist, has extensive experience reading the ultrasounds during a lying-in. Without taking his eyes from the screen, he reaches across to tinker with the transducer. Barely five minutes go by before he calls, "Now."

Evie starts to change.

And this is why the last weeks are the hardest. Early on, the pups change into babies, and the babies turn into pups in response to their mother's hormones. But toward the end, the tiny cretins become self-aware and start doing it themselves, responding not to their mother's hormones but to one another's.

So back and forth they go, and Evie has no choice but to change too before her body rejects the aliens inside.

Gabi adjusts the harness so it will stay fixed to her contorting belly. How they ever managed to survive before all the medical technology is a mystery. Or not. They often didn't.

If Evie hasn't delivered by the Iron Moon, she will be induced, because we can't risk her trying to deliver when she's turned. If she changes and the babies don't, they're too large. They will all die, and there won't be a thing anyone can do about it.

"They're changing back."

And except for short exhausted interludes, this is the way it'll be for the next three and a half weeks.

Chapter 23

"YES?" TI SAYS TO THE KNOCK ON THE BOATHOUSE DOOR.

"Is Quicksilver there?" asks a tremulous voice.

Ti opens the door and says nothing. Just stares at the naked man standing at the bottom of the stairs, shuffling in the snow.

"Hey, Kyle," I say, pulling off my thick socks. "Come on in while I get ready."

Ti glowers furiously at the naked man now standing in our quarters. Kyle's head drops nearly to his chest, his hands fold over his crotch, his toes point in. He looks just like one of Leonora's illustrations of human submission. Except those are never naked. Humans are funny that way.

I pull off my sweater and T-shirt. "Where should we go?"

Kyle mumbles something to the effect of "grumptlywatch?"

Ti doesn't say a word, just stands there, his huge arms folded over his massive chest, his bare foot rapping an angry *ptt!…ptt!…ptt!…ptt!* against the floor.

Quickly peeling off my jeans and underwear, I squeeze past the scowling bulkhead. "I won't hunt anything big, okay? So I'll be back in time for dinner?"

Ti's nose flares, and a soft growl rattles around his throat until I pull at the collar of his fleece with one hand, then at his head with the other. I kiss him full on his lips, and his hand runs slowly over my naked shoulder and down my spine and around the curve of my ass. He holds me tight against him so that I feel exactly what I'm leaving behind. "It's just a run, Ti," I whisper. "It's what wolves do."

Kyle stumbles as quickly as he can down the stairs and toward the snow-dusted forest. I will watch over him in his change so no coyote eats him when he's vulnerable. He will do the same for me.

In the silence of a run, we move as one. Under the snow, we feel the decline toward the moose wallow and swerve together. We smell the tree where a buck rubbed the velvet of his antlers and move closer. We follow the ragged ends of low branches that mark the beginnings of the deer's browse line. We hear an unusual noise upwind and turn, ready to fight or hunt.

Kyle skids straight into a wall of black wolf.

Ti towers over Kyle, his lips curled back again from those sharp teeth. Kyle pulls everything in that can be pulled in—ears, tail, legs, chin, balls—before creeping backward. I slide my muzzle next to his, because Kyle shouldn't be bullied, but he stinks of salt and old leather and is already skittering away.

Ti watches until the last trace of Kyle's fur has vanished deep in the trees. He turns in that awkward, shuffling crappy-wolf way and stands beside me. Pushing off with my front legs, I give him a big, open-jawed kiss. He gives me a sidelong glance and squares his already broad shoulders.

And I run. Even with only three legs, I'm fast enough to make Ti work for it. He falters and gets up and falters again. I swat him in the face with my tail to remind him that his tail shouldn't be dragged behind like toilet paper on the bottom of his shoe.

It's not until we reach the upper slopes that he is at my shoulder, following and leading as we thread our way through the beeches and hemlocks.

The sky is gray with the promise of the first real snow of the season, one of those thick snows that generous nature uses to cover and protect wolves when they sleep. For now, the flakes sit like powdered sugar on top of branches and leaves and on the dried heads of grasses the color of old bronze. The snow erupts around us in little flurries when I jump on him and tumble to the side. I run away and then turn back, running toward him, and he rears on his hind legs, coming down, covering my back, and dragging his teeth gently, gently across my ear.

He bounds, jumping so high in the air that he bumps a branch above him. A tiny kinglet complains, and snow lands on Ti's face. I rub it off with my muzzle. He corners a fisher, which is always a bad idea, and the foul-tempered rodent bites him. He holds his leg up to me, and when I finish debriding it, he props his head on top of mine.

Finally, we make it past the High Pines and the Krummholz to the scrubbed, mottled stone right under the heavy gray sky. Ti collapses on his back, and I flop down next to him, my nose buried in his fur. I breathe deeply, luxuriating in the scent of crushed bone and evergreen and damp fur, totally free of any hint of steel or carrion. And when I put my head to his chest, I no longer hear the slow, shallow sounds of the man in the wolf suit, because Ti has discovered the depth of his lungs and the strength of his heart.

He stretches his neck out long, looking out toward

the upside-down horizon. I think…I think he means for me to take it, but I hesitate, because the last time didn't turn out well. Still, he holds his chin high as though he's waiting, so very carefully, I put my teeth on either side of his throat. It's what we do, and it means *trust me*. It means *I see you at your most vulnerable and will not hurt you.*

He tenses slightly but doesn't move.

I rub against his jaw, and he rubs against mine, and I keep going until I am covered in his scent. I rub against the stones and scratch into the earth, advertising to everyone that he and I were here together. Wild.

I throw back my head and howl. A handful of howls respond from the misty dark violet down below.

From the black wolf beside me, there is only a polite cough.

I wish we could stay longer, but we really can't, because tonight is the New Moon, which all wolves avoid because, even wild, it's hard to see on an overcast night with no moon.

As soon as we're outside the Boathouse, I plop down on the cold ground and pull my shoulders back. After the squishy cacophony of the change, my skin settles against the cold, brittle ground.

Ti hasn't changed. He is rolling his shoulders and shaking his massive head and jumping in all sorts of peculiar ways. As soon as I have my voice back, I squat next to him, suggesting various combinations of rolling and stretching and folding and curving that we use to get the phase started, but nothing works. Every time he emerges from a fold or curve or stretch or roll, he looks at his still fur-covered paw with disgust.

Left outside naked in the snow and dark, I feel my body starting to get cold, so I head inside with Ti following sullenly behind. I squat down and take his big head between my hands, rubbing my cheek against his muzzle. "I love you like this, and I swear on my own wolf that you will never be chained again. But I love the man who thinks he's human too, and I need you to let him come to me now."

He rolls his shoulders distractedly, like a child shrugging out of a jacket, then trots back and forth, his claws clacking against the floor.

Fingering my clothes distractedly, I decide to leave them where they are and turn off the lights. Inside under the new moon, it is pitch-black except for the still-glowing lucidum of Ti's hypersensitive eyes. Staring at the glowing green pools, I lie back on our bed and begin retracing all the paths that Ti's hands have traced on my body. I start in earnest, running my finger across my chin and up to my bottom lip, gently opening it and slipping my finger inside across my fangs. I suck it deeply into my welcoming mouth. With a pop, I pull the finger out and trace cool circles around my nipples until they stand upright, hard as apple seeds.

A soft sigh from a damp nose hits my arm.

My hand drifts lower in those long, languorous strokes. My fingers are cooler than his and smaller, but closing my eyes, I work my imagination hard, trying to re-create his big, strong, warm hands moving over my hips and belly and slipping between my thighs, making my back arch like I'm going to touch the ceiling.

Invisible in the blackness of the room, the black wolf throws himself on the floor. I smile to myself at the elastic thrum of stretching muscles, the hard creak of bending bone, the slurried swish of organs changing places.

Both the bed and I groan when he jumps on me with his full weight. The dustings of black fur settle around me, and I sneeze.

Chapter 24

THE DAY BEFORE THE IRON MOON, EVIE IS PUMPED FULL OF oxytocin. Now she is contracting and changing and contracting and changing. I swear the one time I caught a glance of John through the open door of the Meeting House, he'd lost ten pounds and gained twenty years.

Evie delivers two live pups and a third who didn't make it. But the important thing is that the Pack grows and Evie can finally sleep.

No one wants to tell John that we're also down a wolf. There was an accident on I-87, and Nikki's stuck in the resulting traffic jam. We all watch the progress of her cell phone on Tara's iPad, but by the time Nikki can make any speed, she's only got thirty minutes to get home. She can't step on the gas, because the absolute worst thing she could do is get pulled over by the police.

Last time that happened, we lost a wolf and had to eat a state trooper.

The phone slows to a stop not far from the outer limits of our territory. The Pack sloughs off clothing, and we all wait together, naked in the cold, and pray that Nikki can make it, because there's nothing more we can do.

Ti is with me this time. He sits behind me, shivering despite the blanket wrapped around his shoulders. We watch the fading of the dull-gold stripe between the thick clouds above and the dark mountains below. John is in the Meeting House with his mate, so this time, Tara closes the door to the Great Hall.

The thickness is just building in my sinuses when a crack reverberates through the night. I topple over, terrified among the contorting bodies of the Pack. If someone comes across us with a gun, we are all dead.

Ti stands bolt upright. He says something that, *of course*, I can't hear and then goes somewhere I can't see because my eyes and ears are still changing. When my senses finally come online, he's gone, but I hear the pups whimper. They nuzzle Tara, looking for guidance, but the other adults are still phasing, and I'm the first one up.

Usually we would take the pups to the High Pines, but without adults to guide them, we cannot chance a meeting with coyotes or, worse, bobcats, so I snap at them to hide in the basement of the Great Hall. Even the most fractious pup knows what a gun is and obeys immediately. Small ones are already tumbling through the hinged door. The few nurslings go immediately limp as the juveniles carry them in their jaws.

I make a stumblebum rush toward the access road and the gunshots.

There is someone coming. More than one. Two voices, but at least three sets of footsteps. It's hard to tell.

"What did you see?"

"Don' know. Something."

"You sure they're not here?" I can now smell the oil and warm plastic and wrinkled carrion sticks of Anderson, the junkyard man.

"Nobody answers," says another man whose rough

voice gives way to a smoker's hack. His lungs smell like coal and rot. "The machine says they're at a yoga retreat."

"Yogurt retreat," says the third, a dry, subtle humorist I don't recognize but who sounds young.

The Smoker coughs again.

"You okay?" asks Anderson.

"The cold air," the Smoker wheezes out. "Just got to get used to it."

I finally sight the threesome coming around the curve. A juvenile, slightly younger than I am. Anderson. And the man from the gas station with the dying lungs. All of them armed, like humans always are when confronted with trees.

"Second fucking time they call the DEC on me. Second fucking time. It's my fucking land. I can do whatever the fuck I want to with it," says Anderson.

"Zed thinks they've got a meth lab up here."

"Shut up, Trey. Zed's a moron, same's you."

"But if they've got a meth lab, then we can tell the police and they've got probable cause, right?"

"Jesus, Trey. Those shows you watch are a pain in my ass," says Anderson.

"Nobody wants the police involved," says the Smoker. "We're just taking a look around. Wanted to see what the neighborhood's like."

"So," says Anderson, "up there, they got this fucking huge fence. Easiest to cut through here to my—your— land. You sure they're not here?"

"Doesn't matter. We'll say we've got that easement of necessity."

"Yogurt retreat," giggles Trey, the wry humorist, again.

Humans talk way too much.

"Did you see *Breaking Bad*?" asks young Trey. "Those meth guys… They're some scary people."

"What's that supposed to mean?"

"I'm just saying. If these are meth lords…"

"They're not meth lords, dickhead. They're hippies. Do you think meth lords would go on a fucking yoga retreat?"

"Quiet, both of you. This time, I really did see something," says the Smoker.

"I didn't hear anything. Trey, did you hear anything?"

I hear the swish of a gunstock on Gore-Tex, and Anderson looks through the sight and fires. "He's right. There's something moving out there."

"I thought they were all at a yogurt retreat."

"Some *thing*. Maybe you came out of my sister's cunt, but there is no way you're related to me."

The "thing" is Nikki. I can smell the waves of her desperate fear coming like a heartbeat. All three now have sights up and start shooting. Wood explodes from the trees as the bullets fly, but then I hear the soft involuntary whimper of an injured wolf.

Having finally reached the Homelands, Nikki had gotten sloppy or unlucky. Though sloppy and unlucky are usually the same thing if you're a wolf.

"I think I got something."

"You? Why you? We were all shooting."

"Jesus. Fine. I think *we* got something."

Nikki is a brindle, and her season is past. Just a month ago, the ground and the trees were wet and dark and she would have been hard to see. Now it is my season, when early snow cover is still stippled with dried grasses.

I run at an angle that takes me toward the hunters, hoping to draw them away from Nikki.

A hunter hit Gran Ferenc one Iron Moon. The bullet lodged in his thigh, and it took like a hundred moons before the thing finally worked its way out. Gran Ferenc said he panicked, and when he ran away, he ran straight. "Guns shoot straight, so you must never run straight." He forced us to practice running in a zigzag, back and forth and back and forth, so that when we weren't thinking straight, we wouldn't run straight either.

He forced me too, though those turns are a bitch with only one working hind leg.

There's a shot and then another, and the bark explodes from a birch near me.

"*There it is*. Looks like I got it in the leg."

A shot hits the ground, but they're following me away from Nikki, away from the Great Hall, away from Evie, and away from my vulnerable Pack. Toward Beaver Pond.

The ice at Beaver Pond is thick and covered with snow. Easy to cross. Not that I want to be out in the open for long. I don't want to give them a clear shot when they come crashing through the underbrush like rutting moose.

"Check it out, Trey," says Anderson, pushing at the edge of the ice with his boot.

"Uncle Al?" the juvenile says, his voice shaky. "Why me?"

"Because you're lighter, dickhead."

They don't notice me sheltered behind a winterberry. If you want to keep watch on your prey, shelter near something that misdirects the eye. If they notice anything, it will be the bright-red berries encased in ice, not the patch of white and gray blending into the winter's monochrome.

Beaver Pond is still and not so deep, and the ice is plenty thick. Trey heads across cautiously at first, then as he becomes more sure that it's safe, he jumps up and down before slipping and landing on his butt. Anderson follows him onto the ice, laughing.

"Is this all Torrance's?" asks the Smoker.

"You see up the mountains there and parts east go almost to Lake Champlain. They've got the biggest chunk of land in private hands in Upstate New York, and they just keep on buying. And for what? They don't do a fucking thing with it."

I creep away, moving slowly until I'm sure that they are across the pond. Then I move toward the pines. This part of the forest is not good for me. The snow is in the canopy, and the needles underneath are damp and dark. It shows me to worst advantage.

"There it is," Anderson shouts, pointing his gun in my direction. I bolt for Clear Pond.

Now, there is a reason it's called Clear Pond. Not just because the water is so clear. It's also a mnemonic for our pups. From their very first winter, they are told that it's called Clear Pond, because you *stay clear* of it in winter. But for anyone who doesn't know, in the winter it looks like a continuation of Beaver Pond, a broad plain of ice covered by snow.

It isn't. The water is much deeper, and the ice here is almost always gray, thinned by the relentless churning of the springs underneath. There's a thick layer of snow that not only disguises it, but insulates the friable ice below from the cold air above.

I splay my legs to distribute my weight as widely as possible until I get across. Then I limp into a stand of pines on the opposite side.

Trey is smarter than his uncle gives him credit for. He looks at the orange rescue sled and hesitates. Not Anderson or the Smoker, though. They see the hunt coming to an end and follow my tracks across snow that crunches under their boots and disguises the sound of ice groaning underneath.

A new smell of evergreen and crushed bone wafts through the air, and the cloud-dimmed moon picks out the enormous dark outline of my bedfellow.

Damn it, Ti. Don't you go telling them about the ice.

"What are you doing here?" he says tersely. I follow the green glow of his lucidum to the Smoker. There's a glint from the heavy dull-gray gun held lax in his hand.

"Are we trespassing?" the Smoker asks, though he knows he is. "We're just out doing a little night hunting and winged a coyote or some such. Wanted to finish it off. Don't like to see a creature suffer," the man says. Then he smiles. "Not even a dog."

Ti raises the gun.

A red dot appears on Ti's chest. I growl so that Ti will see Anderson has a bead on him. I smell adrenaline and sweat coming not from my bedfellow but from Anderson. Must be pretty strong if I can smell it this far away. And above the stink of gasoline and carrion sticks.

"Relax," the Smoker says to Anderson. "He won't shoot. You know what they say," he continues, still smiling. "A barking dog never bites."

Maybe that's true, but Ti has said exactly five words, and when he shoots at their feet, the already stressed ice finishes fragmenting, and a huge shard tips forward. Scrabbling backward, the Smoker falls and grabs for the edge of the ice. It bobs up, sending him tumbling in. He claws frantically, pulling himself up on the ice, but each time, it splinters and he falls again.

Anderson's shot goes wild as he flails, the water seeping up and turning snow gray and the ice slick. It slips away from him, and he falls into the slush, screaming for his nephew.

Trey hesitates and then tentatively walks onto the fragile ice edge weakened by cattails. It gives way under him almost immediately, first one foot, then the other. He grabs on to the weeds, his teeth chattering, and pulls himself to shore.

I feel a little for Trey, who is a juvenile. The adults should have taken better care of him on the hunt. He is too deep into our territory; he will not be able to find his way out before he becomes sluggish and gives in to the cold sleep.

I watch the adults' last efforts carefully so we will have a better idea of where their corpses are at spring thaw and can fish them out before they rot.

But then Ti pushes his gun into his waistband and throws the orange rescue sled through the slush to the flailing men. I bark angrily, but he says that he knows what he's doing.

After he strips them of their guns, he drags the shivering, clattering, hacking load over the rough path to the Boathouse, which is closest to Clear Pond and farthest from where Evie and her pups lie vulnerable.

Chapter 25

AT THE BOATHOUSE, TI HELPS THE MEN OUT OF THEIR frozen clothes. He seems to linger over the Smoker, whispering angrily until I approach. I had things under control, then he came along and screwed everything up. "I would have let you drown," he says. Though he addresses the chattering men, I know his words are aimed at me. "But I didn't want the police coming up here. Disturbing things."

As much as I really think they should have been left to freeze, Ti does have a point, what with our Alpha mate just having delivered and in no shape to make the trek to the High Pines. I chuff a little but then pull myself up with my front paws on the tiny counter and nudge the red switch hidden by the pineapple-themed curtains above the sink.

After a little cough, the generator starts up, and before long, hot air fills the Boathouse, along with the smell of burned dust.

Ti stops pulling at the pants of the frantically shivering Anderson and stares at me.

"There's heat?"

I cock my head to the side. If he's still talking to me when I can talk back, I'll explain what it means to heat a place that isn't winterized.

"Every morning, there's ice on the inside of the windows. *On the inside*."

When he's done, Ti leans back in the chair, his gun on his thigh and one hand on my ruff and waits until the men have warmed up. I sneeze, because the Boathouse now stinks of human and Gore-Tex and will have to be fumigated.

Finally, the Smoker stops shaking and shoots a bleary look toward Ti.

"This is posted property," Ti says. "Don't come here again."

"Thaz my land," Anderson says, waves his hand vaguely toward the junkyard. "And I have an...an..." He looks toward the Smoker.

"Easement of necessity," says the Smoker to Ti. "Gives the owner of that plot—" He stops and begins hacking; we all wait for him to finish. "Gives 'im the right to traverse this land so he can get to the public road."

"There's an access road. Stick to it."

"Fuck you, asshole," chatters Anderson. "I don't know where you come from, but my family's been on this land for generations. I know it like the back of my fucking hand, and next time, I'll be here on my own, and you won't even know it until you feel my fucking muzzle at your fucking back. You're just a man with a gun, but *I* am a fucking hunter."

The adjectival richness of his speech stuns me. Humans really do talk so much and say so little.

Ti's nose flares. He opens his mouth just slightly, his tongue held to the roof, creating an echo chamber of scent.

"This evening, you had a steak, iceberg lettuce with blue cheese dressing, an IPA, and a tequila. You sat with your nephew and another man who is not here. Your nephew had a hamburger. The other man had chili. You shared onion rings. Two...no, three days ago, you screwed the wife of the man who had the chili. She has two small children. You are sterile and have irritable bowel syndrome."

The Junkyard Man's face slackens, and he slumps back, his mouth slightly open, but for the first time, he has nothing to say.

"You only think you're a hunter, because you've never met a real one." Ti turns to me. "Silver, I think it's time for these men to go."

I stretch out my front legs and then my back and wait near the door.

"Silver?" the Smoker croaks. "Well, *Silver*." He lifts his hand, and holding two fingers out like the barrel of a gun, he sights me. "Eat lead."

Before he's even finished with his pantomimed recoil, a hollow crack hits his face, and he lands halfway across the room with a dull thud and a muffled scream.

"Gear up," Ti says, throwing their partly dried clothes and boots in front of each man. "I'm walking you to the road."

"Uncle Al?" Trey says. "I'm not sure your friend here can walk."

"He broke his jaw, not his legs," Ti says, his gun to the Smoker's ear. "He can walk just fine."

The man flinches when the safety comes off.

"Uh, mister?" Trey says. "Only the shirt's mine."

"Wear it or don't," Ti says, pulling up the hood of his anorak and strapping the three rifles across his back. "We're leaving now."

The men work quickly to pull on clothes, except for

the Smoker, who can't get the shirt on over his broken jaw and pulls on a coat that must belong to Trey, because it's too small and exposes a stripe of pale, hollowed-out chest above his pale, distended belly.

When Ti flicks the red switch, the soft wheeze stops. He opens the door, letting in icy air.

"On the *inside* of the windows," he mutters again.

We lead the shivering men toward the access road, surrounded by scores of silent, invisible wolves. I smelled them earlier and heard them scenting the air, watching and waiting.

They pass like the shudder of dry sycamore leaves in the quiet left by the cowering of everything else in our land.

I fall into step beside Ti. We have no trouble negotiating the darkness, but the three men stumble under the dark cover of the woods and the unreliable light of the moon. We can tell when the Smoker stumbles because of the strangled scream.

Ti must've found keys in one of the men's pockets, and after placing the three rifles on the ground, he climbs into their vehicle. I hop up, my front paws on the wheel well so I can watch. Twisting to the back, he lifts a camouflage tarp and throws it to the ground near the discarded rifles. He pulls four more rifles from the gun rack and, checking each quickly, tosses them out too. I eye the men, see if they're going to try anything stupid. Trey is too scared. The Smoker's in shock, both hands holding his face. Only Anderson makes a halfhearted shivering lurch that I cut short with a quick bark.

Not that I'm worried: there is a wall of enormous,

furious wolves standing feet from the great and oblivious hunter.

Once Ti finishes feeling around the back, he sits in
the driver's seat. He checks around the glove compartment and the visor, and then feeling the passenger seat,
he works his finger into the side seam. The rip of Velcro
sets my teeth on edge, but a second later, he pulls out a
very large, very mean-looking handgun.

"You got a concealed-weapon permit for the
Beretta?" he calls to Anderson.

"Fuck you."

"Didn't think so." Ti points the Beretta at Anderson.
"Get in and get out."

The road is long and very rough, and the Smoker's
stifled screeches echo in the quiet until miles later, the
trio reaches the paved road.

Tara howls the all clear. The pups join the adults, and
the silence becomes a fraction less quiet.

Tiberius sits on the tarp with the pile of guns and
methodically opens each action. Before long, he has
built a hillock of ejected cartridges and shells.

A pup dashes out from the woods, his nose close to
the ground until he comes near the pile. He clambers into
Ti's lap to get a closer look at a gunstock, but a sharp
bark from the blackness calls for him to return. He jumps
from the summit of Ti's knee and scuttles away from the
guns and back into the protection of the dark wood.

Once he has disassembled all of them, Ti wraps them
in the camouflage tarp and tosses them over his back.
His eyes blaze into the shadows.

"These will be in John's office."

There is no reply, except for the gradual winking out

of the luminous eyes as one by one, the Pack turns to go in a shiver of leaves.

Growling, I slap my muzzle against Ti's leg and stalk toward Home Pond.

"Just don't say it."

I look pointedly at the moon. Like I'm going to *say* anything.

"I know. So I got it back. You don't want guns because you don't want to be dependent on something you can't use during the Iron Moon. But I'm not you and I can use a gun and I'm at least good enough with one to protect the Pack from hunters. Isn't that what you want?"

I growl. *What I want is for you to stop fighting what you are and be wild with us.* Yes, we're vulnerable when we change. And maybe Ti could stand guard over our Iron Moon. But our first Alpha was adamant that when we were wild, we embrace that wildness. That we be self-reliant. Those who guard you in your weakness, she said, will always end up exploiting it.

Ti goes to John's office. I go to the front lawn. The pups are bundled in a roiling pile in the middle, surrounded by a warm carpet of whatever adults aren't out hunting.

Tomorrow, I will hunt, but for tonight, my gut is clenched, and I can't imagine eating anything. Except always bear heart; I could definitely eat bear heart. I turn round and round, carving a little nest for myself in the snow. I'm starting to drift off when John appears. Even as a wolf, he looks thinner and older.

I jump back up to greet him, and he rubs his muzzle next to mine, and I am instantly comforted by his scent. Then from the woods, a huge, black wolf lopes toward us, and John…John lays his muzzle against Ti, marking him too. I tense slightly, watching Ti, worried that he won't understand, but he stands stock-still, his eyes on mine, until John is done.

Then he curls next to my snow nest. I fluff my tail over my nose. When Ti does it, he sticks his tail in his eye. He blinks furiously.

Still kind of a crappy wolf.

Chapter 26

"John?" I poke my head into his office. "You wanted to see me?"

"Come in. I'm just packing up some things so I can work in the Meeting House with Evie and the pups. Can you unplug the adapter?"

He wraps the cord around his laptop.

"How is the Boathouse working out for you?"

"Fine. It's getting a little cold for Ti, but he's managing."

John nods. "You know," he says as he slides his computer into a messenger bag, "when you were little, Evie and I would stay up waiting for you after every Iron Moon. Those were exhausting days. But you always came back. Limping and wheezing, you always came. We called you the tiny Terminator."

There's a knock on the door, but before John can say anything, Tara comes in, a sledgehammer balanced easily on one shoulder.

"It's right here," John says and toes the camouflage bundle that Ti brought in that first night of the Iron Moon. Tara picks it up, wrapping the ends twice around her fist so the bundle won't fall.

"Tara, you know to—"

"Smash 'em and trash 'em," she says and lifts the sledgehammer. "I'm going to do it right now."

"Thanks, and, Tara? Maybe we should close up

the Boathouse." She nods with a quick smile in my direction.

John watches his Beta's retreating back. "There's something I'll never understand. One rifle's not enough? Why do they need two *each*?"

I pause a moment.

"Humans," I say. "Can't live with 'em, can't get Showtime without 'em."

John chortles with his sad eyes. "Sometimes you really do remind me of my brother."

Thing is, I was there and I can count. There were *seven* rifles and *two* handguns.

So tell me, Ti... Where are those other guns?

I'm pretty sure that John was trying to tell me that we were in. That we'd made Pack. Closing up the Boathouse can only mean we're moving out. Hopefully getting a cabin with insulation and a little stove and no ice on the inside of the windows.

There's not much time for me to tell Ti. Besides, if someone objects at the last minute, his disappointment would be that much worse.

At Iron Moon Table, Adrian, the juvenile who likes marking John's boots and is fast enough to get away with it, yips a warning to the assembled Pack.

The scrape of benches and chairs, a final slurp of coffee, and the high, sharp yelp of a pup falling down the stairs are the only sounds as the Pack gets to its feet, huge and silent.

Ti pulls on my hand, his brow furrowed. "What...?"

I always forget how little he knows. "First Marking," I whisper, but then Evie enters, and I hold up a finger to my lips.

Evie is so thin now, sucked dry by the past month, but her back is still tall and straight. Except when she nuzzles her cupped hands and a furry tail moves a little. The pup in John's cupped palms sticks her nose over the rim of her father's hands. She sniffs the air curiously and yawns, but her eyes won't open for a few days yet.

They are followed last by Gran Drava, our eldest wolf. Her cupped hands tremble a little.

Nikki is nearest the front door. She hobbles to her feet and puts her hands under Evie's before bending down to the tiny pup, sniffing carefully to find his scent and memorize it. She leans in and rubs a cheek against his tiny, furry body; it is the beginning of a lifetime of being marked by the Pack. She does the same with the pup in John's hands.

She repeats it with Gran Drava, even though her hands are empty. It is a sign of mourning for the pup who didn't make it and a recognition of the void left in the Pack.

Each member will mark and scent the pups. It's a long process, and by the time they come to us, Evie's face is drawn. A trickle of blood stains her ankle. When she stumbles against the corner of the bench, Ti starts toward her, but I pull him back. However much she may distrust him now, if he makes her feel weak, she will hate him more.

She lifts the pup up to the wolf next to us and murmurs his name for the zillionth time. Nils Johnsson. Torrance is a name we use for legal documents. I have no idea where it came from. But our real names, our Pack names, are derived from our highest-ranked parent.

I am Quicksilver Nilsdottir. Because I am the

daughter of the former Alpha, John's brother and this tiny pup's namesake.

Ti reaches out for his turn with the pup, but Evie walks past without a second look, and his face freezes.

I tug at his arm. "Only Pack can mark him," I whisper, my heart breaking as she passes me as well. Still, there is no law that can stop me from breathing in little Nils's scent, committing it to memory.

I do the same for Nyala Johnsdottir. Ti keeps his hands tightly clasped in front of him as Gran Drava walks by. Her airy burden is named Hannah Deathsdottir, because Death holds the highest rank of all.

After the last of the Pack scents and marks the pups, Evie and her children will return to the Meeting House to rest. Usually her mate would accompany her, but for now, John must stop being the nurslings' father and must be Alpha again.

The Pack sits once again and digs in.

"Any Iron Moon that marks the increase of the Pack is a happy one," says John, once Evie has gone, "but this is doubly so. Not only are we welcoming two nurslings, but we welcome back Quicksilver Nilsdottir"—I turn to Ti with a big smile that dies on my lips as I see his horrified expression—"and her bedfellow who will be known from now on by his Pack name, Tiberius Malasson."

Ti leaps to his feet so fast that the bench tips backward. "Your mate," he says. "She has to be here. We can't... She has to be here—"

"I would never go behind Evie's back. You helped protect us when we were vulnerable, Evie most of all. And you did it without killing, even after you got one of their guns."

I admit, I may have fudged that bit. There's no telling what John would do if he knew that Ti had sieved through the bog and hidden a gun for a moon or more.

"Whatever concerns there might have been about this Pack claim"—John's eyes hold those of a disgusted-looking Victor—"have been addressed. As there are no against-speakers, the only thing left is to make arrangements for your *Bredung*. Your mating."

Ti's big body weaves slightly under my hand. I look up, hoping for a clue, but he focuses on the ground, and for the first time, I scent the unmistakable smell of salt and old leather, the smell of fear.

His breath is coming fast, and he swallows convulsively. The circles under his eyes appear almost black against his dark skin, and he starts to shake. Grabbing his arm to support him, I quickly blather something about "gratitude?" and "this unexpected honor?" and everything comes out as a question like I'm hoping someone will tell me why my unflappable bedfellow is having a full-fledged panic attack.

John nods at me with a sad smile and pity, because instead of greeting the news of our *Bredung* with joy, Ti looks like he's going to vomit on the floor.

There are more goddamn sad smiles and pitying eyes as I stumble out, dragging the numbed Ti behind me. Kayla catches my sleeve as we leave, her expression somber, like she is going to miss me. I pull my arm away.

As soon as we get outside, Ti leans over, his hands braced against his knees. I keep my hand steady on the base of his skull, rubbing absently with my thumb while I wait for him to explain, but he stands shakily and walks away. I watch as he breaks into a jog, then a run, racing toward the woods. I let him go. Let him escape into the filigree of bare trees.

We were supposed to be celebrating our upcoming mating with a move into a cabin. A place with proper heat that would be our own. Instead, I return alone to the frigid Boathouse and collapse onto cold sheets that still smell like sex.

I wish I'd known that the night before the Iron Moon was our last night. I wouldn't have slept at all. I would have memorized how his hands moved across my body. I would have lingered over the taste of his sweat and his seed. I would have kept him from coming so I could revel in the feeling of his thickness buried inside me and the staccato thrumming of the veins that warned me he was getting close. I would have listened harder to the throttled cry he always makes at the end.

Made.

Better yet, I'd go back further to a time before my heart got involved.

Ripping off my clothes, I pull the sheets that don't smell like steel anymore between my legs. I rub my face into the pillow that smells of crushed bone and ever-green, but it's too late to mark him.

What was it Lear's Fool said? *He's mad that trusts in the tameness of a wolf or in a boy's love*.

Chapter 27

I DON'T REMEMBER FALLING ASLEEP, JUST WAKING UP. THE sun couldn't be bothered with more than a lazy visit above the horizon, and the sky is the color of mercury, and the waters of Home Pond are the color of lead, and the skeletal fingers of spruce have turned from evergreen to graphite.

There's something warm against the curve of my spine. I take a deeper breath, feeling the shape of his shoulder blades. I turn onto my back and pull the blankets tight over my body.

"I'm sorry, Sil, but I had to think."

There's a wasp's nest in the highest reaches of the pitched roof.

"I did some thinking too. I don't want to be exiled, so why don't we just go through with the *Bredung*, but then you cover whatever viable—"

"*Stop*," he says wearily. "Just...stop." Pushing himself off the floor, he climbs in next to me. His hands, so warm and rough, soothe my aching skin. I turn toward his body, dark and big and scarred as an old oak.

"Those 'viable females'?" he says. "They're like beautiful humans. Always confusing luck with birthright and expecting everything to come to them as their due. Not like you: you assume nothing and fight for everything. You fight for yourself. You fight for your pack.

"And you fight for me," he whispers, his voice as

rough as his bearded cheek. "*You fight for me*. No one's ever fought so hard for me. No one's ever tried so hard to make me feel like I might belong. That I may need to be cared for.

"And that this divide in my soul isn't fatal."

He curls his legs and his shoulders tight around as if he's trying to make his body small. Trying to fit in the circle of my arms. He's too big, but I hold him close anyway and whisper to him that I don't understand what's wrong, but that I love—

"Don't," he says harshly. I try to turn my head, to look at him, but he traps me. "I have something to say, and I don't want to see your face when I say it. Please just listen. I didn't come here because I was trying to escape, Silver. I came here because I was sent."

Sent?

Shifters, he says in a whisper like a dragonfly skimming over summer water, may pretend they're human, but they aren't. They don't grow old the way humans do. They can't go to doctors, because, like us, their bodies are alien. Their paperwork is forged, making legitimate business and public life difficult, because eventually someone starts to get suspicious. It always happens. So they survive on the fertile border between legality and criminality, cocooned in a combination of money and intimidation and the particularly nasty class of humans attracted to that combination. And at the head of it all, at the head of all the Shifters of North America, is a man named August Leveraux.

"My father. I didn't lose any challenge. The whole thing—the challenge, the clawing, everything—was thought up by my father, because he knew no Pack would trust a Shifter, even one whose mother was Pack."

My eyes keep drifting to the wasp's nest. *How is it that I never noticed it before? Had the males all died before we moved in?*

A Shifter at one of the border casinos scented a wolf, he says. "Lone wolves come through occasionally, searching either for a place to belong or a place to die. But this one was marked up, like he was still part of a pack." The Shifter reported it to August, and August sent his best tracker to follow him. Which was how Ronan led Tiberius straight to us.

Where is the mated queen? Is she buried all alone in the frozen ground, her mind and body numb, waiting?

Tiberius pulls at a strand of my hair that's stuck to his lips.

As furious as I am with Tiberius and Ronan, it is nothing compared to my anger at myself. Because I didn't want to be a *nidling*, I kept Ronan's Offland visits secret when I should have told John. Because I didn't want to be a *nidling*, I brought a Shifter into our Pack.

"*Get off of me!*" I curl and twist and struggle to get away from him, but Ti refuses to let go. "Shifters always believe we have money. But you've seen how we live. We're not rich; we—"

"You said you have fund managers, Sil," he murmurs quietly. "They must be managing something. Besides, it would hardly matter. There's a massive shale play extending through the Great North. Yours is the largest holding outside the Adirondack Park, and Washington is offering too many incentives to leave this land alone."

Held in the steel cage of his thighs and the pinion of his thick arms and by the weight of his chest, I slash out at his face with my fangs. He doesn't flinch when I gouge his cheek.

He lifts his head. Blood wells up along the gash left by my canine.

"You told him, didn't you?" I turn away from those gold-flecked black eyes that took me from the very beginning. "I trusted you, Tiberius." A single warm drop burns a trail along my cheekbone.

"I know, Wildfire. Please. I'm telling you everything— *everything*—because I need that trust again. Yes. I told him. The man with the dying lungs? The one you didn't like? That's Daniel Leary, my father's right-hand man. You have to know I was already so conflicted when I met him at the gas station, but yes, I told him. Then he dared to come onto your land and threaten *you* and—"

"*And you kept his guns*. I know you didn't give them all to John. Why? So when the moon comes and we are helpless, you can kill—"

"*No!*" he shouts. "No. No...god no. I did keep them, but I did it because I know my father, and I wanted to be able to protect you. I told you I was a terrible shot, but that was a lie too, because the truth is, Sil...I am a fucking miracle." There's no pride in his voice, just disgust and deep weariness.

"I was my father's enforcer. You know how I said I managed human resources? I did it by hunting them down and killing them. I'm the reason they say no one can escape August Leveraux. But not anymore. Not ever again."

He lifts his hip and slides his hand into his front pocket, reaching for his wallet. He hands it to me. "There's a receipt in there. Read it."

I pull out a receipt from the U.S. Post Office, 10 Miller Street, Plattsburgh, for a priority envelope to the CRA in Ottawa and another to August Leveraux care of a PO box in Halifax.

"So?"

"That's what I was doing. I went to the safe-deposit box in Plattsburgh where I keep—kept—things from my old life. I sent a copy of a zip drive with the most intimate details of August Leveraux's financial holdings to the CRA and a letter to my father telling him what I had done."

I stare a little uncomprehendingly at the receipt. "And what exactly is the CRA?"

"Canada Revenue Agency. Like the IRS. I didn't want you to have to trust the promise of a man who had lied to you so often. I had to make it real. There is no changing it now. Even if you reject me, I have nothing left to go back to."

A drop of blood falls from his face to mine, warm and smelling of iron and salt and mutely tragic.

"Do you remember? At the Clearing? When I told you I didn't want to die? That was a lie too, because the truth was I really didn't care. But then I found you. And you made me realize that it didn't matter whether I was a real human. What mattered was that I was a real man."

In the morning, we are summoned to the Alpha's office, and all the way there, I imagine telling John about Tiberius. But then I imagine never seeing Tiberius again. Or never seeing my pack. Or more probably both. And I can't.

So instead, we find ourselves in John's office with

more wolves than there are carrion beetles on week-old roadkill. Victor is here. Tristan. Leonora. Tara.

Ti stands with his back against the wall nearest the door, his arms tight around my waist. His gaze is cool and impervious, but his body is cautious and needy.

"Tiberius, I understand from Leonora that you suffer from a fairly common human affliction called frosted feet?"

"Cold feet, Alpha," she says and slurps on a stick in a mug of coffee.

"Yes, well." John looks pointedly at the stick. "I'm not going to find that blowing around Home Pond, am I?"

"No, Alpha, I keep it in my handbag. I am simply trying to instruct the Pack in the proper use of straws. The juveniles' field trip to Chipotle last week got out of hand."

She sucks up another long swig of coffee before putting the mug on a coaster of the waxing quarter moon, one of a set sent to John by an Offland wolf. She crosses her arms, and I cower into Ti's chest. I just know that she's going to ask me something I can't possibly answer, like the difference between a brasserie and a brassiere.

"Tiberius," she starts, and my body relaxes. "Our Alpha has asked me to explain the *Bredung* to you. Perhaps you are under the impression that it is a Breeding? If so, I'm here to assure you that they have nothing to do with each other. Unlike with humans, any child born to us is a wish child, whatever the circumstances of their birth."

I reach my hand around to cover his fingers tight on my waist.

"*Bredung* is Old Tongue for Braiding. It symbolizes"— Leonora knots her fingers together—"an intertwined commitment not just to each other, but to the land and to the Pack as well. Through it, we mingle blood and earth and seed, and for us, all three parts are fundamental. Once you are braided, you are part of this Pack, part of this land, part of Silver. You cannot untie one without untying everything. I am telling you this so that you will not mistake it for marriage. It is not simply about keeping faith with Silver. It is about keeping faith with us all."

Absently, Leonora toys with the thin braid of leather around her neck. Her mate, Boris, was hit by a car years ago, and though it didn't kill him, he wasn't the same. A few moons later, he didn't make it back from a hunt. She never took another mate.

"I have studied humans for years. They get restless. They feel it is their right to use something and then discard it when it no longer suits them. That is not our way. When a wolf commits to something, there is no end, except in death.

"So this is your last chance to decide what you are: Are you human, or are you wolf?"

John tears off a chunk of the dark roll he nabbed from breakfast and butters it slowly.

Ti stares at the floor, and I worry that maybe he's gotten frosted feet for real this time. But when he lifts his head, his lips are drawn back from his fangs, and he dares each of the wolves with their smooth, human teeth to doubt how wild he is. I can't help but smile too.

John's eyebrows quirk up as he glances from Ti's mouth to mine. He runs his tongue over the points of his own dull canines and nods.

Chapter 28

I KNEW THE GENERAL OUTLINES OF WHAT HAPPENED AT A *Bredung*, but it is a silent, private affair, mostly conducted by the two participants, so I met with Gran Jean to go over the details, while Ti met with Gran Tito. We have to understand going in, because it is our most sacred ritual, and there are no words. Words would show preference for the skin over the wild, and we would never do that.

I was calmer when I knew less. I drop the long, coiled strand of leather. It's stiffer than bought leather, but it is from a Pack-hunted deer and was tanned with oak bark from our woods. So it carries with it the DNA of our land.

Ti catches it before it falls and twists his fingers into the thin length as we wait for John in the forest next to the Clearing. I pull the blanket tighter around us. He tells me about human weddings, held inside or outside if the weather is mild. The couple wear clothes that are painfully uncomfortable and make their friends do the same. An officiant says a few words that neither party has really thought through—sickness and health, richer and poorer, better and worse—or at least don't believe will be put to the test. Family and friends toast the couple, eat a little, drink too much, give vases, dance badly, and then run for the exits.

I think he's just trying to make me feel better when he

says that so far at least, sitting naked at night in a blanket on an icy stump is way better. Then John comes.

Our Alpha knows it's cold and that we have more to do, so he doesn't waste time stripping down to his jeans. From the worn, oil-darkened sheath on his hip, he pulls out an ancient seax, narrowed by centuries of sharpening. Without hesitation, he pulls the knife down the center of his chest from clavicle to navel. I'm not sure Ti realizes the honor John does us in the prominent placement of the cut.

Blood starts to run as he holds out his hand for the leather lash. He puts it in place inside the cut. With my splayed hand on John's chest, I hold the lash in place. After a moment, Ti does the same. John puts one hand over ours and then pulls the lash through with his other, until the full length is coated with his blood, symbolizing our bond with the Pack.

It's a bitch, being Alpha.

When we're done, the wound is red and angry and will scar, an emblem of what it really means to be Alpha: power built on sacrifice.

Gran Jean showed me how to tie on the lash, but it's harder to do now that we're both shivering in our bare skin. Ti holds one end in his hand while I thread it over his shoulder and mine, down my back, between my legs and between his ("always being careful of his testicles, dear"), and then crisscrossing to the other shoulder and back between our legs. John helps tie a special knot that won't loosen but has a loop that will allow us to get free after.

Then John leaves, and we are alone.

I circle my legs around Ti's hips as he squats down,

careful not to drop me. There's a reason the *Bredungs* almost always take place in the warm months, one I didn't mention to Ti, because, well, the whole thing is awkward enough without putting the idea of cold-induced impotence in his head.

It turns out not to be a worry, because I can feel him, steel sheathed in silk, against my stomach. His arms cage me, his hands cupped around my head. He curves his back high so he can take both my mouth and my sex.

I knew the braiding was all about symbols—Land + Pack + Mate—but there's something about the damp cold of the earth bleeding through the blanket under me and the miraculous trail of the heavens above me, the smell of John's blood, and the deep thrusts of the man I love. There's something about mind and body dissolving limits in an endless expanding and contracting that braids everything together. I see Ti's seed spilling through the infinite sky above me. I smell my body in the cold, damp ground beneath me. And in my mate's steady strokes, I feel the pulsations of blood and oceans and dark matter and everything else in the universe that moves in currents.

It all twines together, contracting tighter and tighter until the whole universe is a tiny seed of infinite mass. Inside me. Inside us. A scream tears from my throat, and it explodes.

"Open your eyes, Silver," Ti whispers.

He drives into me one more time, his eyes focused on mine as my contractions pull at him.

"Because that is where I see the man I want to be."

—◦◦◦—

"Don't do it too tight."

Gran Jean clucks irritably. I *know* I'm being irritating, but I don't want this to remind Ti of any earlier band around his neck. Gran Jean adjusts the neck ring she has braided from the thin lash of deer hide tanned with oak bark, earth, John's blood, and our sex.

"Quicksilver," she snaps, "in six hundred moons, I've never made it too tight."

"Of course I trust you, but I'm just saying if you have to choose between tight and loose, make it loose."

"Sil, it's okay," Ti says when she's done. "It's fine. It doesn't feel anything like…well, it doesn't feel like what you're afraid of."

Standing between his legs, I unbutton his Henley to see how the new braid sits on the old scars. It does nothing to obscure them, but bursting out from under the thin leather, they have a wild beauty.

My hands slide up from chest to neck to cup his face.

"*Min gemæcca*," he whispers with an accent that makes me laugh.

"What? Gran Jean told me the word for mate. If this is going to be my home, shouldn't I learn the language?"

"*Gea, min coren*."

Yes, my chosen, my fit, my beloved.

So all that's left to complete our full membership in the Pack is the paperwork. The Homelands are covered by some elaborate trust document that all Pack must sign. Ti because he is new, me because I am now an adult and will replace John's proxy signature with my own. The document is the work of generations of lawyers, and it seems as if many of those generations have gathered in the Meeting House. There are Kayla, the 14th's lawyer, a first-year law student, and Reena, the 2nd's Delta, who sits on the Second Circuit Court of Appeals. And of course, Elijah, who is the keeper of the Trust and the most aggressive defender of the Pack's legal protections.

Ti listens carefully to the lawyers' explanations and looks through the sheaves of paper set in front of us. Looking at line after line of numbers, I remember when I was a pup and crawled into the tiny space between the wall and John's desk because at Iron Moon Table, he'd called a meeting of all the Pack's "fun managers." I was stuck there for what seemed like hours, having less fun than I've ever had in my life. When the last of the no-fun-at-all managers left, John leaned over the back of his desk and scooped me up. He'd smelled me the second he'd come in but figured making me sit through the whole tortured meeting was an appropriate punishment for skulking. I've been allergic to money talk ever since.

I watch Nils and Nyala enviously. Nils is busily gnawing a cheese chew under a bookcase, while Nyala bats at him until she finally retrieves it. Nils pops out, and they tussle for a while, the cheese chew ignored on the floor beside them. They only stop when the howl of a perimeter wolf brings them up short. Cocking their heads to the side, they listen to the Pack responses and then reply with their own squeaky, staccato howls.

When we finally get around to the actual signing, Tara takes out a small, heavy glass jar filled with black ink and a slim, dark box burned with a kind of stylized tree. With its upraised fletching, the Eolh rune is almost the opposite of the Tiw I have on my hand and symbolizes the defense of what one loves. Opening the ink,

Tara struggles to fill the pen, wipe it on a rag, and write a few scribbles on a piece of scrap until the ink runs.

Evie starts, signing on behalf of Nils. John signs on behalf of Nyala. Tara refills the Eolh pen before handing it to me.

This doesn't really seem like us, and seeing my expression, Tara must know that's what I'm thinking. "Bartholomew had it made up," she says, naming an earlier Alpha. "Thought it gave the process gravitas."

But a thing either has gravitas with a Number 2 Ticonderoga pencil, or it doesn't. What this outsized, poorly weighted tool gives the process is repetitive stress syndrome, and after all the signing and initialing, my hand cramps horribly.

So maybe it's my fault that when I pass the pen to Ti, it rolls from my hand and doesn't land in his but instead hits the table and then falls to the floor on one end and flips to the other before breaking apart in a puddle of ink.

No one says anything. Nils bats at one silver half, chasing it as it twirls away. When he runs after it, little black paw prints smudge across the scrubbed wood. Evie chases after him, and Nyala jumps from the table to see what the excitement is. Finally, Evie picks up her children, holding the squirming, furry little bodies far from hers until they get outside and she drops them in the snow.

"I'm...I'm sorry," Ti says, gathering up the broken remnants. The ink runs down his palm like blood.

One of the lawyers has a Bic in the bottom of her bag, and he signs with that.

"I'm so sorry," he says again when it's all over.

But John shakes his head. "I always hated that thing," he says, and once we're back at the Great Hall, he puts the remnants of the Eolh pen in a dusty blue-and-white coffee mug that says:

> YOU WOULDN'T UNDERSTAND.
> IT'S AN ALPHA THING.

We have been given Cabin 97, maybe because some wolves are still nervous about having a Shifter in their midst. It's in the middle of the trees halfway toward the Clearing. I love it because when I leave our bed at night, all I have to do is tumble down the stairs to sleep in the woods.

The Boathouse has been closed up. The boats are on the walls, and as soon as we get our things—mostly just clothes and books—the pipes will be drained, and no one will go in again until spring.

Ti sits on the snow-covered Adirondack chair overlooking Home Pond. It is completely iced over, though when the weather changes, like it has today, it creaks and complains with sharp pops and dull twangs like some giant, soggy rubber band.

"Ti?" I say, perching on the broad arm of the chair. He's been distracted since the signing. "Ti?"

"He was right."

"Who? John?"

"My father. Packs do hoard. You weren't paying attention, but I was. Scattered around various funds. About 1.5 billion."

"Billion what? *Dollars?* And are you saying billion with a *B*?"

"Yes, billion, and yes, dollars. U.S., not Canadian. That's without the land."

I thread my hands into the sleeves of my fleece.

"So we've saved some money. It's just to take care of the Pack, take care of its future." But even as I say it, I shiver and burrow my face in my collar. "Do you think your father knows?"

"No. They're very careful with it. They keep the Trust documents locked away in Elijah's safe in New York. Besides, it is set up so that while new names can be added, nothing can be changed without the unanimous consent of the entire Pack, and my father is just not that persuasive."

Home Pond groans and pops again, sounding for all the world like a giant straining to free himself of chains of ice.

Sten nods his assent for us to poke around among the furniture in the barn behind his shop. "Don't..." He circles his hand higgledy-piggledy in the air.

"Of course not. We'll put everything back where we found it."

In the end, Sten and a couple of other wolves help us carry a mattress, a sofa, two comfy chairs, a small desk, a dresser, and two tables—dining and coffee—into our cabin. All of them have been carefully sniffed for mold or bugs.

Before today, the coffee table was a table table, but then we sawed it down. Badly, as it turned out, and now it thumps and bumps. Tomorrow, we'll measure twice and cut it once, but for today, I search through the stack of summer wolf publications that we brought from the Boathouse, looking for something of the proper thickness to keep it steady.

"*Architectural Digest*?" Ti says, plopping next to me on the big orange and bright-green leaf-print sofa that is hard on the eyes but super nice on the ass. "I'm not sure it's aimed at cabin-dwelling wolves."

"Really isn't." I prop my head on his thighs and my feet on the sofa arm and flip through a few more pages before letting the magazine fall on my lap. "Though it is kind of what I imagine you had before."

"Hmm."

"Is that a yes?"

"Maybe. Why are you asking?"

"Just curious. I wonder sometimes what you gave up to be here."

He takes the magazine from my lap and starts to look through it. "Why don't I tell you what I had," he says. "Then you can decide for yourself what I'm giving up."

He opens the magazine.

"I was seventeen when I got my own place in Montreal. Well, I didn't get it myself. My father paid an agent to find me something 'appropriate.'"

He turns a page.

"It was a newly remodeled three-bedroom duplex with marble and copper and travertine and bronze and a terrace and a Jacuzzi and a fireplace that came on with the click of a button. The lights were so bright and the walls were so white that they hurt my eyes. But it was definitely 'appropriate.' It sent the right message about who I was, or rather who my father was. For a long time, all I had there were a blow-up mattress and boxes of clean shirts in the bedroom. Soap and toothbrush in the bathroom. Batteries in the refrigerator."

I can't see Ti, just the back of the magazine with a picture of a large watch on a fine and featureless wrist with carmine-tipped fingernails that looks nothing like my own hawthorn- and weasel-ravaged hands.

"Then I started entertaining, and the women I entertained expected more than an air mattress at a good address for their services."

He must feel my head on his thigh tilt toward him. "They weren't prostitutes, Silver. But there was an unspoken transaction: Money for beauty. Power for sex. I don't know why it isn't prostitution, but apparently it isn't."

A rough stripping sound is followed by the sudden overwhelming acridity of artificial resin and citrus. Ti angles the perfume ad toward me.

The call of the wild, it says.

I flail furiously at the air in front of my nose until he crumples it up and throws it away.

"Since my father compensated me well for my invaluable contributions, I had the money to pay someone a ridiculous amount to fill the shell I'd spent a ridiculous amount to buy.

"So there were more 'appropriate' things: a leather sofa with no arms that was angled so deeply, you couldn't sit on it—or get out of it, if you did. Barstools of carbonized steel hexagons. Tables of clear acrylic that needed to be cleaned if you breathed near them.

"Since the ceiling was dotted with spot lighting for artwork, they covered the walls with big paintings of beautiful women, their eyes part closed and their mouths part open."

He flips to the end of the magazine.

"As for the actual beautiful women, I had to warn them to close their damn mouths and open their damn eyes and focus, because my king-size mattress floated on a platform of stainless steel so sharp, it could cut glass. And when they sliced open their shins, there would be blood and tears, and I would have to pretend to care.

"And I hated that most of all."

He reaches down to the side and slides the magazine under our wretchedly tilting table.

"So now talk to me, Wildfire, about what I'm giving up."

Chapter 29

TIBERIUS IS TRYING SO HARD. HE'S LEARNING TO DISTIN-
guish the scent of a sick deer, the torn-up stumps that
mean bear, the shorelines that attract raccoon, the gnaw
marks of muskrat (nummy) vs. the gnaw marks of a
porcupine (pointless).

Because he won't ever be a real wolf until he learns
to hunt. But he won't ever learn to hunt until he learns
to hunger.

It's not easy.

"You said they tasted like chips," he says, washing
out his mouth again.

"I said voles *are* like chips. They're crunchy. A little
salty. And nobody can eat just one."

He leans down, pulling his lip away from a flat
bicuspid.

"There's something stuck between my teeth. Do you
see it?" Before I can look, he coughs. "*And* there's hair
in the back of my throat."

I find myself afraid to look into the mirror, afraid
to discover that I've stepped into someone else's life
and love and luck. We are officially the 14th Echelon's
Theta pair. I'm not strong enough for a higher position,
and Tiberius can't hunt. But Theta is a good position,
hitting that sweet spot in the hierarchy between grim
pathos and seething envy.

Our little cabin is perfect. We're working steadily

with the silent Sten. There are a *lot* of voles. And most of all, I am mated to a man I love more than I can express in words.

There are times when we run that everything seems like a metaphor for that love. The root wrapped tight around an inopportune rock. The black tree dusted with a silver shimmer of snow. The low sun piercing through the netted forest canopy. Love and greed. The two great catalysts of human endeavor. I don't understand greed, but I fear it, because if human greed is half as strong as my love, then all the safeguards of all those generations of Pack are worth nothing.

Last week's strong winds mean blowdown. Wolves search the forest for likely looking trees, while others take turns chopping before the wind-thrown wood turns to ice.

Ti and I are the ones doing the chopping now. Both of us have stripped down to muscle shirts. There is something hypnotic about the winter quiet, interrupted by nothing but the *thunk* of the maul, the crack of the split log, the dull stuttering fall of wood on snow-muted earth, and wolf howl.

Deep-Deep-Deep-Deep

I startle at the unexpected sound. A furrow appears on Ti's brow. Then John passes at a run. With a quick look at each other, we follow.

"What is it?" I ask Sara, the wolf on gate duty.

"A truck."

"I can see that. I mean, what's it doing here?"

"Not sure, but John's called for Tara and Josi."

Then the wind shifts, and even though I can't see into the cab of the truck, I smell oil and heated plastic and carrion sticks.

Anderson jumps to the ground, his voice growing louder. Two burly, beer-gutted men emerge from the back, one with his hand reaching to the back of his waistband.

Josi, the 3rd Echelon's lawyer, arrives, racing past in oversize rubber boots and an anorak. Her legs are covered with fleece pajamas that mark her as someone who has an office and a life Offland. Still, Josi is our go-to for leading the second prong of a pincer attack and New York property law.

Sara opens the gate for her.

Josi begins talking with Anderson, softly and urgently, while John looks on. Other members of the Pack arrive, cleaning under their nails with seaxes, knocking mud from their boots with mallets, scratching their calves with oversized adzes.

A door opens on the passenger side of the cab, and a man jumps down. His lungs react to the first bite of sharp, cold air with dry, expulsive barks.

"Mr. Torrance?" says the Smoker, holding out his hand as he walks around the front of the truck. "Daniel Leary. I represent the new owner. We're clearing out Mr. Anderson's lot here." He taps his chest and coughs again. When he stops, a line of silver glimmers at his gum line. "Sorry," he says. "My lungs."

He must see Ti standing huge at the front of the gate, fisting the enormous maul, but he ignores him, reaching into an inner pocket of his jacket and pulling out a pack of cigarettes. He taps it firmly against the heel of his hand.

"Only one left," Leary says quietly, almost to himself. Ti's eyes narrow. A single cigarette slides out. "But legally, it's still a pack of cigarettes. Even if there is only one left. It is still a pack."

John and Josi and Anderson all look baffled for a moment while he cups his hands around his lighter, drawing hard on his cigarette until the tip glows red. "This kind burns real nice," he says before dropping his lighter into his pocket and turning back to the huddled conversation.

Ti stands frozen for an eternity and then, without taking his eyes from Leary, lifts his maul high over his head and brings it down on a pale granite boulder embedded in the frozen earth. A chunk shears away into powder.

Leary doesn't react at all, but Anderson puts his hand to his chest, and the one beer-gutted man puts his hand to his waistband again.

John signals to Tara. After a few whispered words, she returns to the gate.

"Your Alpha says you are to leave," she says quietly. "These are nervous men with guns. He will not see any of you hurt."

And because John spoke not as himself but as our Alpha, the Pack disperses in the wind like the seeds of a dandelion.

Except for my furious mate, who has to be dragged and pushed all the way to our cabin. By the time I slam the door and block it with my body, he is panting and pacing like a caged wolf. He slams his fist into the door beside my shoulder, making me jump. I wipe the tiny slivers of wood from my sleeves.

"That's enough, Ti." I hold out my hands to his, to see the flayed meat at his knuckles. I start to pick out a few odd splinters. "So your father bought that land. So what? It's not like he's going to drill on five acres."

He tightens for a second as I pull on one last splinter buried deep in the valley between the last two knuckles. As soon as I spit it out, I close my lips gently over his shredded skin and let my tongue swirl gently across it.

Ti has changed. He doesn't say anything now, just lets me. He pushes my hair back with his undamaged hand.

"He was sending me a message."

"Hmm?" I ask, my mouth otherwise occupied.

"That's why he bought that land. To send me a message." He sits on the sofa, pulling me after him. I curl my knees up on either side of his hips and lean my head on his chest, listening to his wolfish heart. "Somehow, my father has seen the Trust. Must know that it can only be altered by a unanimous decision of the Pack. But what makes a Pack? That's what Leary was saying. Legally, it's still a Pack even if there's only one."

I lift my head. Only one? Only one wolf? No wolf would betray the Pack. Maybe he's thinking Tiberius?

"*You* would be the Pack of one?" I almost laugh. I know my mate well enough now to realize he has no love for his father. "Why would he think you'd do *anything* for him?"

"He doesn't *think*. He *knows*. You missed the true meaning of that performance. You weren't supposed to understand it. It was meant for me alone. I'm the one who knows that Leary always smokes Marlboro Red. *Always*. It was no mistake that this one time, he was smoking Marlboro Silver. And when he said..." Ti props his chin on my head. "When he said, 'This kind burns real nice,' he was threatening *you*. I broke his jaw for pointing his finger at you. And because I didn't kill him then, my father knows how to control me now."

Licking my teeth, I still taste Tiberius's blood, rich and bittersweet on my tongue.

In England, right before our founding Alpha left, they say one of the greatest Packs was destroyed. It had been wealthy and powerful with scores of strong wolves. But one Iron Moon, Shifters and humans came on them during the change and bludgeoned them. Shot them. Cut off their heads and hung them from the branches of the great oaks, their blood soaking into their land.

Now all I can see is *our* trees festooned with the sightless heads of *our* wolves. *Our* land soaked with *our* blood.

"Where are you going, Wildfire?"

I hadn't realized that my hand was on the door handle. "Hunting. I need to hunt. I need to think."

"I'll work this out. You know that, right? It's all going to be fine."

"I know, *min coren*. It's all going to be fine." I reach up to slide my cheek against his. He holds me tight, rocking me, reluctant to let go.

At the Great Hall, I take four prepaid charge cards and the ID Tara gave me last time I went Offland.

In the basement, I grab food and clothes and fit it all in the neon-green daypack with a logo that reads, god help me, *Hound for Glory*.

One by one, I close the doors tightly behind me: the warped ledge and brace door to dry storage, the heavy double doors to the Great Hall, the storm doors to the foyer.

I start for the ends of the earth. Once I'm there, I will change and wait for the Iron Moon to pull me over the edge of wildness. Then I will be an *æcewulf*. A real wolf. A forever wolf. And August Leveraux will have lost any control he has over Tiberius or the Great North Pack.

I am ready.

Chapter 30

I WAS SO NOT READY.

Wiping the bile from my mouth, I wait for another chunk to come up. I can tell from the taste that it's still more of William Dunn Crawley's sclerotic liver. The intestine is the worst, though: slimy and filled with fat and decay, it is a meter of carrion sausage that almost killed me going down and is trying to do it again coming back up.

I made it across the Canadian border before shifting to skin. Then I did my best to make my way disguised as human. At first, I did well: I caught a bus to Montreal and a train to Winnipeg, but once I was there, things started to fall apart.

Another section of intestine comes up. I try to keep my throat open wide and pull at it with my hands.

While I was waiting for the train to Hay River in the Northwest Territories, someone stole my daypack, leaving me with no money, no tickets, and no change of clothes. No way I was going to make it all the way from Winnipeg to Great Bear Lake on three legs before the snows made the route impassable, so I'd started the long walk along Highway 16, hoping some kind stranger would give me a ride to Saskatoon. Edmonton, even.

A stranger did give me a ride, but he wasn't kind, and because I killed him, I had to eat him. I did it in his car, which was very tight and awkward, but there were no trees by that section of the highway, and anyone seeing a wolf eating a man along the Yellowhead Highway would have shot me dead.

Does it count as eating a man if you can't keep him down?

I didn't hear footsteps, but hands are suddenly on my hair. I flail at them. That's what William Dunn Crawley did. He held my hair with one hand, his other hand on that bowie knife. My muscles twitch now like they did then, my anger rising.

But I don't think I can do it. Eat another man.

These hands are different, though. They don't push me anywhere. They comfort me, one hand smoothing my hair away from my sweating face, the other stroking the back of my neck.

"Shh, Wildfire."

I had explained to William Dunn Crawley—I saw his license when I stripped down the body—that I wasn't receptive, and he still insisted on pushing my head down on his naked cock. He seemed shocked when I ate it, but really, what did he think was going to happen?

I manage to get another bit of Crawley fat out before I crawl away from the mess. Ti holds out a bottle of icy water.

"We need to go now," he says and lifts me up, kissing my sweat- and blood- and bile-smeared face. "Someone is going to check on the car soon." I look up blearily at the scrubbed, gray, empty Manitoba vastness and doubt it.

Then I smell the burning plastic, and when I lean back against the headrest of his rental car, I see the tall plume of black smoke.

"Do you need to stop again?"

I wave my hand frantically, and Ti stops. Even with the windows open and the cold, fresh air, we haven't been able to get more than twenty kilometers without pulling over to let me purge.

Each time, he squats next to me, making sure I don't tumble over and murmuring words of encouragement. He doesn't say anything else. Nothing about why I ran or how he tracked me or anything. Not that I could answer.

When I finish, I crawl away and curl onto my side. Each time, Ti pokes through the steaming meat with one of the takeout chopsticks he has stuffed in the glove compartment. I don't know what he's looking for, maybe to see if I've finally gotten around to vomiting up my own guts.

"There it is." He jams the chopstick into the pile and pulls out William Dunn Crawley's chewed and partially digested penis. He throws it to the road.

He cleans me up as best he can with rough brown towels that still smell like roadside bathrooms and herds me back into the car. This time, he fastens the seat belt and pulls it tight. "Hold on," he says before hitting the gas. He jerks the steering wheel, pulls on the hand brake, and the wheels spin.

Leaning my head on the cold window, I watch the smear of flesh on the asphalt retreat in the side mirror. It is all that's left of William Dunn Crawley.

Tiberius drives into the night with his hands clutched around the steering wheel, his teeth grinding together. "Stay here," he says when he finally unlocks his jaw at a motel near Portage la Prairie. After getting the keys from the night manager, he pops the trunk and hands me my daypack. I don't know where he found it, but

I'm guessing—from the blood that stains the neon-green black—that he took it from someone who hesitated before giving it up.

"Shower?" he asks.

"Toothbrush?" I reply.

He rummages through my daypack.

I'm in the middle of washing my hair for the second time when he comes back in. I miss our "dog shampoo," but I'm not in a position to complain that the shampoo smells like disinfectant.

Ti stands stiff, staring at my back, my toothbrush upright in his hand like the lance of a palace guard.

I know what he's looking at because it hurts like hell, and when I crane my neck, the view in the mirror doesn't look much better. The bowie knife slid along my back, peeling away the skin and revealing the ribs, but like Tristan says, if it doesn't shatter bone or damage internal organs...

"It's just a flesh wound."

The bathroom door closes softly, but the outer door slams so loudly, I swear the cinder-block wall starts to crack.

He doesn't come back into the little bathroom while I brush and re-brush my teeth and finally rub against them with the rough towel until my fangs squeak.

The room is small, with a double bed and a single dull lamp with a plastic shade bearing a bumpy, mottled spot from a too-strong bulb. There's a Bible next to it. Ti sits completely still, a pair of scissors, a big roll of gauze, and a tube of antibiotic beside him. He pats the bed.

"Hold your hair up," he commands. "No, both hands."

When I have both hands above my head, Ti fits the

flap of skin back in place. Next, he gently layers on antibiotic and folds a piece of gauze over it.

He wraps his arms around me, holding one end of the roll under my breasts, and binds it slowly around my rib cage until the roll is done. He ties the ends firmly and helps me into a T-shirt (*Paul Smith's Bobcats*) that drags to my knees.

I sit next to him, but Ti doesn't say anything, just stares at the floor until finally I say his name. He looks up, startled, and keels over, pulling one of the thin pillows to his face and howling furiously.

Someone bangs on the wall behind the bed and makes the painting of evening pine tree shiver in its plastic frame. "*Hey, asshole, keep it down.*"

Lying on my good side, my whole side, I try to pull away the pillow.

"You weren't outside," he chokes out. "And you didn't come back from hunting. I tracked you as far as the stream near the sap house. I walked south and then north along the banks, but you never got out."

"It hits a bog a few miles up. There's another stream to the east."

He shakes his head and starts to crumble. I doubt he's slept since I left the Homelands. "I remembered what you said about musk ox and going someplace where there are no people and turning wild forever. I picked up your scent on a westbound platform of the Gare Centrale in Montreal and then again in Union Station in Winnipeg. I got distracted by your backpack, but I finally tracked you to the Yellowhead Highway, and then I didn't anymore, because someone"—his voice drops so low that I strain to hear—"someone had picked you up.

"You were running away from me," he starts softly, but with each word, his voice rises again. "And someone picked you up along the *fucking Highway of Tears*."

The volume of those last words bothers our neighbor again, but Ti is not his normal unflappable self and thrusts his fist through the plasterboard. He grabs something, then gives it a sharp pull. It hits the wall with a sloppy thud and a whimper.

Ti crams that painting of the evening pines with its plastic frame into the hole.

I slip into bed, lying on my good side, and lift the blankets for him. He crawls close and pulls me closer. I put my head on his shoulder, and he lifts my leg across his thighs. He carefully shapes my hair into a channel across the black plain of his chest. It reminds him, he says, stroking the silver course of my hair, of the moon on Home Pond.

"I can deal with my father, with anything else, but not with that. Promise me, Silver. I will never trap you. I know what happens when you try to break a wolf, but promise me that you'll never run from me again."

I'm about to say that I'm a wolf, and we don't make promises because we say what we mean, but in the needy, jumpy heartbeat against my cheek, I start to think that when I was balancing my love for my Pack against my love for Tiberius, I hadn't considered this third love that wasn't mine but was his.

The only vow I know is an ancient one that Gran Sigeburg said came from long-dead wolves who lived in the long-vanished forests of Mercia. It's what I whisper now to my own worried and worn-out wolf.

"*Mid min clawum ond fængtoþ wille ic scieldan þé.*

Mid min flæsc wille ic retan þé. Mid min fyrhþ wille ic gehamian þé."

"What does it mean?" he whispers into my hair.

"With my claw and fang will I shield you. With my flesh will I comfort you. With my soul will I make you a home."

And in the flimsy bed in the cinder-block and particleboard room of the motel off the highway near Portage la Prairie, my Shifter love cries.

In the morning, the radiator cranks up, and I wake to the smell of overheated plastic wafting through the vents. It smelled like William Dunn Crawley's car. I struggle up from under the covers, but Ti's arm is on my hair. I don't like that either, because it feels like William Dunn Crawley's hand.

I pull my hair out from under Ti's arm and stare at the ceiling of variegated white squares set in metal struts. Loading my toothbrush, I open the blind onto the back parking lot, the one that doesn't face onto the walkway, and brush my teeth.

Ti hears me and heads into the bathroom, then sits on the bed, rubbing his face and his scalp with his big hands. He jumps a little when I kneel down in front of him and begin to pull down his shorts.

"What are you doing?" he says, clutching the waistband.

"What do you think I'm doing?"

"Just wait, Silver. I think...what with everything, I don't think this is what you really need."

"Actually, it's exactly what I need. A man did

something that I didn't like. I killed him and ate him and purged him and washed him off and brushed and spat and rinsed and repeated, but it's not enough. In my mind, I still feel *his* hand in my hair, I still smell *his* scent, I still taste *his* body.

"I don't want him in my mind. I want you."

He shakes his head. "I—"

"Ti, please. If you want to help me, don't tell me what I need. *Do* what I need."

Finally, he releases his shorts and leans back, one hand covering his forehead. I can feel the tension as I strip him, but oh god, the relief as I slide between his dark, ropy thighs, so different from Crawley's pale, flaccid legs.

I take Ti's hand and move it to my head. He refuses at first, but I coax him, and he holds my hair so carefully, following the motion of my head as gently as a thistle seed on the breeze. I breathe out and breathe in the smell of crumbling wood and musk coming from the narrow thicket of black curls. Ti's reluctant sex grows harder under my tongue. Ti's twinned weights tighten as I hold them carefully and firmly in my palm. The drop that glistens like amber in the low morning light tastes like salt and smoke and Ti. Ti's hips tighten and tremble as he tries to hold back. Ti's solid arms lift me carefully onto his lap. It's Ti's voice that whispers to me before he sweeps the hair back from the cord of my neck and takes it between his sharp teeth.

It is Tiberius whose every iron inch slides thickly into me.

It is Tiberius who splinters me, his body straining to give me everything he has, and by the time he has emptied himself inside me—rich and hot and smelling like crushed bone and evergreen—I can't even remember that fat shit's name.

Chapter 31

IT'S BEEN NEARLY FOUR DAYS SINCE I SNUCK ACROSS THE border somewhere north of Perry Mills Road. And except for the unpleasant interval needed to eat someone, I've been in skin.

As a wolf, the world is filled with cues: the dry crack of a branch under the weight of snow, the smell of fungi, a quiet rustle of a nest that once housed a sapsucker and now a squirrel in a tree that is dead and not just for the winter.

As a human, the world is filled with commands: YIELD, DO NOT PASS, WATCH FOR CHILDREN, KEEP CANADA CLEAN, IT'S CHOCOLATE TIME AT TIM HORTONS.

In skin, my mind is being dulled by the constant onslaught of headlights of cars coming west from Montreal, by the deadening drone of our tires on blacktop.

"You're going to scratch yourself raw," Ti says somewhere east of wherever it was we were before. "I think it's best if I drop you off at the edge of Homelands first and then return the car."

An hour later, he drops me off at the border of our territory. He gets out and crouches beside me and says something that starts with "Remember..." but it's too late. I've already started to change. I'll have to ask him when he comes home. I tumble down a decline, dislodging damp needles. At the bottom, my still-useless and contorting body lands against a spruce. Soft snow sifts down, cooling my half-furred skin. I want to scream at the relief of it, which of course I can't.

Instead, I run, sniffing the markings of my pack, and struggle to make my way through the thick snow, which is especially hard with only three legs. I've just dislodged a redpoll when a perimeter wolf emits a sharp huff, a kind of witheringly dry cough. It's what we do when we don't have words and need to say *Alpha first; cavorting later*.

John raises his eyebrow at my damp hair, still-grubby nails, and motley collection of oversize, yellow-and-purple Saxons athletic gear. "Tiberius asked if you could come with him to settle his affairs Offland, but you should have asked too, Quicksilver."

"I-I… You talked to him?"

He waves me off as he picks up his Rolodex and a sheaf of papers. "He called. Said you did well at first, but that he didn't think you could last much longer in skin." John's eyes narrow skeptically. "So you didn't change for nearly four days?"

I nod dumbly. I guess Ti called on his way to the rental place? It would have been helpful if he'd told me that he would be talking to John.

"Good. Anyway, he says he'll be finished by the Iron Moon."

"What? But that's—"

"Yes?"

"—a while," I end lamely.

He nods, tired and distracted as he continues sorting through the sheaf of papers. He doesn't notice when I leave.

I track Ti's most recent movements from the access road back to the sap house, and under a couple of loose floorboards, I find the rags soaked in turpentine and lavender oil he used to cover the stench of his guns. The Beretta and the rifle are gone. But the gun he brought when he came here is still there.

I track him back to our cabin and the hastily scribbled note on our coffee table.

Wildfire… The paper in my hands shakes badly.

> *If you're reading this, you're home. And you probably already know where I've gone. If I'm not back the afternoon of the Iron Moon, then my father may still be alive, but he has lost his Pack of One.*
>
> *I never expected to find love. I didn't really believe in it, the way they said it would come. That it would be sudden. Inexplicable. Mystical. It wasn't. Not for me, anyway. I fell in love with you because you took my hand and walked me there. You took me as you found me, and step by step, you walked me there.*
>
> *I would never have been able to find the way by myself, but I'm here now and this is where I will stay. Always in love with you.*
>
> *Tiberius*

The junkyard is empty now, just a scrubbed rectangle of dirt. Leelee's hole is gone, as are the old TRESPASSERS WILL BE SHOT signs. Our markings around the barbed wire have been disturbed as well, so several male wolves drink gallons of tea and head over to trace the perimeter once again.

I spend too much time here, pacing and waiting. There are no trees nearby to block the snow, and no animal will cross it because the edges have been marked by wolves, so it's a pristine white parallelogram, a sterile breeding ground for my troubled imagination.

The Iron Moon is coming, and I feel the humans circling.

Even before my foray into humanity and Canada, I'd been getting tired easily. I thought it was just the sudden fullness of my life, but it's been worse recently. I tried to say something in passing to Tristan, so it wouldn't seem like I'd actually come to see him.

He sniffed at my ear, pushed his hand against my belly, and fingered my breasts.

I told him I wasn't receptive and nipped him.

He dragged me to medical and hooked me up to the ultrasound. As impossible as it seems, I'm pregnant. Conception is usually so hard for us that I wouldn't have believed it, except I've seen the four miniscule bodies nestled inside me.

Tristan didn't offer me a Tic Tac.

The day of the Iron Moon, I walk back and forth along the perimeter nearest the access road, carving a dark dirt path in the snow. Every wolf coming home sends my heart racing.

But with each wolf who passes through the gate, my anxiety grows. I run for the sap house, worried about deserting my post, and then push Ti's gun, the one that he left, into a squirrel hollow not far from the gate.

By late afternoon, I'm clinging to the chain link, praying for a glimpse of black. I beg the gate wolf to let me lock up. He looks divided, then nods and heads back to the Great Hall. He must have passed John on the way down, because it's only a few minutes until I hear John's boots.

He stands next to me, looking out on the quiet ice- and snow-frosted woods beyond the fence. "Maybe he got held up in traffic," he says.

I can't bring myself to respond with anything but a nod.

"Lock the gate before you come," he says after a few quiet minutes. "But don't be too long. Remember: Death and the Iron Moon wait for no wolf."

He rubs his cheek against my head and walks back the way he'd come. I watch him leave, grateful beyond words that on this, his first real Iron Moon with Evie and his pups, he took the time to mark me again and remind me that whatever else happens, I belong.

I take my hands out of my pockets, hoping that in skin, he couldn't smell the bitter scent of steel and gunpowder.

John is long gone, and there are only maybe thirty minutes of light left when I finally hear the sounds of tires grumbling over the snow and gravel. I rush to the gate, feeling for the latch, and then stop, listening more closely.

It's a car, sure, but why is it moving so slowly? Ti would know to hurry. He would know that I was waiting and that the change was coming.

It's also a layered sound: some closer, some farther

away. I think—no, I know—there is more than one car. I dart back into the dark, back for the elm with the emptied knot that holds the gun. The cars turn off at the junkyard.

Doors open carefully, followed by urgent whispering. Something bangs against the doorframe, and a flashlight comes on and then quickly shuts off. These accents are strange, and the tones are alien. One voice hisses something and starts to cough.

Something heavy falls to the ground with a muffled groan and goes silent. I creep along the forest floor, keeping hidden by the understory until I am directly upwind, then I strain every nerve of my poor human senses, sieving through the smells: steel, carrion, dying lungs, the varying scents of so many humans. Two—no, three—bear the teasing trace of wild that marks them as Shifters.

Then the smell of evergreen and crushed bone and iron and salt and old leather. Tiberius is bleeding and afraid, but I'm not about to run into a herd of healthy animals armed with nothing but hope and a gun I'm not sure how to use.

Leary hisses out his instructions. One Shifter will take a group north. The other will take a group south. The third will go up the main path, all converging on the Great Hall.

"*Allons-y. Commençons la chasse. Et n'oubliez pas. Tous les chiens. Meme les p'tits. Mais pas l'avorton d'argent,*" Leary says before translating for the Anglophones. "We start the hunt, and remember: all the dogs. Even the little ones. But *not* the silver runt."

"What about him?" says a voice.

"Chain him up before you go," Leary says.

"Chambord and I will stay here. This cold, dry air"—he hacks twice—"is not good for my lungs."

Winter dusk is already too dark for human eyes. Leary points the flashlight, and for the first time, I see Ti. He slumps forward as they chain him to a tree. Then the man pulls on a rope, and Ti's head jerks back. The light reflects from tiny rivulets of blood glistening below the line of a prong collar. From the steel grill across his mouth.

My tongue darts over my sharp fangs, and my body shivers with the need to tear apart the men who dared muzzle my mate.

As soon as the Shifters have taken their teams, I move silently to the little hollow behind Ti's tree. Neither Leary nor Chambord are Shifters, so they don't hear me or smell me, even though I am now downwind. Ti does. I know because he stiffens suddenly, and he turns his head, his nose flaring.

The closer I get, the thicker the scent of blood, until I am at his hands, shackled with a loose chain looped around the back of the tree. The smell of blood is almost overwhelming around one hand that is swollen and crusted and hangs at an odd angle.

He makes a soft, pleading sound.

"Shut up," Leary says. "What you destroyed would have been your inheritance. You owe your father restitution. Personally"—he spits—"I would have crucified you, but August reminded me that we need your signing hand."

Ti doesn't make another sound as I lift the gun, plant my feet, and aim carefully. Then I pull at the trigger. Nothing happens. I try it again. There's something about a safety? I start feeling around for it.

"Oh, Jesus fuck," Leary snorts, his own gun at the ready. He nods to Chambord. Both of them search the dark near me. "You call this a rescue party? A man who can't even use a gun?"

Of course, he's right. I was never meant to be a man with a gun. I move as quietly as I can around the other side of Ti's tree, pausing for a moment, brushing silently against the warmth of his uninjured hand.

Each step I take sounds thunderously loud to me, but Leary keeps staring into the blackness where I had been until he feels something hard in his back and stiffens. The air stinks of salt and old leather as he waves Chambord off.

"Now," I whisper tightly. "Let him go."

The moment I speak, the scent of his fear fades, and his spine relaxes against my touch. "Well, that's a problem," he says coolly. "See, I don't have the key."

Leonora says humans fear men but not women. Which I don't understand at all. How is it possible that they alone of all animals don't know that there is nothing more ferocious, more deadly, more willing to die than a female protecting her own?

"You were right about the gun," I say softly, my lips against his scruffy cheek, "but not about the other thing. I could never be a man. I am not even human."

In a flash, I sink my wolfish teeth into his face. Not my fangs, which would only tear through. I use my carnassials, and in two slicing bites, the whole side comes off. *One. Two.*

Judging by the way Chambord freezes, staring at Leary's screaming partly exposed skull, I don't think he was told exactly what he would be hunting.

That moment's hesitation is too long, because Tiberius does know how to use a gun, and the chain has enough play in it to let him angle the one I slipped into his "signing hand."

I crouch over Leary, holding two fingers out like the barrel of a gun. "Bang," I say and throw his gun far away. I don't want to kill him. I need his screams to alert the Pack.

Reaching behind Ti's head, I gently unfasten the muzzle, and he takes a deep cracked breath. "They'll hear him," he says, his lips dried and split against mine, his breath sour and bloody. "They're going to come back. You've got to go." I drop the muzzle and start to work on the prong collar. I can't go too fast; some of the metal is still embedded in his neck and sticks as I pull at it. He just keeps whispering for me to go. As soon as it's loosened, I carefully pull it up, raising myself on my toes to make sure I don't scratch his eyes.

"Do you know who has the keys?"

He shakes his head. "Please, Silver."

I put my knee on Leary's writhing chest to hold him steady while I look for the keys. I know he said he didn't have them, but he's human and they lie.

He tries to say something but lacking lips and one cheek, it comes out garbled, incomprehensible.

In his jeans pockets, I find his lighter. And a set of small, square-topped keys. Leary splutters again, blood bubbling between his teeth. The keys start to shake, almost slipping through my fingers. I clutch them in both hands and stumble back to Ti.

"I can hear them. *They're coming*," he hisses. "*Get out.*" I steady myself against the tree as best I can, but the Iron Moon is pulling me inexorably toward wildness. My hands shiver badly, and my eyesight is failing. I scrape the key along the surface, searching for the keyhole. It sinks into something, and I turn the key. I don't know if it was the keyhole or just air, but it doesn't matter. I'm done: my eyes are useless, my hands misshapen. The bones in my feet fuse and lengthen, my legs contort, and as my body begins to fall, I wrap my arms around the little beings nestled in my belly.

"Silver!"

Then it's over, and I hear nothing beyond the milky stillness. Except gunfire. Gunfire has an unnatural percussive power that hits even my changing ears like a shock wave.

A hard push against my ribs sends me falling back into the hollow. My arms and legs flop helplessly as I tumble down until something catches on my running pants. I scrabble as best I can, moving whatever muscle obeys me at that moment—a toe, a finger, my shoulder—until gravity takes over and sends me careening to the bottom of the decline. I can tell from the cold on my legs that my pants, loose around my changing body, have come off.

Shaking my head, I try to clear my ears. There are two more gunshots. Four. Finally, my ears clear and I hear humans running, surrounded by the small pandemonium of animals cowering, the crack of sapless winter branches, and the thick fall of snow dislodged from the forest canopy.

A car starts and peels off.

Struggling up the hollow sideways, I keep my two healthy legs always on the downward slope so I don't fall back. The chain is slack at the base of the tree. Chambord, three other humans, and a Shifter lie dead. Leary is gone. So is Ti, but I can't follow him now, because howls and gunfire and high, sharp barks are coming from the Great Hall, and then the wind brings the thin smell of accelerant.

As I near the Great Hall, I hear Adrian's howl reverberate from the basement, followed by the high staccato sounds of the pups. I skid into a turn, running for the two spruces, one big, one small, the tip of Whiteface centered between them.

Another gunshot, and the crackle and acrid smoke of arson. My claws hit wood under the forest carpet, digging hard until I find the rope handle and pull and push. It falls with a thump to the hard ground.

Squeezing through the roots that have dug down from above, I yip as I run so the pups will know that someone's coming. They must hear it, because their claws scrabble at the trapdoor. It would be hard for them to open from the other side, of course, but I can just push—

Except that after Ronan broke in, John had the trapdoor covered with shelving, and it won't open wide enough, not even for the littlest. I slam my shoulders against it again and again, trying to topple the damn shelf. Adrian seems to have figured out what I'm trying to do. He barks and barks some more, and then with one more push, I hear something crash. Now when I push, the trapdoor opens a little.

The floor is covered with gory-looking puddles, but it's just the sour cherries we put by in the summer. I can't open the trapdoor wide, but it's big enough. The little pups are confused and hesitate until I yip for

Leelee, who trots over and bends to look into the darkness beside me. I smack her in with a twist of my head, and as soon as she lands, she barks so the others know it's not deep. Some jump bravely, some waver, but not for long. Juveniles at the back push them in.

Then Adrian, the final juvenile, jumps in with Nils in his jaws, but Nils whines worriedly, and I suddenly realize that I haven't seen Nyala.

I curl up tight, my good hind leg wedged high into the wood slats that keep the tunnel from collapsing. With one big shove, I push through, the hatch falling on the tip of my tail.

I remember Nyala's smell from the First Marking, but there's too much confusion—smoke and fire and sour cherry—and my senses are muddled. She's too small to climb up, so I push my nose along the base of the floor, scenting her almost immediately. I stick my muzzle farther under the potato bin and yip softly, hoping she'll come to me. Maybe because I didn't scent-mark her at the presentation ceremony, she isn't sure I'm Pack and holds back.

Too damn bad. I lie on my side and reach under with my paw and slap her out. She mewls in complaint, but when I grab her withers between my jaws, she does what every instinct tells her to do and goes slack. Standing with a mouth full of pup, I realize that I can't leave by the door, and the trapdoor, blocked by the toppled shelves, is impossible to open from the inside.

Like any Pack, my eye flickers toward the moon, just an instinctual need to track the pattern of my life. But now when I do, I see not only the moon, but its light running down where the shelving struts broke through the single tiny, narrow window high in the wall.

I growl at the limp thing in my mouth, warning her, because I have to jump. Jumping requires coiling the muscles in both thighs, in both hips for a simultaneous release. I don't have both, I only have the one, so when I jump, one goes off properly, the other doesn't, and my body does a semi-spiral. Clinging with my claws, I scrabble awkwardly up the shelves.

Shoving my head through the break, I spit Nyala outside. The hole isn't really big enough for me, but I have no choice. Glass cuts lines along the length of my body as I push my way through; still, my bones and internal organs are in one piece, so it is a flesh wound.

Another gunshot.

Terrified, Nyala creeps forward, pressing her shivering body against me as I hang my head, trying to find my balance again, before I pick her up once more and race toward the mouth of the tunnel in the forest. Gran Moira, who was hiding in the woods, joins me, keeping pace next to me. At the mouth of the tunnel, I drop Nyala and smell for the other pups. Nyala barks softly, and Nils stumbles out. Gran Moira pushes the little pup toward her brother. Laying my muzzle beside hers, I give over responsibility for our young. Gran Moira turns and snaps, herding them toward the protection of the High Pines.

Another shot.

There's a dead human lying halfway in the water. The huge, red jerrican in one hand is leaking gas onto the ice of Home Pond. His gun is still holstered, but his throat is ravaged. A few feet away, a big, golden-brown wolf with dark gray markings lies dead, a hole in the back of her head. The Iron Moon is reflected in her open eyes, and human blood stains her mouth.

Wolves are not like humans. We do not wait for death to find us. We die hunting.

Solveig fulfilled her destiny as a wolf and her duty as an Alpha and died hunting.

My nose close to the ground, I follow the stench of steel and carrion into the woods and toward the Clearing.

A heavy footstep crunches through the snow nearby. It isn't Ti; even wounded, he would never be that loud and clumsy. I bury myself in the snow behind a patch of dogbane and wait for the hard boots with thick treads. The hunter reeks of salt and old leather and startles when one foot sinks into the brittle undergrowth. A shot rings out from a few hundred yards, and he pivots toward it, pulling frantically at his leg, his gun trembling in his hands, like a vampire hunter with a cross, terrified that a death he doesn't understand lurks in the dark.

Once my jaws crunch hard into his wrist, I pull myself up, my one strong hind leg tearing into fleshy stomach just above this man's belt.

Death does lurk in the dark, and I am it.

His gun goes down; with my hind leg buried in his intestines, I push up and crush his windpipe. He claws at me with soft hands, like a raccoon.

More gunfire erupts at the edge of the woods, flash after flash of it, and the man holding the gun screams furiously. I don't think he's attacking. I think we share this with humans. When we attack, we are silent. We make noise when we're worried or confused, and I think this man is terrified. There's another shot. Another single soft *pop*, different and distinctive, then silence. I race toward it, coming to a stop at the body of a man with a bullet so perfectly placed, it looks like a third eye in the middle of his forehead.

The rifle with the big magazine smells like burned metal, and the barrel is warm.

A man at the other side of the Clearing screams over and over and over and will not shut up.

A wind from the mountains brings a soft unleashing of snow and the distant promise of my mate's scent. I run toward him, my heart beating so fast that it almost blurs with the fluttering of a wood grouse dislodged from its blanket of snow. Almost. I skid to a stop, because I didn't disturb the grouse. A Shifter did.

The agony across the Clearing subsides to one final choked scream and then stops.

Unlike humans, the Shifter senses me. Unlike Pack, he is presumptuous and careless.

"I hear you, dog," he says. He swings around and shoots at the ground.

So. He can hear, but if he could smell me—see me—he wouldn't have aimed where he did. I crouch behind a low, snow-encased bush, trying to remember everything I've ever learned about winds and land and the acoustic properties of snow. The hunter starts walking in ever-widening orbits, hoping to dislodge me like he did the grouse.

I stay still as he circles closer, his gun held in both hands, his head moving slowly from side to side, listening. He's so close that he is almost on top of me. If my legs were whole, I'd take him down, but as I am, I can't take any chances. I know he doesn't see me, because he keeps squinting into the woods. Just one more pass and—

Pop.

The Shifter teeters before falling onto his back, a shocked expression on his face.

The man lies on the snow, his arms outstretched and a hole placed so perfectly in the middle of his forehead, it looks like a third eye.

The seeping blood steams slightly in the moonlight.

It's barbaric, killing this way. Pushing a button in the distance. We at least see our victims. Taste their blood. Feel the incoherent spasming. Hear the final gurgling pleas. Death is real for us.

Ti stands next to me, his leg against my shoulder. He holds his damaged hand close to his chest. His good hand still holds the gun.

We both listen for hunters or gunfire, but there's nothing. Everything in the Homelands is afraid, and that fear has a quiet so profound that it reaches to the very edge of silence.

But there is one thing in the Homelands that isn't afraid, and when Evie screams, it is as only a wolf can: cracked and haunted and primal.

Twisting away, I stumble into the Clearing where Evie stands on the Alpha's rock, a dark shadow howling her fury and loss.

The Pack is already gathering at the edge of the woods, and that's where I go, creeping low through all of those huge bodies. Whimpering, I nuzzle my head under John's slack chin, begging him to get up. I lick at him, begging him to put me in his pocket and keep me safe when that makes no sense. Begging him to be waiting for me when I finally make it home. Begging him to mark me again. Make me belong.

He didn't even have a chance to fight. There is such a tiny hole in one side of his chest. That opens up into a huge chasm on the other. All of John's strength and skill meant nothing, because the man who killed him saw him in the distance and, from that distance, shot him.

Then Evie ripped out his intestines and calligraphed them across the snow. It had not been a clean kill, and until his heart dropped into the cavity left by his viscera, the man suffered.

Demos stumbles into the clearing with what looks like a broken leg, but even though it must be painful, he plants his feet into the ground as always. Blood is already stiffening on his muzzle. He stands still while the others sniff at him and smell that Solveig is dead too. After a short bark, he adds his own mournful howl.

Evie's dark eyes reflect the flames at Home Pond that light up the sky like sunrise. Then, scenting something new, she turns toward the man as big as night who stumbles and then lowers his body into the center of the Clearing. He crosses his jeans-clad legs.

Evie leaps from the Alpha's rock and tears toward him, but Ti sits utterly still, his hands on his knees, his gun on the ground beside him.

I race faster with three legs than I ever have with four. Tendons tear, bones scrape, nerves scream. I lower my head and throw myself at Evie, at my Alpha, my jaws open and ready to fight because Ti won't, and I can't explain that things are complicated or that her pups are alive.

Surprised, she falters, and when I put my teeth on either side of her neck, she scrapes into my torso with her hind legs. My spine curls tight, trying to protect the little lives inside me as I clamp the back of Evie's head in my jaws, hard enough to hold her but not to hurt her. She struggles and scrapes, and then she slows. Her nose flares again and again as she scents my muzzle. She has to smell Nyala, who I carried in my jaws, but she should smell the other pups too, who left their mark as they squeezed past.

Her ears perk up, her head whipping away from Ti, and I let her go. The others are already racing toward the north edge of the Clearing nearest the High Pines. Several elder wolves emerge, accompanied by the quiet, frightened, questioning yips of the tired fur balls with them.

The whole pack nuzzles them, sniffing them and licking away the smoke and sour cherry and kerosene. When they are done caring for the pups, the adults circle around and begin the long keening. Without quite knowing why, the pups join in, mourning our dead.

"We are," they say, "less."

I can't mourn. I don't have time. The crumpled man in the center of the Clearing is going to die if I don't get him sheltered. I push my nose under his head. *Get up, damn it. Get up.* He mumbles something but doesn't move. I fasten my teeth to his jacket and start to drag him, pulling and fighting for every stupid inch across the Clearing.

Then starts the hard part—bumping him over the crowded, uneven ground toward our cabin. He lifts his hand. "One minute," he says. But that's what people say when they're about to give in to cold and exhaustion, so to hell with your minute. I snap at his finger and start to pull him again.

"No, I know. I just mean give me a minute to get

up. That's all." He pushes up from the ground with his good hand and stumbles precariously. I move closer, and he braces against me, using my shoulders to push himself upright.

Behind us, the trail of his blood stands out bright against the moonlit snow.

We hobble slowly, the two of us, through dark paths until I see our cabin deep in the woods and Ti slows.

He staggers those last few rough feet up the stairs and in through the door. As soon as the door closes, he collapses. I drag all the pillows and blankets and towels and pile them around and over him, like a snow nest, then curl my small body around my mate's big shivering one. He holds his pierced and broken hand to his chest. Tristan will have to see to it later, but for now, I lick at it gently, carefully cleaning away the embedded rust and dirt.

I can't sleep, worried about Ti. Listening to the Great Hall collapse around its burned timbers. Listening to the coyotes calling for their packmates to eat our dead.

Hearing John's last words to me: "Death and the Iron Moon wait for no wolf."

Ti wakes with a shudder in the middle of the night. When I move my paw gently against his shoulder, his glowing eyes find mine, and he sighs. I don't know what he was dreaming, but he smiles at me sadly before crawling toward the kitchen.

The water runs. Ti opens a cupboard, and when he comes back, collapsing once again into the pillow nest, his face is damp. He is silent for a long time, but by the rise and fall of his chest, I know he isn't sleeping.

"Carrion and steel." Ti's voice is halt and slurred.

"That's what it smelled like. My father's compound. I'd never noticed it before. I doubt my father did either. It was just the smell of our lives."

He grunts in pain as he shifts his hips, trying to get comfortable. I sniff at his back to see if he's bleeding here too. "S'ok, Sil. Just broke something. Rib, I think." He shuffles one more time and stops. "But it isn't. It's the smell of *human* life. There was no wood or earth or grass or rain. No blood or bone. Nothing that I recognize now as wild. That's how I knew that my father—that all the Shifters—were gone."

He turns his face to my fur, taking long, gulping breaths like a drowning man. "I needed this," he says, his breath heating my skin. "I need this."

Ti tracked the scent of Shifters north. But his failure to fall into the trap August had left at the compound had clearly made his father nervous. He added more Shifter guards, because while everyone knew the rumor that no one ever escaped August Leveraux, only August knew the truth. That no one ever escaped Tiberius.

It was on the side of the James Bay Road that August opened the blackened window of his car and tossed out an apple core. And Ti shot him above the bulletproof vest and below the Kevlar helmet.

Then it was the Shifters' turn to hunt Ti. There were too many, and he'd been going for too long, and when they caught him, they were not…gentle. That's what he said. Not…gentle. More than once, he thought he was dying. He said his mind clung to the vision of the silver wolf leaping from the rock overhang into the night-black water of Clear Pond. Clung to the knowledge that whatever happened to him, he had saved her. Saved me.

He didn't die, though. Instead, he woke up tied again to the overgrown chain-link fence where he'd spent the Iron Moons of his childhood, while Leary shoved papers at him: postdated, transferring controlling interest in the Trust once the Pack was gone. When Ti refused, Leary had him secured to a fence post with a spike through his left hand. "Not just any spike. A *dog* spike. Even before he said my father's name, I knew he was somehow alive, because there is nothing that man likes better than torture with a side of irony.

"I'd saved nothing."

———————

There is no Iron Moon Table when we change back, because we have no table, no roof, no walls. Nothing is left of the Great Hall but blackened wood around the ruin of the main fireplace. Digging through the wreckage, the pups find a few kitchen pots and three first-kill skulls.

And the Eolh pen, protected in its cracked coffee mug.

YOU WOULDN'T UNDERSTAND.
IT'S AN ALPHA THING.

It is not in the nature of the Pack to accept change quietly, but for now, the Alphas of the other echelons gather with Evie in the Meeting House. I found Tara and explained to her as best I could how Tiberius came to be in the company of a small army of Shifters and humans. I didn't know what to make of her expression as she promised to explain to the Alphas and disappeared through the door of the Meeting House.

There's nothing for us to do but wait, even though Ti desperately needs food and medical attention. He weaves unsteadily against my shoulder until Tara pushes back through the door and signals to us.

I help him up.

All the Alphas are standing, ignoring the chairs as resolutely as the Year of First Shoes. No Alpha—not Eudemos with his broken leg, nor Evie with her broken heart and body still weak from her lying-in—will sit. Now more than ever, we cannot coddle weakness.

Evie stares out the window and doesn't move when we come in. The forest starts a few yards out, but I think her focus is beyond it, on the empty place where she left John's body.

"So, Shifter," she says eventually. "You betrayed us after all."

"Yes," he says, and just like in the Clearing, he doesn't defend himself.

"I told you that the second I knew you were lying to us, I would rip your throat out." Her finger caresses the braid hidden below the collar of her shirt. "What's to stop me from doing it now?"

"Nothing, Alpha."

The other Alphas stand ready, muscles taut, hands on seaxes, eyes on Evie. We don't use the Meeting House often, so the space is cold and thin clouds stream from their nostrils like so many dragons. All it would take is one word, one gesture, from Evie, and Tiberius would be ripped to pieces.

All we have to defend ourselves are words, but Tara's already talked to the Alphas, and clearly they aren't in the mood for words. I know wolves when they're in this frame of mind, when listening is hard and acting is so easy.

Pivoting on my heel, I grab at Tristan's seax, because the 5th's Alpha knows my secret, and I know he would never hurt the tiny bodies inside me. The other Alphas, though... They whip their blades out, their thighs coiled and ready to pounce. Ti pulls me against his chest, his wounded hand crushing me to his chest, his other arm shielding my head.

"Do what you need to with me," he croaks, his voice raw and shredded. "But not her. Don't touch her."

He freezes as the sharp blade of Tristan's seax whispers against his throat. He searches my face with those black-and-gold eyes I love so much.

Trust me, min coren. Trust that I see you at your most vulnerable. And I will not hurt you.

Still holding my gaze, Ti lets go and stretches his arms wide like a crucifixion.

Tristan is a doctor and keeps his blade sharp and clean, so when I strike, it splits Ti's shirt easily down the middle. A button skitters across the floor.

Now every eye is on us. Except for Evie. She never looks away from the ice-laced window in front of her.

Ti hates the pity and the "tragic faces." He's always been so careful not to phase in front of the Pack. But I need them to understand that Ti is not just another Shifter, that this is not just another Shifter betrayal.

"John told me that if Ti lied to *himself* about what he was, he was going to lie to us. And he was right—you were right, Evie—Ti did lie to us."

Ti tries to cover his neck, but I pull his hand away. "But he didn't just wake up one morning and decide he didn't want to be Pack. It took years to break him. Every Iron Moon, when we need to be wild, when *he* needed to be wild, his father collared him. Those scars are the marks of a wolf trying to get free.

"Imagine how you would feel if you spent the three days out of every month that are most sacred to us chained to a fence like a dog. Would you really still believe that your other wild self was holy and deserved to be cherished above everything else? It wasn't until he came here that he understood, and then he did everything he could to protect us. He tried to stop his father, and when that failed, when they tried to kill him"—my voice falters as I brush the wrist above Ti's pierced hand—"when they hammered a spike through his palm, he refused to betray us."

The Alphas look again toward Evie. Her back is still stiff, but their posture has become more tentative, the posture of wolves waiting not for a command but for guidance.

"He could have just taken one of their cars and run, but he didn't, even though he knew the Pack would blame him for what had happened. Yes, he lied to us at first, but in the end, he did everything he could to save us."

Evie puts her hand to the window and smiles weakly at someone outside. Seeping through the windows come the rough-and-tumble sounds of pups playing in the snow.

"Alpha," says the last voice I expect to hear. "I did not lose as much as you did. Still, Solveig was my shielder, my friend, and my Alpha. My echelon," Eudemos continues, "now looks to me for guidance. But I *have* an echelon, one that includes Silver and Tiberius. The

Great North Pack lost four wolves, and the only reason we are here to mourn them is that Tiberius fought for us.

"Wolves killed five, but this man, *this* wolf, killed the rest."

Tristan moves toward Evie and stands beside her, whispering urgently. Our Alpha starts. "Silver?" she says. When I head toward her, Ti limps out in front, still trying to shield me. "Not him. I don't want to see him," Evie says to the window.

I draw Ti's worried face to mine, stretching as tall as I can so he can lean into my lips without having to bend his broken body. Then I stand before my Alpha, my head down.

Evie breathes in my scent and holds it inside her. She hesitates only a minute before folding herself in half, her cheek sliding against mine. Marking me. Because she is a good wolf and will be a great Alpha, and she knows her duty to the four new lives that will never fill the holes ripped in our Pack, but might someday patch them.

"Deemer," she says, turning for the door. "He must be punished; I leave it to you to decide what is fit." Then she leaves. It will be a long time before she can bring herself to look at Ti or say his name.

When Tiberius has healed, he will take the stone like I did. But where I was marked with the Tiw, to remind me to uphold the law, Ti will be marked with the Ur rune to remind him to cherish the wild.

Epilogue

This moon is the last Iron Moon before my lying-in. I am still carrying quadruplets. Our doctors always advise culling if there are more than three.

I finally told Ti, and he stood with me while Tristan and Gabi let him know all the possible complications. He held my hand when I said no to culling. The one they wanted to cull was, of course, a runt.

As soon as they left, Ti bent over the trash can, racked by dry heaves.

For now, the loose dress I've taken to wearing is carefully folded in the unfinished hulk of the new Great Hall, next to Ti's clothes. He sits on the warm grass, looking at the fading sun, while I nestle between his knees.

Evie, the last out, closes the door behind her.

My mate helps me through the change as he always does. As soon as he finishes phasing, he races me toward Clear Pond. I nip his tail, he nips my leg, and he gives me openmouthed kisses and lightly slaps my muzzle with his until we reach the big rock overhang above cold, night-dark water.

We both fly from the rock.

What a glorious wolf.

For more of Maria Vale's powerful writing,
unique mythology, and heartrending romance,
read on for a preview of book 2 in the
Legend of All Wolves series

A WOLF
APART

Available soon from Sourcebooks Casablanca

New York Times, *USA Today*, and international
bestselling author Jeaniene Frost on *The Last Wolf*:

"Wonderfully unique and imaginative. I was
enthralled by both the world and the characters.
Sign me up for the sequel!"

Chapter 1

I'VE DONE IT SO OFTEN, I DON'T HAVE TO THINK ABOUT IT anymore. My hands hardly seem to belong to me as they unfasten my cuff links. A quick twist to the left, then to the right. One after the other they plink into the silver Tiffany tray beside the sink.

The tray is engraved in flowing eighteenth-century script, an absurdity for the plastics industry.

> *To Elijah Sorensson*
> *with Gratitude from*
> *Americans for Progressive Packaging*

The platinum chain links with a bar in between were another gift. This from Aldrich Halvors to mark my first day at Halvors & Trianoff, nearly twenty-three years ago. Our Alpha, Nils, had just died. Shot along with his mate. And now another bullet has taken his successor, John.

Aldrich told me they were a reminder that no matter where we found ourselves, we were still crucial parts of the chain that bound the entire Pack.

Halvors. His real name, his Pack name, was Aldrich Halvorsson, but he gave that up. Just like he gave up any rank within the Pack hierarchy. When he died, he was the Omicron of his echelon even though he had once been so strong. Being Offland—being away from our Adirondack territory, being in skin for twenty-seven days at a stretch—does that to you. Leaches your strength. Leaches your will. Leaches your soul.

Aldrich had already been Offland for years when I first met him in New York City, representing the Great North Pack's interests in a firm founded with Pack money. Lori, who was Aldrich's assistant before she started to work for the surviving partner, now *my* partner, Maxim Trianoff, says that at the end, he'd become increasingly withdrawn and would stare out of the firm's huge plate-glass windows for days at a time.

He needed to go home.

An hour after he stared out of that window for the last time, Maxim got a call from the police. Aldrich had wrapped his car around a lamppost on the West Side Highway. He wasn't wearing a seat belt.

Wasn't wearing any clothes either.

It was a simple accident, but if the coroner had gotten involved, they'd have found that the corned beef hash in the driver's seat had been a man halfway to becoming a wolf.

He just couldn't wait another minute.

Almost makes me wonder if there's something in the HST offices. I gave two wolves a ride down to the City this moon who have been Offland as long as I have. Reena, who sits on the Second Circuit Court of Appeals, and her mate, Ingmar, who does something I couldn't quite figure out for the New York Department of State, only go home for the very rare holidays. And, of course, for the Iron Moon. For those three days out of thirty, when the moon is pregnant and full and her law is Iron and the Packs have no choice but to be wild.

Subordinate wolves in the 2nd echelon, Reena and Ingmar seem unaffected by the tearing alienation of Offland. They yacked the whole way about lawyers and restaurants and real estate and *Hamilton*. It was like being trapped in an enclosed space with humans for five hours. Except without that horrible smell of carrion and steel humans always have.

I would've bitten them, but they're not in my echelon.

I toss my shirt (Turnbull) into the dry-cleaning bag and hang my suit (Brioni) before stepping into my marble-and-copper-tile shower stall.

My. Nothing in this apartment is *mine*. It was bought sight unseen from floor plans by Pack money managers who had determined that it was likely to appreciate, so when it came time for me to leave New York, the Great North would be able to net a tidy profit.

Remember that things Offland break easily, they said, as though I hadn't been warned repeatedly. As though the Pack hadn't already had to pay to replace various Pixy Stix constructions that pass as furniture out here.

Don't do anything that will damage the resale value.

So I'm particularly careful when I scrub off the last remnants of my change, because I've already had to replace the showerhead once. The shower stall may be generously sized by human standards, but by Packish standards, it's a tight squeeze.

Then I carefully wipe out the drain strainer, scraping the fur and leaves and prickles of my home into the trash can.

In my bedroom, I can hit a switch that changes the

floor-to-ceiling windows from opaque to transparent. And when I stand here in skin, I have unobstructed views over the East River and can watch the moonrise and calculate how long it will be before I can go home again.

I am not like Aldrich. I did not give up my name—my Pack name—so Halvors, Sorensson & Trianoff is acid-etched on the glass doors.

And I have not given up my position either. They've tried, but I am too strong and have fought too many wolves for too many years. Even the most powerful, most belligerent wolves of the Great North have begun to realize that there is no one powerful or belligerent enough to unseat me as Alpha of the 9th echelon, the age group I have controlled since we made the transition to adulthood.

The Pack has been in turmoil since September when the badly injured Shifter came to us. All Packs hate and fear Shifters. Shifters can change, but unlike us, they don't *have* to, and that single difference has allowed them to become almost human, to become as corrupt and self-serving as humans.

The Iron Moon, those three days when we must be wild, is a sacred time for us, but like anything that is truly important, it comes with risks.

The risk that humans will come upon us by accident and, thinking that we are *æcewulfs*—real wolves, Forever Wolves—kill us. The risk that Shifters, with their almost Packish senses, will come upon us on purpose and, knowing exactly what we are, kill us.

If it had been up to me, I would have left the Shifter for the coyotes that first night, but he was half Pack, and our Alpha, John, was soft. Soft on him, soft on Quicksilver, the runt who is now his mate.

It turned out he was a lie. He had been sent to infiltrate us, find our weaknesses, by the head of all the Shifters, August Leveraux, his father. The fact that Tiberius changed allegiances from Shifter to Pack is in his nature. In the Old Tongue, Shifters are called *Hwerflic*. Changeable.

He killed many of the Shifters and humans who descended on us during the Iron Moon. I killed one. But the Great North Pack lost the Great Hall, our main gathering place. We almost lost our pups, our future. We lost four wolves, all of them highly placed, because the true meaning of leadership is sacrifice.

At the end of this Iron Moon, we laid the stones for the wolves we lost at the *Gemyndstow*, the memory place: Solveig Kerensdottir, Alpha of the 14th echelon. Orion Tyldesson, Alpha of the 5th. Paula Carlsdottir, Beta of the 8th. And John Sigeburgsson, Alpha of the Great North, the Alpha of Alphas.

But John's stone, like all of the others, is marked only with his name and the date of his last hunt. The Pack is a thing of hierarchies, but there is no hierarchy in death.

The ritual was silent, as our most important rituals always are. A nod to all of those times we are wild and speechless. At the very center of the widening circle of stones are the worn ones of Ælfrida, the Alpha who dragged her unwilling Pack from the dying forests of Mercia to the New World all those centuries ago, and Seolfer, her Deemer.

The dozen or so pups run in and out among the stones, understanding only that this place is important somehow and that every important place must be marked. So they do.

The stones are set. There are no bodies here; those were quickly consumed by the coyotes. The *wulfbyrgenna*, we call them. Wolf tombs. So death has been honored and now we must get on with life.

As we walked back toward the Great Hall, I fell in step beside Evie, John's mate and the new Alpha. The fourth wolf I have addressed by that title.

"Alpha, it's time for me to come home. The 9th needs me. I have been Offland for thirty years"—it slipped out, but I quickly correct myself—"360 moons and—"

"And we need you protecting our interests Offland more than ever." She picks up a pup who is jumping at her ankles and rubs him against her jaw, marking him. He lies on his back offering his belly to be rubbed, but as soon as he hears another pup, he twists and turns, anxious to get back down. They are like that. They need love, but they need freedom too.

"The Pack is vulnerable now, and no one knows better than you how to protect us from the human world. I agree with you that the 9th needs its Alpha, but it doesn't have to be you. It is time for you to let your Shielder take primacy; Celia's been holding the echelon together for years, and it's time, Elijah.

"It's time for you to let go."

Long after she left, I stayed staring down into the foundation being laid on the still-blackened smoke-scented foundation of the old one. It is cavernous and complicated because we need storage and because the frost line is so deep.

What Evie doesn't understand is that I am blind in a maze, with only this thread to hold on to. If I let go, I will never find my way out again.

—⁓—

At 3:00 a.m., when the city that never sleeps finally does, the twenty-four-hour fitness center of my luxury condominium building is finally empty.

That's when I drag out the cambered power bar that I store in my hall closet. Turns out that the cheap things they have at the gym develop a permanent kink once you load on eight hundred pounds.

Evie refused my request, and Evie is immensely powerful, but females take at least three moons to recover from lying-in. It has been only two. Meaning she will still be weak for one more moon.

I have spent over ten thousand days Offland. That's ten thousand days in skin. Ten thousand days without the earth of home under my paws, without the pine-scented breezes rolling down the mountainside and through my fur, without the bones of prey breaking in my powerful jaws.

But I refuse to end up like Halvors: corned wolf hash, wrapped around a streetlight on the West Side Highway.

One.

I am going home.

Two.

I am going home.

Three.

I am going home.

Four.

I am going home.

"What are you looking at?" I bark at the balding man staring at my overloaded bar. He stumbles backward over the threshold to the gym. The lid to his water bottle trundles across the floor. He leaves it.

Five.

I am going home.

Chapter 2

JEANS (D&G), T-SHIRT (ARMANI), JACKET (CUCINELLI). A quick squint in the mirror for the state of my shave. Left side, right side, lift chin. My hair is long and red-brown, though the tips are banded a darker color. Agouti is common enough for a sable wolf. Less common for corporate lawyers.

The one time I cut it, I spent two moons fighting wolves who made fun of my crewcut hackles and a near-constant chill across my withers.

I wonder if this was how Aldrich felt toward the end. If he felt a little sicker with every breath that came from the HVAC system. With every drink of water that tastes like chlorine. With every meal of denatured things from half a world away. With every cab that stinks of human.

"Keep the windows open, please," I say, leaning forward so the driver can hear.

I wonder if he was as desperate for the hunt as I am. Did he indulge in the same pathetic stopgaps that I do?

Nothing marks Testa but a dark-green door, a brass number, and a prime spot on the narrow New Street in a location that is convenient to the courts, City Hall, and the Financial District. There are a handful of clubs like this scattered through lower Manhattan that offer privacy, exclusivity, and smoking. Testa charges five hundred dollars for a single night's membership; there aren't any other kinds of membership, because the owners want to be able to refuse the man who's already wasted and likely to be an embarrassment. The man who misbehaved last time. The man who is under investigation by the SEC.

Men. Women—if they're young enough, beautiful enough, trim enough, and well-dressed enough—get in for free. Members then stand them drinks.

The lights are always low. There are no large tables, only booths with high, tufted backs to mute the sound. It's all about giving the illusion of privacy so we can hunt our prey without distraction.

I've learned that I don't need to bother with the booths. The bar is just fine. My back is to the room, but I can see as much as I need to in the mirror behind the brightly colored bottles of gin.

"Hey," says a voice. The voice's long, blond hair falls in carefully blown-out waves down either side of her lightly tanned face with perfectly regular features. Dressed in a white, backless dress with a low-draped collar showing supremely full breasts, she promises the warmth of summer in the dead of winter.

"Hey."

"My drink's a Moscow mule," she says, swinging onto the empty seat beside me.

I nod to the bartender and tap my glass for a refill.

"Wow," she says, putting her hand on my arm. "D'you play football?"

I shake my head, then throwing my chin back, I bolt down a handful of wildly salty nuts.

"Basketball?"

"No. Not much for sports."

"Are you, like, in financial services?" she asks.

When you're hunting, all sorts of things happen. Without making a move, your heart starts to pound faster, your muscles tighten, your senses become razor-edged. Adrenaline-primed, you are so ready to leap that the real strength, the real power, is in holding back until the moment is absolutely right.

It used to be like that—watching a beautiful woman, knowing that beneath the tape on her breasts, her nipples will be tightening, that she will be feeling an uncomfortable warmth.

Or will she? I can't really tell anymore.

"Lawyer."

"Oh," she says, a slight tinge of disappointment in her voice. Noah, one of Testa's owners, comes over and hands me back my credit card. I lean up on one hip, retrieving my wallet. As she watches me slide in the black-and-pewter card, she brightens. "Oh," she says. "That's interesting. I haven't seen you around here before."

"Hmm."

Tomas, the "mixologist," slides me my seltzer with bitters and lime. Wolves can't really drink. Does something awful to our livers. Tomas is discreet about my drinking habits because it's his job to be discreet, because the ownership certainly doesn't mind customers who don't use the bar as an all-you-can-eat buffet, and because I tip him well.

"Thanks, I guess," she says, lifting her Moscow mule toward me. She slides around on her seat, scanning the room, looking for someone who might be more responsive.

"Elijah Sorensson?"

In the mirror caught between the tall, emerald-green

bottle and the square, blue bottle, the woman in white pauses as a sloppily drunk man I'm supposed to know slaps my shoulder. Pale-gray tweed jacket with black piping and a black shirt. Elaborately stitched jeans. He smells vaguely familiar. Like wild onion and rubber. I didn't say pleasant, just familiar.

"This man…" he slurs. "You remember, we bought Alacore? In 2015, we bought it. But the big abattoir around our neck"—I'm assuming he actually means *albatross*, not *slaughterhouse*—"was a busted-up cement plant up near…I don't know where."

Now I remember. His name is Dante something. "Fort Miller," I say.

"I think you may be right. State says we're goin' to have to clean it up. For a lotta money." He rests one foot on the rung of my stool. "I don' remember how much, because this genius, he makes it out so that we don't have to do shit. Says the rotting concrete is good for climate change."

I'm not in the mood to explain the mechanics of concrete carbonation to Dante Something from the Mergers and Acquisitions Department at LMSC. It's part of my job. I'm very good at my job, and when I'm good at my job, I make money. Money that is used to protect another piece of land and a different wilderness up there. North.

"Well, anyway, the thing is still rottin' away." He guffaws again. "Rottin' from the inside out. Being good for the environment." He removes his foot from my stool but doesn't slap me again. Humans don't. They do it once to be comradely, but there's something about what they feel under my bespoke jacket that makes them nervous about doing it again.

I take another drink. The woman in white stands closer, her breast pressed against my arm.

"I haven't seen you here either," I say. Now I'm just going through the motions, mouthing the words to an old script. "I would certainly have remembered. No man could ever forget you." She looks exactly like half the beautiful women in this place. The other half have dark hair.

When she finishes her Moscow mule, I order her another. She's jabbering something about some start-up. An app that does something I don't have any use for, so I hear but don't actually listen. When her voice goes up in a lilting question, I nod or frown slightly, concerned. When conversation lags, I look intently at her irises for a beat or two past the norm and say something about the sky or storms or chocolate, depending on their color. It's a body part humans set great stock in.

"Your skin is so soft." Lifting my arm is like lifting lead when I brush her hair back from her face and my fingers trace her cheek. "You should never wear anything but silk."

Her bleached-blond hair is dry and crisp and feels like late-autumn sedge against the back of my hand.

I don't know when the thrill of the hunt died. My cock is so jaded now, but I can't help myself.

In the end, I am left looking at the ceiling, waiting for her breathing to even and slow. I don't know how many Moscow mules this one had, but it must have been a few. Her breath is sickly sweet, and she snores in the way women do when they're chemically relaxed.

I can't take this anymore.

Chapter 3

WHEN I GET BACK TO THE BUILDING, THE NIGHT PORTER IS busily polishing the brass.

"Nice evening, Mr. Sorensson?"

"It was fine, Saul. Thanks."

And I lope past the acrid smell of polish, through the elevator that smells of take-out carrion lo mein and into the apartment. Because I bought a model unit that no one had ever lived in, it didn't take long for the stench of carrion and steel and artificial sweeteners to dissipate.

Humans don't come here. The only thing I changed was the mattress. I left the queen in the hallway one Tuesday afternoon so that the men came and knocked and rang and eventually left the California King in its place. As soon as I was sure no one was around, I carried it into my apartment.

The only thing that is truly personal is the photograph, sandwiched between two pieces of UV resistant glass, of my echelon the summer before we divided up.

There are eighteen of us in the 9th echelon. All born within five years of each other: Celia, my shielder, who runs things day-to-day, frames the left side; I frame the right. Between us are the other sixteen. Eight standing, eight crouching down, all side-facing and squeezed tight together. Genetics as well as centuries of breeding to power mean we are very big on the human scale. One at a time, the reaction is dully familiar: "You play football?"

There's a reason we never leave Homelands in groups.

Some of us would go on to college and come back to run Pack businesses near Homelands. Some of us would stay away longer. I remember staring at the shield on the acceptance letter to Yale Law School, with its crocodile, dog, and staples and thinking with dread that from now on, I would be that dog, fastened far away, protecting my Pack from that crocodile.

The photograph shows a happy cluster of newly minted adults but so much has changed. Nils was the Alpha at our *Daeling*, our Dealing. He was the one who watched as we fought for position within the hierarchy and cemented our transition from juveniles to adult. Not long after, he and his mate were shot by hunters. His brother John took over, and now, another bullet later, he is dead too, leaving his mate, Evie, as Alpha.

It has hit us all hard. I don't think humans could understand the ties that bind us. They have family, but the longer I live Offland, the more I realize that it has nothing to do with Pack. Parents do horrible things to children. Children ignore parents. Spouses divorce. The loss of an Alpha goes beyond the loss of a parent. An Alpha is like the woody trunk of a grapevine. Everything spreads out from it. Yes, you can graft the vine onto a new rootstock, but not without consequences.

Sarah and Adam, the 9th's Gamma couple, seems to have been particularly hard hit by John's death. This past moon, they huddled close to Home Pond and the burned-out remnants of the Great Hall.

Carefully setting the photograph back on my bedside table, I reach into my pocket for my phone. Then

I open the little app that is designated by a full moon sandwiched between a black star-speckled square and the spine of our native mountains. Called Homeward, it is not available in the Play Store or on iTunes. It was developed three years ago by one of our wolves so that Offlanders who sometimes get caught up in the rhythms of the lives of humans do not forget our own.

Each morning, a wolf—the developer, I presume— intones *"Hámsíðe, ðu londadl hǽðstapa"* in the Old Tongue, before a computer-generated voice counts down the days until the next Iron Moon. "Homeward, you landsick heath-wanderer, in 27 days."

Whoever devised this must have known firsthand how desperate Offlanders became for the Homelands. How "landsick" we gray heath-wanderers, as men once called us, became.

If Homeward calculates that a wolf is too far away to make it back before the change, it chirps out one last phrase in the Old Tongue.

Ond swa gegæþ þin endedogor.

And so passes your final day.

Who says Pack have no sense of humor?

Usually I set Homeward for a single reminder one day before the Iron Moon, but this time I set it for a daily countdown so I won't forget just how important this particular change is.

Hámsíðe, ðu londadl hǽðstapa, in 26 days.

Homeward, you landsick heath-wanderer, in 26 days.

From inside the elevator, I hear a door open, followed by tiny claws skittering on the carpet. My thumb is pressed so hard into the brass Door Close button that it bends. We were told to be careful with human things—they are delicate and break easily—but it's hard to remember when you're in a rush.

"Hold the elevator?" says a lilting, questioning voice. My finger drops from the elevator button and my heart falls with it. I smile at the woman with the black Dutch boy haircut, yoga pants, and a raincoat. Amanda is in her thirties. Her husband, Luca, is nearing sixty.

He travels way too much.

Usually I would have been smart enough not to screw someone who knew where I lived, let alone lived where I lived, but the day I did it, she was wearing a raw wool poncho that smelled like sheep and made my mouth water.

"Elijah? How have you been?" She leans one hip against the wall of the elevator and smooths her hair over her ear. Left, then right.

"Well. And how is Luca?"

"Well?" she lilts again. She swoops down and picks up a fluffy gray doglet whose hair has to be clipped from his eyes so he can see and away from his underbelly so he can walk and who is apparently full-grown but is named, for some unaccountable reason, Tarzan.

Pulling Tarzan to her nose, she eyes me over the faux-fur collar of the dog's trench coat. "But Luca? He's out of town? In China?" she says as if to ask whether the distance is far enough to revisit our infidelity.

That damn poncho.

Before the implicit invitation becomes explicit, the elevator door opens and Amanda is pulled into a conversation about lobby improvements while I glare at Tarzan.

"You," I whisper to the little ball of coyote meat

dressed in beige-and-black plaid, "should be *ashamed* of yourself."

Tarzan lowers his eyes, then whimpers piteously. The little bit of wild that has not been bred out of him, recognizing that submission is his only option.

I know it's not his fault, but still, a little dignity. Please.

As soon as the elevator hits the ground floor, I mutter something unintelligible and race for the street, hailing the first car that will take me. The driver motions for me to wait while he pulls the seat forward, but I throw myself in along the length of the back and slam the door closed just as Amanda extricates herself.

Halvors, Sorensson & Trianoff is housed in a tall yet squat postmodern building overlooking the last feet of the Hudson before it transforms into New York Harbor. It is undistinguished except for its proximity to a huge, green-glass atrium holding sixteen palm trees. It's odd that humans will pay so much for exotics as though that makes up for the native trees they are so profligate with.

There is a man at the top of the curved atrium entrance. Looking up, I see his feet and the thin pole he uses to pull at a wave of soap. A line tethers him to the wall of glass above. I wonder if he's ever thought of sliding down the slick of soap and leaping off, flying toward the not-so-distant smell of the ocean and the sound of the seagulls. But then the leash would tighten and pull him back and he'd end up back where he started, bumping against the glass.

"Elijah? Are you coming?"

The window washer starts toward the next tier of glass.

"Max." I nod to the little human before opening the door into the expansive lobby with its high wall of shaded glass, its marble floors and brass fixtures. The security guards behind their white desk wave us through the turnstile without demanding ID.

Maxim Trianoff is in his late sixties. He'd spent his early legal career as a brilliant member of the SEC's enforcement division. He'd been, I heard, a Democrat who believed deeply in social equity. Then in the middle of his first very expensive divorce, he left the SEC for Zoerner, Marwick. By the time he was done with his second very expensive divorce, he was a Republican, committed to holding on to whatever money he still had and ready for something new. Ready to see his own name acid-etched in glass. That's when he was approached by Aldrich Halvors with a proposition from a silent partner who wanted to fund a law firm with lobbyists who would represent its interests and turn a profit.

Great North LLC.

"And how are our silent partners?" Max asks as he always does when I come back from trips up to the Great North. He has no idea how silent our silent partners are. Gliding through the great tangled swaths of pine-and-loam-scented hardwood that his firm, our firm, was created to protect.

"Fine, though John Torrance has stepped down." I hadn't been able to say it last time; it was still too raw then. I stare straight ahead at the bronze elevator.

"Well, he was there for a long time. Have they chosen someone new?"

Two elevators arrive at the ground floor.

"Hmm. Evie Kitwana."

We get into the second elevator, the one with fewer people making fewer stops. Looking down, all I can see is the thinning top of Max's scalp, but in the high shine of the elevator, his face is reflected clearly. Worn, with puffy eyes and cheeks that hang low like a bloodhound. Taking out a large handkerchief, he blows his nose.

I look younger than I am, because left alone, we live a long time. We rarely do, because eventually the most powerful wolves take a bullet, trying to defend the Pack.

Still, I'd rather be shot during the Iron Moon than to deflate soufflé-like as Max is doing.

"And does Ms. Katana—"

"Kitwana."

"And is she looking for any changes to our arrangement?"

I can see my jaw tightening, and the door slides open onto Halvors, Sorensson & Trianoff.

"No. She wants things to stay exactly the same."

From her place within the white circle of the reception desk, Dahlia calls out to tell us that the associates are already in Conference Room A.

Six associates are seated at one end of the long oval table in Conference Room A, leaving the two at the very end free for Max and me. I slide my tablet into the slot designated for it and plug in to the USB so we can talk about bonuses without putting anything up on the big screen where potentially envious not-associates might see it.

Of course, Max and I already knew that last year was a banner year for HST. The three equity partners—Max, myself, and Great North LLC—have all done exceedingly well. Max will be able to not only pay his three ex-wives, but also make a down payment on a fourth.

"That's a lot of money," Max says, once the associates are gone. "What are you going to do with it?"

I don't know. The Pack pays for whatever expenses aren't covered by the firm. I don't know what they do with the rest. I have no money. I have only the facade of wealth.

"I don't have any real plans."

"I'm going to be honest with you. You've seemed off your game for a while now. You work hard, Elijah, and there is no one who knows how to reel in the clients like you do. But you've got to be on and be focused. You should do something. Travel. Buy a boat, for Chrissake. My brother-in-law over at Morgan got a boat a few years ago. Swears by it."

Lori, Max's assistant, knocks softly at the door and Max waves her in.

"Mr. Sorensson, your eleven o'clock is here?"

"What eleven o'clock?" I always block out the entire morning for associates' meetings.

"Tony Marks apparently—"

"Oh, right," Max says. "I've got this, Lori. Just send her to Mr. Sorensson's office."

"Sorry about that," he says, pouring himself one more cup of coffee before walking through the door propped against my foot. "I meant to tell you about this before you went Upstate, but it slipped my mind. Our great friend and client Tony Marks is very fond of his gardener, even though he lost him when he lost Southampton to Susannah. Now, apparently, the gardener's niece has found herself with some kind of legal problem. If what Tony says is true, it should take no time, so just take care of it, will you? Pro bono, of course. Neither gardener nor niece have any money. And, Elijah? Be as charming as you want, but keep your clothes on. Hard to credit from a man on his third alimony, but still, I'd appreciate it."

"You really need a divorce lawyer who can stand up to women," I say, starting for the southeast corner of HST.

Chapter 4

"MR. SORENSSON." SINISE FROM ACCOUNTING SCURRIES INTO step beside me. "That was a super presentation. But you always do such super presentations." It wasn't a super presentation. It was pure bullshittery. But then Sinise from accounting puts her hand on my arm and bends her leg behind her, leaning slightly to fix a strap of her shoe. When she stands back up, she shakes her head, tossing her long, oddly burgundy hair first left then right.

So.

It has nothing to do with the quality of my presentation and everything to do with indicating that she is receptive.

My assistant, Janine, quickly insinuates herself between us, her back to Sinise. She tells me that a client is waiting and unnecessarily adjusts my tie, thereby marking me. Telling Sinise that I am already fucking *her*.

Having defended her *cunnan-riht*, Janine points with her chin toward my office and the client Tony Marks sent who is waiting there. I can only see her from behind. Her thick, black hair hangs down wild, like flames pointing to the curve of an ass like a Japanese pear. Her strong, slim legs are encased in jeans, one leg of which is caught in the top of a pair of mud-spattered hiking boots.

Janine has returned to her office, which is really a windowless interior cubicle across the hall from my own. She has her hand on her mouse and her eyes concentrated

on the screen. Unlike Sinise, this woman poses no threat.
When she turns around, I see why. She is not beautiful
in the way Janine recognizes. She does not have the tight
symmetry that every cosmetic surgeon and every patient
of one aspires to. She has a long nose in a face that is
broad and soft below high cheekbones. Strong chin. Her
mouth is wide and straight and unsmiling.

She is probably four inches taller and eight years
older than Janine, and since she is not like Janine, Janine
not only doesn't see her as competition, she doesn't see
her at all.

This woman doesn't flick her hair or coyly lower her
eyes with a half smile. She doesn't angle her hips or
finger her collarbone or bite her lower lip. She is con-
tained, quiet, still. And when I take a step closer, she
smells nothing like carrion and everything like cold,
damp earth.

"Elijah Sorensson," I say, holding out my hand. Her
hand has cropped nails and no ornament. Calluses in the
grip between thumb and forefinger.

She sizes me up quickly with eyes the color of ironwood and just as unyielding.

"Thea Villalobos," she says, and it takes me a
moment to get my breath back.

"I'm sorry?"

"Thea," she says slowly. "Villalobos."

Wolves laugh about the madness and mutability of
men. About how they are prey to the sudden whims
of fate and their own emotional instability. From my
jaded and indifferent perch, I have laughed about it too.
Laughed about Max and his sudden passions.

But now, confronted by this woman with an ass like

a Japanese pear, hair like night, eyes like ironwood, skin the color of gold rye, the ground shifts and topples me into a rotation around her.

Thea Villalobos. Goddess of the City of Wolves.

"Elijah Sorensson," I repeat, stalling while I try to remember what Maxim had said about her. Tony Marks's something. Daughter? No, that wasn't it. She'd have money if she was Tony Marks's daughter.

"Have a seat?"

I hit my toe on the corner of my desk and stumble into my chair, the Titan. That's what my chair is officially called. The Titan.

I discovered it after four years at college, three years at law school, two years clerking for Judge Baski, and two more years at Halvors & Trianoff, crammed into tiny human-size chairs. Then when I became partner, my assistant at the time—Barbara, whose pubic hair was waxed into an arrow as though most men she'd had were too drunk to know where to aim—suggested the Titan.

Ever since then, each new piece of furniture has been upgraded, even the two chairs facing across from my big desk. Sitting with their feet dangling loose above the floor helps whether I need to intimidate or impress. And everyone who comes into my office has to be intimidated or impressed.

Thea Villalobos shrugs off her backpack and pulls out a file and a flash drive before settling into the corner of one arm of the chair, her knee propped against the other. I want to see her do it again. I want to see that economy of movement, deliberate and smooth.

"I think you'll find everything you need here. I didn't want to waste your time," she says, "but my uncle felt that a letter from a firm like yours would send a stronger message than something downloaded from LawDepot."

As I take the manila folder and flash drive, she settles back, almost motionless. Almost but not quite. Her ring finger gently pulses against the upholstered back of the big chair. There is, I think, a restrained sensuality in Thea Villalobos. I feel that long-lost prickling in my thighs, and my Pavlovian part stands up and remembers.

Leaning over my desk and her file allows me to adjust the suddenly awkward side tuck. My mind is only half there as I look over the papers she's typed up.

Thea Villalobos is an environmental conservation officer living in Buttfuck, New York. Robert Liebling, lunatic, is suing her for springing the body grip traps he'd set on his land but right across the border from the wilderness she patrols. He set them again, and Thea tripped them again. The third time, he took video and decided to sue her for trespass. As she points out, by the time he'd taken the date-stamped video, trapping season was over.

"You'd done it before, though? *During* trapping season."

"Maybe." She watches me eject the flash drive. "But his case against me is based entirely on that video."

"It would still be useful to know the history."

She says nothing.

"You do know that everything you say here is privileged?"

"It's not germane and I don't think you would understand."

I follow her unyielding eyes to the two shelves of my bookcase that are empty of books and filled with photographs of me with various high-profile clients. The head of the United American Energy Commission, the board of Northeastern Developers Association, the CEO of Consolidated Information. A line of men, none of whom will ever make it into *Us* or *People* or *InStyle* and must make do, instead, with ruling the world.

"I am not my clients," I say.

She leans back, pulling an errant strand of hair away from her forehead. When she bends forward again, she sits closer to my desk.

"Have you ever seen an animal in a body grip trap?"

I shake my head. Hunters come during the Iron Moon, but we've only had one man set a trap on our land. Marked so heavily with wolf urine, no animal would go near it until the Iron Moon was over, and John had the opposable thumb he needed to trip it. And once she had the words she needed, Josi, the 3rd Echelon's lawyer, took care of the silly little human.

"They say they're humane, but they're not," she says, fingering the flash drive. "I've released animals when I can, but mostly you just have to kill them.

"Liebling claimed he was a trapper, that he needed the money and had the right to trap furbearers on his land. Furbearers. Like they're nothing but the keratin on their backs. It'd be like reducing everything you were to 'hair bearer.'" She leans back into the corner of the chair. "See, I knew a man like you would think it was funny."

"No, not funny. Not funny at all. I agree with you completely. It's just the part about 'hair bearer.' I can think of a few men who would say that was an apt description of me."

"Bald men?" she asks, a cool half smile hovering around her lips.

"Mostly."

"Anyway, Liebling claims he's a trapper, but he doesn't have a license. I took pictures of the skins he's taken. They're shredded and unsellable. It's just so much pain and waste. So yes, I triggered those traps, and yes, I will do it again."

I like this woman.

"You don't like him much, do you?"

"No, he's a shit."

It's one of the things you learn about humans early on. They're always hedging their bets. Always putting things in the conditional, always making concessions. Leaving their options open.

Thea doesn't, and it makes me like her more.

I tap the edges of the papers she's given me, as though to even them up.

"Unfortunately," I lie, "there are complications you haven't accounted for here."

She doesn't say anything at first. Then she pulls out a pen.

"What kinds of complications?"

"He claims to be a farmer, so he doesn't need a license to trap on his land."

"He's no farmer. I put some stills on the flash drive. Every month for five months during spring and summer of last year when he first brought up this 'farmer' idea. He put some plants in old plaster buckets that never got big enough to identify before they died."

"I really am happy to do this for you, Ms. Villalobos—"

"Thea."

"Thea. I'm just saying it may take a little longer than we originally thought."

"And I'm saying I'd rather take care of it myself."

"It's all pro bono. Won't cost you a thing. We owe it to your…to Tony Marks."

Her ironwood eyes focus on mine. It is all I can do not to look away. "My uncle's employer's ex-husband?"

"He's a big client. Look, you live in Arietta? We have an office in Albany and I have another very important client up near Plattsburgh that I visit…frequently. I could meet you in town and—"

She laughs at that. It's deep and throaty and untamed, and I have to hear it again.

Everything I knew about Arietta came from a road sign on one of my more meandering drives home for Iron Moon. Turns out that Arietta is 330 square miles with a population of 304. Her physical address is a set of coordinates. Her mailing address is a post office box near Piseco Lake over forty-five minutes away.

But she agrees to meet me at the HST offices in Albany. Next week. I'll have something drafted for her by then.

She pulls on her coat. Her eyes catch on my photographs again before she tosses her backpack over one shoulder. Then she slides her left hand in her jeans pocket, her anorak caught behind her forearm, and takes my proffered hand with a smooth slide of her palm against mine.

After she goes, I look at my photographs. How is it that I never noticed before? Never noticed that my pose is the same in every one of them: left hand in pocket,

jacket on that side behind my forearm, right hand taking that of my powerful client.

Holding my hand to my mouth, I breathe deeply the scent of Ajax and black earth, while from the office window I watch the stretch of sidewalk that gives onto Vesey.

After a few minutes, Thea Villalobos emerges from the building. She bends down to loosen the pant leg from her boots. A little beyond her, the leashed man continues to work on the glass.

In Liebling's jumpy movie, a woman in jeans, shit-kickers, and a cable-knit sweater carries nothing but a long, thick branch. Standing far back, she pokes the thin metal trigger until it snaps. Her makeshift staff snaps on the second one. She picks up another branch and heads for the most distant one, the third.

"Janine? Tell Albany I'm going to need an office next Wednesday."

Liebling waits for a little and then starts to move, whispering softly that he's going to the third trap so the GPS on his phone will record that she was still on his land. "And, Janine? Where exactly is the Albany office?"

Then I message Samuel, the investigator I use most often, to stop by as soon as he gets back. Two hours later, I slide him a copy of the video and a piece of paper with Robert Liebling's name on it. "Find out everything you can about him."

He pauses, looking at the other side.

"Yes. About her too."

Acknowledgments

Acknowledgments seems like such a pale word. A nod of the head. A token. It does not begin to cover my gratitude to the women of Sourcebooks—Susie Benton, Heather Hall, Beth Sochacki, Stefani Sloma, Laura Costello, Dawn Adams—who took such great care and never complained once. Or my utter amazement on finding that my great editor, Deb Werksman, and my magical agent, Heather Jackson, said yes in the first place.

Thank you.

About the Author

Maria Vale is a logophile and a bibliovore and a worrier about the world. Trained as a medievalist, she tries to shoehorn the language of Beowulf into things that don't really need it. She currently lives in New York with her husband, two sons, and a long line of dead plants. No one will let her have a pet.